A
CITY
DIVIDED

A. B. Levin

CHAPTER ONE

It was a warm September evening when Melvin Jackson stepped out the front door of his row home at Fifty-Seventh and Blackstone, just a few blocks from the University of Chicago's main campus. He had recently moved in and was enjoying the tranquility of the treelined street.

His business had been flourishing, and moving into the bourgeois South Side neighborhood of Hyde Park allowed him to enjoy the fruits of his labor and rub elbows with a class of society he never thought he'd be a part of as a child. He grew up just southwest of his new home in Englewood, one of the poorest, most crime-ridden neighborhoods in the city. It was only three miles away, but in Chicago's heavily self-segregated neighborhoods, three miles may as well have been twenty.

Nearby church bells tolled to signify the time—6:00 p.m. on the dot. Melvin stepped out the door and turned to lock it. Most of his neighbors didn't need to lock their doors except to give them peace of mind, but in his line of work, he didn't think twice about it. The three custom Schlage locks he had installed on the steel-framed door would be enough to thwart any would-be robbers from breaking in to look for cash, guns, or drugs.

Only once had he been robbed, and it was most likely by a few addicts who were looking for a quick score. He didn't keep drugs in his home, though—always fearful of a midnight raid by the police. He kept his profile low enough, but that would only work until some overzealous badge decided Melvin was getting too big for his britches. He learned well from his mentors about all facets of the drug trade, including raids. If you were lucky, they'd be looking for a payoff, but even that came with baggage. There always seemed to be someone else in line that you owed if they caught you with enough weight.

He kept his product off-site, in the back of a warehouse owned by an LLC that would never be traced back to him. At his house he only kept money, and he had it well hidden. No one would find the cash unless they already knew it was there. He also kept guns, but having never caught a felony conviction, those weren't illegal for him to own.

Things were looking up for Melvin as he started down the street toward his car. A kid from nothing who outsmarted his rivals, the cops—hell, the whole system—to become a real entrepreneur. It was a success story by all accounts, even if his business was an illegal one.

Unfortunately for Melvin, he was too preoccupied reflecting on his success to look up at the third-story commercial rooftop a block and a half away. Otherwise, he may have seen the glint of waning sunlight bouncing off a VX5HD Leupold scope mounted on top of a custom modified Springfield M1A rifle. It was a rare tell for the man on the other end of the gun, but his original perch had been compromised by some unexpected rooftop maintenance. He knew the sun could give away his position, but he was careful not to uncap the scope until his target emerged. Besides, this wasn't Fallujah. No one would be shooting back.

Just as he expected, Melvin didn't even notice as he fumbled in his pocket for his keys outside his all-black, fully loaded Range Rover. The sniper took aim, lining up Melvin's head in the cross hairs, having already adjusted his scope for windage and distance. His breathing grew slow and steady. Then, as he reached the bottom of his breath, he paused. His entire body froze in place except the tip of his index finger, which gently squeezed the trigger.

There was no crack from the silenced rifle. Just a tap of the firing pin striking the primer on the .308 Winchester round and the sound of the shell casing tumbling, absent of malice, to the graveled rooftop.

The bullet screamed out of the barrel at 2,600 feet per second, closing the distance to the target so quickly that it looked instantaneous to the untrained eye. The sniper watched as Melvin Jackson's head snapped back and his lifeless body crumpled in the street. After waiting several seconds for any movement, the sniper, satisfied there was none, dropped the magazine, ejected a round from the chamber, and started breaking down his rifle. It only took thirty seconds to place the parts in a small case and then drop the spent shell in an exhaust vent with his gloved hand before sliding down the fire ladder in the rear of the building.

He traveled a full three blocks before he heard the first sirens.

CHAPTER TWO

Crack!

The sound of the telephone receiver slamming down on the cradle could be heard down the hall.

"And if it's not here in thirty minutes, there's going to be hell to pay!" was still reverberating off the walls.

Naomi Archer had no time for screwups. She was under a deadline, and she wasn't about to miss it. As a partner at the prestigious Chicago law firm Sloan MacIntyre, she had rarely missed her deadlines, even if it meant pulling the occasional all-nighter. Such was the life of smart, sophisticated, and successful attorney who had been voted a rising star six years in a row—one for every year since she'd graduated from Michigan law.

Sure, she had missed a few deadlines, but with her caseload, it was inevitable. Then there was the time she got snowed in while on a business trip to New York. "The blizzard of the century," the *New York Times* called it. Every flight into and out of the city was canceled for three days straight. The lost productivity was estimated in the billions. Not to be deterred from getting home, though, Naomi marched into a Hertz and rented the last car in the greater New York–New Jersey area.

It hadn't been easy, or cheap. She had to give the man who held the reservation three hundred dollars just for the privilege of renting the car, but getting home was her top priority because she had a very special appointment that she couldn't afford to miss—dinner with her father for his birthday.

Every year on the Saturday of his birthday they had a standing reservation at Sapori Vincenzo. It was a local Italian joint. The kind where the chef is the owner, the food is cheap but good, and they make a great martini. Not exactly a place you'd expect a successful attorney to take her dad to celebrate in style. But this was their spot. Cozy, no frills, and the perfect speed to get away from her stressful job and catch up on some long overdue family gossip over comfort food.

On that day, Naomi was not going to miss it. She had planned to do work on the plane, but now that she was making the 750-mile trek from LaGuardia to Chicago via car, that work would have to wait. If the snow held out enough, she figured she could make it in ten hours flat, just in time to drop off the car, change her clothes, and walk over to meet her dad for a plate of pasta Contadina, a house specialty and her favorite.

Of course, with grit and determination, she made it with fifteen minutes to spare—but those who knew Naomi would have said that outcome was never in doubt.

About today's outcome, though, she was unsure. She stood at her desk, anxiously biting her fingernails, a habit she had tried to kick with gum on many occasions. She looked at her computer screen, which was raised to meet her five-foot-six slender frame so she could stand while she worked.

Sitting for long stretches had recently become difficult. Years of an active lifestyle had taken its toll. She loved to run and held a black belt in Tang Soo Do, a particularly aggressive form of martial arts. As a style, it didn't win any points for grace or beauty, but it fit Naomi's personality well—unadorned and brutally effective. If she was ever going to need to use her skills in a fight, she wanted to learn the form that would guarantee her a win.

Her legs may have been average in length, but when she got her heel going in a spinning back kick—well, let's just say that many taller men have woken up on the mat having foolishly believed they were safely out of range. The years of training and torque took a toll on her hips, though, and she was forced to hang up her Gi after tearing both labrums a few years prior.

Naomi had recovered well. It was nearly a year of recuperation and physical therapy. Even if she could no longer perform a high kick like she used to, she could do nearly everything else, and she was just fine with that. Besides, she didn't have as much time for it anymore. She had made partner on her time off, even interviewed on crutches and in a leg brace. Unsurprisingly, she was unanimously voted in despite being out for four months, which the doctor had assured her was the least amount of time he would consider she take for two major hip surgeries.

Things were falling back into place for Naomi, but sitting for long stretches wasn't one of them. She never much liked to sit, anyway; always being on move, she hardly had time for it. Now that she had the standing desk, she wondered how she ever lived without it.

Shifting her attention from the twenty-seven-inch monitors in front of her, she stared out her floor-to-ceiling glass window towering over the green-tinged Chicago River. Something about these documents just didn't add up.

Naomi hoped that she was wrong, but deep down she knew—if these documents were what she suspected them to be, it was going to be an all-nighter.

CHAPTER THREE

The call came in just as Detective Patrick McCauley was about to end his shift. He was walking out of the bureau of detectives' homicide division at Fifty-First and the Dan Ryan Expressway when the cell phone rang inside his left pocket.

He checked the number and thought, *They always seem to call at shift change*. He listened to the caller, then acknowledged he was on his way before ending the call and immediately dialing another number.

His wife, Emily, picked up the phone. "Let me guess. Work called, and you won't be home for supper. Why does it always happen just when you are about to come home?"

"It doesn't happen all that often! It just feels that way because you like seeing me so much."

It was true—she was thrilled now that he had switched to days for the past few years. At first it was almost strange having him home such regular hours, but she genuinely loved spending time with him. And now with the kids out of the house, that sentiment only grew stronger.

"Okay, I'll fix something for dinner that you can heat up. If you get home fast enough, you may just have someone to enjoy it with."

"Thanks, Em. I'll keep you posted. Love you."

"Love you too."

He closed the phone and made for the department-issued Crown Vic. The address wasn't far away, and with his police lights on, he made it on scene in just under ten minutes.

Already patrolmen had set up a perimeter of yellow caution tape and were pushing back the crowds that were forming at the macabre scene. McCauley could see legs sticking out behind a black Range Rover. They waited for him before disturbing the scene, which meant leaving the body uncovered. He parked his car just outside the perimeter, exited, and ducked as a young officer lifted the tape for him.

McCauley had a reputation as a heavy hitter in the department. Just shy of fifty years old, he had the scars of a physical job hidden all over his six-foot-two muscular frame. Despite a reconstructed knee and rough-skinned hands, his face was that of a man ten years younger. The grays that peppered his dark black hair made him look more his age, though he wasn't one to dye them.

Like every officer, he started in patrol. Armed with an undergraduate degree in criminal justice from Loyola and raw athletic ability, he had excelled at the academy but quickly found out that his success there meant very little on the streets of Chicago.

His field training officer once quipped, "That's great that you can run a mile in six flat. You do that, and I'll chase the perps down in my car."

Pat wouldn't hear it, though. His high school hockey coach had always said to put yourself in good position and take good shots, and good things will happen. He applied that to his police work and stayed in peak physical condition. He was also aggressive, never one to nap the last hour of his shift in a dim Walgreens parking lot like some of the veterans waiting for their pension to kick in. He was always moving. Staying constantly mobile gave the drug-corner lookouts fits and made him tough to spot. It wasn't long until he was in a position to use his six-minute mile to run down a winded midlevel dealer, who had enough heroin on him to send him away for a long time, a mistake he chalked up to one of his soldiers being a no-show for a prearranged deal. Of course he flipped, and three other mid- to high-level busts came out of it. McCauley's detractors would call him lucky, but that would be the first of many "lucky" busts.

He levered his rising star to move about the department. He wanted to get as much experience as he could in every area —narcotics, gang, vice. He even did a stint in the marine unit for a few weeks one summer when they were short on man power. It was mostly writing tickets to boaters, but he wasn't one to complain. The bikini-clad passengers were beautiful, and when they had been drinking enough they'd often flirt with a man in uniform. Pretty good way for a young cop to break up the gruesome side of big city policing. For all his moving about, though, he always had eyes for the bureau of detectives. The rotations were just his way of making sure he was well prepared for when he got his shot.

Once he did, he never looked back. As he had done in patrol, he quickly rose through the ranks, first tackling petty crimes, eventually moving up the ladder to robbery, arson, then finally homicide, where he had been working the past fifteen years.

His meteoric rise in the department came with its downsides—mostly jealousy and internal politics. One scorned officer who was upset at having been passed over for promotion spread a rumor about how McCauley was the king of beating confessions out of suspects and that he had a nasty habit of sending innocent men to jail. None of it was true, of course. McCauley was as straight as they came—no bribes, no coercion, not so much as a uniform violation, just good police work.

Like any good legend, the tall tales grew and took on a life of their own. At last telling of his career highlights, he had busted three gangs out of existence, arrested half the Russian and Italian mobs, been in five gunfights, and shot seven suspects officially and scores more unofficially. McCauley never denied the rumors; in fact, he kind of liked them. The clout made it easier to cut through red tape and secure resources from the veteran brass who admired that type of hard-nosed police work. He particularly liked the gunfighter persona—so much so that he played it up. On his right hip he carried a pearl-gripped .45-

caliber Colt 1911 as his primary weapon and Smith & Wesson Model 66 Combat .38 special revolver as his backup. He kept the S&W in a cross-draw holster on his left side so the butt of the pistol would peek out from his sport coat, revealing a matching pearl grip.

Neither pistol had been department approved for at least a decade, but he had been grandfathered in. And even if he hadn't been, who would have stopped him? The grips were a cheap investment, a subtle detail that added credibility to the tale. The truth is, he liked the older guns because they were reliable. Take care of them, and they will take care of you. He carried two spare eight-round magazines for the Colt and six in the cylinder of the revolver. All told, he had thirty rounds on him while on duty. It was less ammunition than the modern polymer pistols afforded, but one thing he learned early on was that the guys who were quick to draw their guns were policing incorrectly. Besides, if it really came down to it, thirty rounds would be enough. He was a crack shot and figured if he couldn't hit the bad guy after thirty shots, it would be time to hand in his badge.

He wasn't thinking about any of that, though, as he walked up to the crime scene. His focus was taking in every detail around him.

As he strolled under the yellow police barrier, the young officer holding up the tape gave an awkward nod before his eyes darted away back toward the crowd.

He's heard of me, McCauley thought, chuckling to himself. *At least he made eye contact. Most of 'em don't even do that.*

CHAPTER FOUR

The sun was beginning to set, leaving only thirty more minutes of daylight. Sensing the impending darkness, the street light's sensor fired an electrical signal to the bulb, which was met with a distinctly audible click. The bulb began to glow, growing brighter until it finally cast a perfect spotlight directly over the body of Melvin Jackson.

McCauley approached the remains to find a young man in an expensive gray pinstripe suit and freshly polished brown oxfords squatting over Mr. Jackson, trying to view the wound at different angles without touching him. He clutched a notepad in his gloved right hand and had a cheap blue pen behind tucked behind his ear.

"Detective Davis," McCauley stated, alerting the young man to his presence. "Anthony, you wear a thousand-dollar suit and three-hundred-dollar shoes to a murder scene but bring a Bic pen? Where's your Montblanc?"

Davis stood to meet McCauley at eye level. "Thanks for the compliment, Pat. I see that none of my style tips have rubbed off on you yet. Let me guess. Your suit is from Macy's? Or perhaps something a little seedier. Is it off the sale rack at Penny's? Don't tell me—I'll figure it out before we're done here. Either way, I recommend picking up an iron. Nothing ruins a cheap suit faster than a wrinkle."

McCauley chuckled at the quip. Few dared to give McCauley guff, but Davis was a sharp young detective who was confident in his abilities. He had only been assigned to the squad for a few months, but already McCauley took a liking to him, a rare feat for a guy who usually preferred working alone. His skill and direct nature reminded McCauley of his younger self, and so he naturally began to take him under his wing.

"The victim's name is—" Davis began.

"No, no, don't tell me yet," McCauley interrupted.

"Right, take in the scene first, then look at the victim. Keeps the scene fresh without any judgment."

"Excellent, you are learning well, young man. I see the wound, pretty good shot. Shell casings?"

"Haven't found any yet."

"Bullet holes from misses?"

"None, just the wound on the vic, directly between the eyes. And no powder burns, so it couldn't have been that close. Also, judging by the size of the entry wound and what I can tell about the exit wound without having moved him yet, it's a large-caliber round. Could be a rifle."

McCauley thought for a minute. A shooting scene was rarely this clean. Many were crimes of rage or opportunity. Shooters didn't stick around to "police their brass," a gun range term referring to picking up one's shell casings—they were too busy fleeing. Even rarer was a one-shot kill that wasn't some sort of execution. Most shooters missed, and missed a lot for every hit they scored on a target. A robbery wasn't out of the question, but the man still had what appeared to be a very expensive diamond-encrusted gold watch on his wrist. Maybe he refused to give it up, the perp walked away, changed his mind, turned, and shot him. It could explain the lack of powder burns and the accurate shot. Far enough not to leave any burns, but close enough for a one-shot kill. Still, the shooter would go back for that watch; it had to be worth at least $10,000 if it wasn't a fake. That theory didn't quite add up.

"The shot definitely came from the south." McCauley turned and faced away from Jackson and pointed his arms out straight, indicating the path of a bullet. "If it is a rifle, it's a perfect shot, right in the T-zone."

"T-zone?" Davis asked.

"The spot that forms the cross of a T from eye socket to eye socket and running down the bridge of the nose. The bullet severs the spinal cord and is instantly fatal."

McCauley had never been in the army. He was hired on the police department right out of college. A group of his friends did join up out of high school, and he had picked up all sorts of army slang on boozy reunions when they'd come back to visit.

"Let's roll him."

Davis stiffened his torso to object.

"I know, I know, but we're losing the light. Let's do it quickly and see if we can garner anything from the exit wound. If there's a round that's not in there, I want our guys to be able to find it tonight."

Davis nodded and took up position, placing his hands over the dead man's ears to stabilize his head. McCauley got on one knee, and together they rolled the man slowly a few inches off the ground. McCauley put his face near the cement to check the back of victim's head.

"Okay, that's good. Let's set him down," McCauley said, carefully returning the man to his back.

"What did you see?"

"Well, I think you're right. Definitely a large caliber and a down angle on the exit wound. Meaning—"

"Meaning it was fired from an elevated position!" Davis was getting excited now, like he was putting his training to good use.

"Or?" McCauley prompted. Despite agreeing with the young detective, McCauley wanted him to explore all options.

"Well, an elevated position if it was a rifle...a handgun would likely mean a tall suspect."

"Right, and this guy must be six foot four. When we rolled him I could see some fragments but nothing substantial. That round is down the street. Let's get some officers to canvass the area one block north of the body. If they don't find anything, have them push toward the next. Call for a wrecker. I want those parked cars moved one at a time in case it's under one. Then bring them to the high school parking lot around the corner. We'll have to go over every inch and see if it didn't get lodged in a door."

McCauley stood and pointed in the opposite direction.

"I'm going to check down the block this way. If we confirm a rifle round, this scene will have a whole different dynamic. I want to start searching for where it may have come from."

"Guess it's going to be a long one."

"Yep, get used to it."

CHAPTER FIVE

Chicago's business district is home to many multinational corporations. Nestled between the winding river to the north and
west sides and Lake Michigan to the east, it's been the center
of the city for the past hundred years. It's known as the Loop
for the fact that it's surrounded by the Chicago train system,
which runs a ring around the district on all sides. Chicago's transit revolves around the elevated train, or the El, as Chicagoans
fondly refer to it, in a hub-and-spoke system that fans out in
all directions save for east into the lake. Nearly twenty-four
hours a day, silver electric trains dutifully shuttle passengers to
and from the outskirts of the city. During the morning rush the
trains draw people into the downtown to start their workday,
then travel around the Loop before sling-shotting like an Apollo
space capsule on a return vector back to the start of their re-
spective spoke.

She had visited the Pennington Corporation many times
before. Named for the founding family that still owned the bulk
of the now publicly traded company, it was known as one of the
preeminent hotel chains in the world. The family diversified
into dozens of ancillary businesses, including laundry services,
catering, food delivery, and restaurants, but most of them were
centered around the crown jewel of their portfolio—the hotels.

This afternoon Naomi Archer was walking into the heart
of the Loop from her firm's plush offices in River North. It only
took her fifteen minutes to walk to the front of a twenty-five-
story all-white building with art deco trim located at Clark and
Adams.

She had visited the Pennington Corporation many times
before. Named for the founding family that still owned the bulk
of the now publicly traded company, it was known as one of the
preeminent hotel chains in the world. The family diversified
into dozens of ancillary businesses, including laundry services,
catering, food delivery, and restaurants, but most of them were
centered around the crown jewel of their portfolio—the hotels.

The Pennington Corporation had been a client of Sloan MacIntyre for years. As a Chicago-based law firm, it was well positioned to secure Pennington's business, as the family had a reputation for supporting Chicago-based businesses.

Sloan Mac had handled many types of matters for them, from contract work to litigation, and even helped with the family's very generous mission of philanthropy.

Most of the work, however, centered around the hotels. With over four thousand locations in a hundred different countries, there was no shortage of matters for the firm. Naomi arrived at the offices to discuss a potentially sensitive one.

It was getting to the end of the work day, but she phoned ahead to Pennington's general counsel, Richard Eisner and let him know that she'd be coming over with an important update.

After lobby security cleared her to enter, the guard called upstairs and alerted the legal team of her arrival.

When the doors opened, a gust of air trailing the elevator up from the shaft blew through the cracks. As Naomi stepped off, the invisible draft pushed her unbuttoned suit jacket open, revealing a white silken blouse tucked neatly into her matching knee-length skirt. Naomi dressed well. Even on jeans Friday she looked the part of a high-profile lawyer. Just because she had to dress like a lawyer, though, didn't mean she couldn't look good. When she made partner she sprung for custom-fitted suits and skirts from the firm's unofficial tailor. The tailor was a nice older woman who lived just over the border of Chicago in Indiana but often traveled downtown for in-office fittings. She outfitted Naomi with an entire wardrobe that looked utterly professional but with enough style to let her stunning beauty shine through. Her body was a tailor's dream, perfect in every way. A more difficult task would have been successfully hiding it.

Richard Eisner was waiting at the elevator banks flanked by a man and a woman. The man's jaw dropped a little when he saw Naomi. Her heels clicked on the white marble floors as she walked toward them.

"Richard, thanks for staying late to meet me," she said, extending her hand.

"Thanks for getting back to us so quickly. I have to be honest—I didn't think you'd have something for us so soon." Richard gestured to his colleagues. "These are two attorneys on our team that are assisting us, Matt Epstein, whom I believe you spoke with on the phone, and Vanessa Dawes."

Matt shook Naomi's hand. "Nice to see your face, er, put a face to the voice, I mean."

Vanessa rolled her eyes at the awkward introduction, then took her turn assertively shaking hands. "Nice to meet you as well. I've heard many wonderful things."

"Thank you, it's a pleasure to meet you too."

Richard reserved a conference room with clean windows and stunning city vistas. The lake views had long since been obscured by a tapestry of skyscrapers, but it was impressive nonetheless.

All three took their seats around a shiny oak table that filled most of the room.

"It's getting late, and I don't want to keep you too long," Naomi began, "so I'll cut to the chase."

"I expect nothing less," Rich responded.

"First, let's start with what we know. Three days ago one your employees in accounting brought to light a potential embezzlement scheme that is being perpetrated against the hotel subsidiary, Pennington Hotels Corp. After you looked into it for a day or so and found merit for a further investigation, you enlisted Sloan Mac to take a deeper dive. Given the scope of the allegations, I've been working on nothing else, first verifying that a crime has been committed, and then if I could confirm it, who was committing it and to what extent."

"And?"

"Well, it's a good-news-bad-news type of conversation. The bad news is you most definitely have a leak."

"How much?" Rich was leaning forward in his seat.

"Manageable. It's just shy of a million dollars. Precisely

$952,353."

"Oh, good. We can handle that kind of number." Richard was already thinking of the positive reaction of the management team. For a multibillion-dollar company, this would barely register a footnote on the filing forms. "And do you know who is behind it?"

"Well, again, it's good news and bad news. The bad news is, no, I don't. The person was very cautious and covered their tracks well. It's not to say that this person didn't make a mistake, but so far, finding them has proven to be...challenging." Naomi was an expert at parsing her words. As a lawyer, she knew never to deal in absolutes.

"So what's the good news?"

Naomi was beaming ear to ear now. "I have an idea on how to find him."

Richard Eisner looked perplexed. On paper it could work, but he was far from convinced.

"Naomi, you know we have absolute faith in your work. You've always been an exemplary attorney, so forgive me for what I'm about to say. Are you nuts? You want us to cut the embezzler another check?"

"Just once more."

Naomi could hardly contain her excitement. She loved these types of cases. That's not to say she didn't enjoy arguing in a courtroom, but investigations spoke to her core. As a product of the '90s she was enthralled with the notion becoming an FBI agent in her teen years. She was an avid fan of *The X-Files*, a show about two FBI agents paired up to investigate the paranormal. Fox Mulder was the believer of the duo, but Naomi connected more with Dana Scully, the doctor who took the approach that everything has a rational explanation. In fairness, Naomi wasn't so straitlaced that she didn't get a kick out of the monster-of-the-week story lines, but Scully set off her desire to join the FBI during her impressionable teen years. When she saw Clarice Starling track down a serial killer in *The Silence of the Lambs* for the first time, it only reinforced the dream.

She was so enthralled with the idea that while her friends were going to summer camp to water-ski and roast marshmallows over campfires, she was running PT drills and shooting guns at the Michigan State Police Youth Explorer Camp. It wasn't easy to get her mother and father to agree to send her. Her parents were educators and reasonably conservative. They had met at work, her father the superintendent and her mother a teacher. Initially they weren't too keen on their little girl training with a department that has a reputation for being a paramilitary organization. Her father gave in quickly, but her mother took some convincing. Naomi left brochures around the house just to spark up a point-counterpoint-type debate. She was always far more rational in her arguments than one would expect of a teenager. Eventually her mother relented, mostly because she was tired of debating it, but also because she figured if Naomi was persistent enough to take it this far, a reward of sorts was in order.

Of course, fancy gives way to life, and Naomi's path changed. She was accepted into the University of Michigan and eventually enrolled in the business school. The job market had soured while she was in school, and the practical advice of her parents told her that the b-school was the best route for a steady job. After graduating at the top of her class, she earned that steady job at Chrysler in the labor relations department.

She liked it well enough, but it wasn't as fulfilling as she had hoped. Her coworkers all shared the same goal—a role in middle management. A good salary with good benefits, but not much else. A job that is designed to keep the machine running, not to reinvent it. That just wasn't for Naomi.

By then the dream of the FBI had long since passed, filed

safely away in the corner of her mind labeled "remember when?" It wasn't a shock when she decided to apply to law school. It was a logical step for someone with her background, skill, and general interests. She aced the LSAT, which was necessary because Michigan Law rarely took Michigan undergrads, as a means of diversifying the background of their student base. Naomi was one of the few exceptions.

Like a movie script of her life, everything went according to plan. She graduated with honors and was offered a job at a prominent Chicago law firm, where she rose up the ladder to become one of the few female partners in Big Law.

Still, these investigations that required all her business and legal training sometimes reminded her of her first passion. Sitting in the impeccably decorated conference room, she felt well prepared for the pitch she was about to give.

Naomi had already had this conversation with herself a half a dozen times. Persuading the client to pay the embezzler was clearly going to be met with resistance.

"Here are the options," she began, counting on her fingers. "One, we go to the attorney general. We hand over our evidence and, with it, control of the case. We hope their investigators can find the perpetrator. They are capable, but they move slowly. In the meantime, you will have an embezzler sitting in your employ potentially cooking up another scheme. Best-case scenario, it takes months; worst case, they never find him."

"It's definitely the safer option," Matt chimed in from the cheap seats.

"It's safe if your goal is to keep your job. It will also safely inhibit you from doing that job, which is to find the perpetrator and stop him from causing further damage to your shareholders." Naomi was glad Matt said it. It afforded her the opportunity to remind everyone of their duty without challenging Rich directly.

Matt's brow furrowed at the shaming, and he slumped back in his chair.

"My proposal is low risk, minimal cost, and has a reasonable chance of success."

Rich took the lead again. "You've identified the department, so why don't we just go in there and sweat the weakest performers? It's got to be one of them."

"Not in this case. Most embezzlement schemes are unsophisticated. Embezzlers aren't always particularly smart—they just stumble upon a loophole in the system and exploit it. For instance, maybe they find out how to reimburse themselves for fake travel expenses. Also, they are usually the instrument of their own demise. They start small, then get bigger and bigger until finally someone notices."

"How do you know it's not the same in this case?" questioned Rich.

"This is more than a loophole that this guy stumbled on. He created it. He's submitting forged invoices from bona fide vendors. Like this one here for Sunshine Cleaning Supplies."

Naomi pulled two seemingly identical invoices from a folder and placed them in front of Rich, who was sitting at the head of the table. She stood to his right and tilted her head to read papers lying on the table. As she did a lock of her flowing brunette hair dangled in front of her eye. Matt suddenly became interested again.

"Notice the difference?"

Rich eyed the documents for a minute, then threw his hands up in surrender.

"The PO boxes. This forged invoice is exactly the same down to the paper it's printed on, except one number. PO Box 78132 on the original, 78122 on the forged copy. The perpetrator identified a weakness—that for a multibillion-dollar corporation, your accounts payable division is woefully out of date."

Rich looked up, a little irked.

"Sorry. What I mean is that you have all business-to-business transactions at the local level verified, paid, and entered into a computer by hand by one person. That one person is literally writing and logging hundreds of checks a week, and one number would be easy to slip by."

"So it's the check writer?" Vanessa asked.

"You mean Karen Day." Naomi pulled out Karen's employee file and set it on the table. She opened the manila envelope and revealed a photograph of a woman in her sixties paper clipped to the top. "By all accounts she was an exemplary employee. It's not her."

"Was?" Vanessa was now fully engaged.

"She retired two months ago. But before she retired, she accidentally processed hundreds of checks for nominal amounts—nothing over three thousand dollars, but all made out to the Sunshine Cleaning Supplies Company, PO Box 78122. In fact, her replacement, Karen Wall, may be the only reason you were able to uncover it. Karen never noticed the difference in numbers due to the volume of checks she processed on a daily basis. In order to process the tens of thousands of checks over the course of a career, maybe even hundreds of thousands, she needed a routine—one that would allow her to work swiftly but that happened to be prone to error. The fact that she was so proficient at her job was actually a weakness in the system."

Naomi took another employee file out, this time with a photo of a young woman who looked barely old enough to drink.

"Her replacement, on the other hand, isn't as proficient, or at least not yet. Karen Wall is much slower, someone who's been doing this job for two months, not twenty-five years. Like any new employee who wants to impress, she's diligent. It's her fear of making a mistake that alerted her to the discrepancy. She's poring over each number for accuracy to make sure nothing comes back in error. When she showed the head of her department"—Naomi looked down at her list of employees—"a Charles McGill, she thought it was just a typo, a minor error in need of correction."

Rich chimed in, "Look, I know Charles, he's the one that brought it to us. If you're about to say he's involved, you better have something concrete."

"He's not. I already ruled him out. Don't get me wrong—he fits the profile to a T, but he hasn't been head of the department long enough. Plus, typically when someone gets a promotion like that, the embezzlement stops. The embezzler feels appreciated, sometimes bad that they did it, and at the very least, they have more to lose."

Matt chimed back in, "So what's the profile, then, for this sort of thing? You said it's not an underperformer, you said they're smart, but don't high achievers have a lot to lose?"

"That's exactly right," Naomi said, watching a coy smile of redemption come over Matt's face. "We are looking for someone with above-average intelligence but is by no means a high achiever. Probably someone in a role that he'll always excel at but never advance."

"There are thirty people in the department that fit that description. They're not exactly doing rocket science down there," Rich said, still unconvinced. "So, is that it?"

"No, there's more. We know this person has been here for at least five years, which is the start of the first invoices. We know this person has knowledge of budgets for multiple local vendors. Sunshine Cleaning is just one. Each time you are under budget for some service, the perpetrator submits a check for the difference, less a thousand or so dollars. Like this one for Dazzle Window Cleaning."

A new invoice came out on the table.

"Your monthly budget is $17,500, but in May you only spent $12,230. A forged invoice was submitted for $4,132, keeping that line item conspicuously under budget. Sunshine, Dazzle, Gourmet Galleries, and Lincoln Audio-Video all have forged invoices. When we narrow it down to those in purchasing who has access to the budgets and invoices of these companies, someone who's been here for five years and is smart but also an underachiever, we get three names."

Naomi placed three more employee files on the table, two men and a woman.

"I can't rule any of them out for certain, but I don't think it's Amelia here—she was on maternity leave several years ago, and during that time, multiple invoices were filed. She still could be part of it, but I think it's unlikely."

Vanessa read the names of two men: "Robert Chadwick and Akash Gahlot."

Both were stocky middle-aged men. The word *unassuming* would be too descriptive an adjective to characterize them.

"Wait, why can't we just trace the PO boxes?" Rich asked.

"Because they don't exist." Naomi had to refrain from smiling; she was impressed with the scheme. "Well, not all of them."

Matt's head was starting to spin. "I thought you said—"

Before he could finish, Naomi continued.

"You can't just pick the PO box number you want. At least, there's no guarantee. For three of the four companies, their PO box is located at a private mail business, not the post office. Mailboxes and More on Clark and Huron hosts all of them except Sunshine."

There was a fifth company, but Naomi wasn't going to mention that just yet. It didn't have the same MO as the others. Could be the embezzler was testing a new scheme, could be something totally different. She had enough to go on for now, though, so no sense worrying the client until there was definitely a problem.

Rich was putting it together. "Take us home, Naomi."

"Sunshine was the first fraudulent invoice we saw five years ago. I think Mr. Chadwick or Mr. Gahlot thought up the scheme and was somehow able to secure that PO box, which is located at the main postal branch a block from here. He did it smartly too—it's registered to a corporation in Antigua. In trying to trace the owner, I got nothing but red tape and dead ends."

Vanessa was getting it too. "A crime of opportunity."

"Yes. He had probably fantasized about doing it hundreds of times, then after a bad day, perhaps, he walked to the post office and checked to see if any boxes with a close number were available. When it was, he took it, maybe even just as a joke at first, but eventually worked up the courage to try his scheme. And after a year of successful submissions, he realized he was sitting on a gold mine. Sunshine was certainly lucrative, but when compared to the other targeted companies, it's small potatoes, by far the smallest monthly budget. So he decided to curate a list of better companies to target."

"Then he got greedy," Matt said.

"He started manufacturing his own opportunity. I'm not sure if there's an accomplice at Mailboxes and More or if he slipped the manager some cash to put the envelopes to the side. I found no connection—no siblings or ex-girlfriends with an employment history there to connect either man to it, so I suspect it's the latter."

"Okay, Naomi," Rich said, "you've sold us. This is fine work. So what do you propose we do now?"

"Catch the bastard with his hand in the cookie jar."

CHAPTER SIX

McCauley walked back to the crime scene. His search down the block turned up nothing. Most of the doors to the businesses in the dually zoned neighborhood were locked. A dry cleaner, which was the only one still open, didn't know how to get access to the roof and hadn't heard any shots. To get to the roof, McCauley would need to ask the residents of the three floors above, but none of them were answering their buzzers.

There's no telling where the round came from. At least they had confirmed it came from a rifle now. Davis texted him that they'd found the bullet under one of the cars they had towed. That part was fortunate. Davis identified it as a larger round, probably a .308, but the soft-point tip had expanded when it hit the victim. The mushrooming would make it difficult to get any usable evidence from it.

McCauley arranged for some recruits from the academy to come back down and canvass the rooftops in the morning, although he wasn't holding out hope the search would produce anything. They'd have to get lucky on which roof it came from, find a shell casing if the killer didn't pick it up, then hope for an identifying mark—best case would be a usable fingerprint. It was a long shot at best. A perfect shot, probably silenced, from a perch two blocks away, using a scope and high-end ammunition. McCauley was sure the killer covered his tracks well.

If they were going to solve it, they were going to have to go through the victim.

A sheet now covered the body, shielding the violence from the news cameras that were lined up and filming the scene from behind the police tape.

McCauley approached Detective Davis searching through the victim's belongings scattered on the hood of the Range Rover. "You have his address yet? He's got a zoned parking sticker for the neighborhood, so it's gotta be close."

"He got a good parking spot, two doors down, and I've got the keys. You ready to take a peek inside?"

"Yep, we may as well. Not sure how much more we'll get out here unless the uniforms get lucky with a witness."

They approached the door, where McCauley and Davis shared a look of suspicion over the beefed-up security on the front door.

"You think there's an alarm?" Davis asked before turning the key.

"I doubt it. Professional hit, three high-end locks on the front door in this neighborhood. This guy was nervous about security, and now we know for good reason. I'm sure there's a security system, but I doubt it goes to an alarm company."

Satisfied, Davis pushed the door open and cautiously entered. McCauley was right. A black semicircle hung in the foyer, masking the faint red glow of a recording camera, but there was no chiming of an alarm warning the homeowner to key in a code. Aside from a slight whirring of the camera panning, the house was dark and quiet.

Both men instinctively drew their guns and announced themselves but only got echoes in response. Their voices bounced off the bare white walls and newly refinished hardwood floors for a few moments before the house went silent again. They pushed forward into the living room to find moving boxes stacked up neatly in the corner. In the center of the otherwise unfurnished room sat a small black leather couch facing large flat-screen television mounted in the corner.

"Glad he had priorities," Davis quipped.

In the kitchen they found more of the same. Except for a small stack of silverware, the drawers and cupboards were totally bare.

They methodically went room to room on the cursory sweep of the house. When they were confident it was empty, they holstered their weapons.

Back in the living room, McCauley sifted through a stack of mail sitting on one of the moving boxes and found an envelope from DirecTV. He tore it open and examined it before declaring, "At the least the search will be quick. According to the bill, this guy's been here almost a year. I was worried we'd have to go search his old house too. Slow mover, I guess."

"Maybe he got it set up early," Davis countered.

"Not likely. This place is immaculate. Definitely a gut rehab. Electricity, water, gas, I'd agree. People wait until they move in to get their TV set up, especially with a premium package like this. No sense in wasting a bunch of money on a service that won't get used. Still, go ahead and check last known addresses just in case. In the meantime, let's start our search. Given the lack of belongings in here, it won't take long."

The pair agreed to start downstairs and work their way up through the house. The basement was seemingly as empty as the rest of the house. It was a nicely finished lower level complete with a wet bar and built-in fireplace. Down a small hallway through the shotgun-style house that was typical of Chicago homes, a door lead to a utility area. It was spacious and complete with a furnace, water heater, washer, dryer, and sink.

Davis took a cursory look and turned to exit, having dismissed any value in any further search of the room. McCauley stood in the doorway deep in thought. His eyes squinted, and he pressed an index finger across his pursed lips.

Something was wrong with this room. For a utility room, it was eerily quiet. No hissing of gas or clicking of the central air. It was as silent as the rest of the house.

"You see something, Pat?" Davis asked, searching the room for whatever was giving McCauley hesitation.

"That," McCauley said, pointing at a gray box mounted to the cinder block, copper piping jetting out of it.

"What is it?"

"It's unnecessary. Or at the very least, this is," McCauley said, approaching the water heater.

"So it's some sort of utility box. What's the big deal?" Davis said, his interest piqued.

"That is a tankless system. It flash heats the water directly in the line, so you never run out of hot water. The guys that installed that would have most certainly taken this," McCauley slapped the old water heater for emphasis. The sound of his wedding ring clanked on the exterior, then reverberated around the interior, revealing it to be empty like the rest of the house.

"Maybe the workmen forgot to take it with them when they installed the new one." Davis almost instantly regretted the comment.

"Anthony, think for a minute," McCauley started, with a hint of disappointment in his voice. "We have what looks to be a professional hit. High-end security in an occupied but empty million-dollar row home. Not just that, a professionally re-habbed million-dollar row home. The people that do this sort of work don't just forget to take an eighty-gallon tank with them on their way out the door. Get my toolbox."

No one would describe McCauley as handy, but it only took him a few minutes to figure out how to pry the top off the all-white tank with the tools Anthony had fetched from the trunk of his police cruiser.

He stood on the top rung of a step ladder that was tucked away in the corner and used his flashlight to light up the interior of the musty tank.

"Bingo!" McCauley said, gesturing to Anthony to move closer. "Grab my legs. There's something at the bottom."

McCauley stretched as far as his arms would go, just barely grabbing a dark plastic garbage bag by his fingertips. Anthony pulled him back, and they set the mysterious package on the floor in front of them.

They tore the outer bag open, revealing the hidden treasure's secret. Two million dollars sat before them, neatly bundled and wrapped in individual vacuum-sealed bags.

"Okay, Anthony. Now, I want to know. Who is this guy?"

CHAPTER SEVEN

Naomi was sitting in her office waiting for the phone to ring. The plan was simple enough. Mr. Chadwick or Mr. Gahlot would certainly be wondering where his check was by now. No invoices had been paid for the past three days as a precaution, which would arouse suspicion. To allay fears of the plot having been uncovered, Naomi manufactured a very public oversight on the part of Karen's replacement, Karen Wall.

That morning the attorneys summoned Karen and her boss, Chuck, to the Sloan Mac offices to talk out of view. They were informed of the plot, and much to Naomi's delight, they were eager to help. All that was needed was a plausible reason for the delay. Turning Karen into a public patsy was the perfect plan. Everyone loves a patsy, plus it kept the rouse contained to just a few people and was utterly believable.

Chuck, who was a mild-tempered man at heart, dug deep and remembered his role as Captain Hook in his junior high school production of *Peter Pan*. He was perfect.

Back at Karen's desk, he tore into her loud enough for everyone to hear but restrained just enough to make it look like he didn't want them to. The nervous eyes of onlookers darted across cubicles at one another. A few people pretended to be on phone calls, but no one dared to look directly at the unbridled reprimanding that was unfolding before them.

Karen, for her part, did well. She was apologetic. Her face displayed fear of firing. The same emotion she had felt her first few months on the job had been summoned for release through her watering eyes.

By the end of the production, the message was clear. Misplacing a stack of invoices like that again would come with dire consequences. She was ordered to cut every one of the checks promptly and have them couriered to their destination with the Pennington Corporation's sincerest apologies for the delay.

The trap was set with an irresistible morsel. Naomi just needed her prey to take the bait.

CHAPTER EIGHT

Two men sat in a black Lincoln town car parked in a delivery zone across the street from the post office. In Chicago, that would usually earn you a big fat ticket, but the older of the two men had already cleared it with the police sergeant on duty. They didn't know each other, but after explaining the situation, the sergeant had no problem with it. A stakeout was as good as any reason to let the men park there. Plus, cops do favors for ex-cops; that's the rule.

Both Pennington Corporation security officers donned black suits and aviator sunglasses. Neither spoke as they observed the exterior of the post office. In the passenger's seat, the younger of the two, who was in his late twenties, fidgeted with a Cannon EOS rebel outfitted with a telephoto lens. Two pictures were taped to the dash, one of Robert Chadwick and the other of Akash Gahlot.

The orders were clear: observe and report only. Take photos of the subject entering and exiting. If they could observe anything that was transpiring inside, even better, but under no circumstances were they to engage him.

A stocky man of Indian descent wearing business-casual attire started down the street. The older man raised his forefinger to point him out, still gripping the steering wheel of the parked car. With his left hand he reached for the handle and cracked the driver's side door.

"Wait," the younger man said, with the viewfinder of the camera up to his eye, spinning the picture into focus. "It's not him."

"You're sure? Look again."

"I can see a pimple on the bridge of his nose with this thing. I'm telling you it's not him."

Annoyed, the older man shut the door and settled back in.

Still looking through the camera the younger man said, "So why can't we grab this guy once he has the check?"

"I told you, the lawyer lady said we are not to touch him. It's illegal to detain him, and she doesn't need us to. We let him walk tonight. Tomorrow he shows up for work, then we talk to him. He comes in of his own free will."

"So it's illegal for us to grab him for stealing our money?"

"Yep, that's about the size of it."

"Great, so in the meantime he gets to go to Gibson's on our dime," said the younger man, referring to the famous Chicago steakhouse.

"It's not your dime, it's not my dime. Just shut up and let me know when you see the guy."

"Yeah, well, I'm not sure how I'm supposed to photograph anything from here. Forget the inside of that place; it's built like a fortress. It may be glass windows and all, but it's a maze in there. I'm not going to get anything of value."

"That's why you're staying in the car, and I'm going in," the older man said, with frustration at repeating the plan for the third time.

"Yeah, well, that ain't exactly a piece of cake either. It's rush hour, there are buses, trucks, vans, you name it, a hundred things that can block my view," the younger man continued to gripe.

"Then you get out of the car if that happens and go down the block. Just don't get made. We need that photo."

Just then, Robert Chadwick turned the corner. Dressed in a plain blue button-down shirt, khaki pants, and tennis shoes for his daily walking commute.

The younger man started to get excited. "Hey, I think I got him."

"Yep, I see him. Okay, start taking pictures, and as soon as he passes the UPS truck, I'm going to get out and follow him in."

The older man exited the vehicle and crossed the street falling into place fifty yards behind Robert. He followed through the revolving doors into the post office, where number two lost sight of him.

The younger man was cursing under his breath at the traffic; he didn't have a clean photo yet of the suspect. Minutes ticked by, and he started to get nervous. How long could it possibly take to pick up a letter from a post office box? He scanned the doors, looking for him, when he glimpsed his partner frantically waving his hands.

How did I miss them coming out, he thought to himself.

As the wheels were turning in his mind, the older security man finally screamed in desperation, "He's out the side exit over here!"

"Dammit!" younger man exclaimed, hopping over the console to the driver's seat. "I told him that thing is a maze."

He threw the car in gear and peeled toward the older man, who quickly entered the passenger side.

"I've got nothing. Were you able to get any photos?"

"Photos? Of what? He never came out the front. You said that side door is locked for security."

"It was supposed to be!" the older man said defensively.

"Yeah, well, maybe you got made."

"Shut up and pull over next to him."

"What? I thought the lawyer said not to grab him."

The older man was out of options, and he wasn't going back empty-handed. "I don't care what the lawyer says. He's not getting away."

They pulled over, and the older man walked around the car to step in front of Robert. The younger man got out as well but stood next to the car.

"Mr. Chadwick," the older man said. "We work for Pennington Security. Please come with us, sir."

The younger man opened the back seat door on cue as Robert Chadwick scrutinized the men standing in front of him.

The older man had been a cop long enough to see the shifting eyes of someone who was sizing up the option to run and shut it down quickly. "Running would be a big mistake at this juncture, Mr. Chadwick. We're just here to clear a few things up, and you'll be home before you know it."

Either out of fear or resignation, Robert Chadwick slowly moved toward the car and sat down in the back seat. The younger man ran around the back of the car and slipped into the spot next to him while the older man retook his spot in the driver's seat. They made their way into traffic back toward Pennington's corporate offices.

CHAPTER NINE

Naomi arrived at the Pennington offices to a chaotic scene. Robert Chadwick was sitting in a conference room with a uniformed security officer standing guard. Down the hall she marched into Rich Eisner's office, where he was letting the two-man security team have it.

They were both tall and reasonably fit men. The younger one looked ex-military with a closely cropped haircut, and the older one had the demeanor of an ex-cop. He reminded her of her days working at Chrysler. Just in case a disgruntled employee decided to get aggressive with her, the company had protocols in place. One of those was stationing two ex-Michigan state troopers down the hall from her in a cramped office. She had a panic button under her desk that went directly to them if she found herself in trouble. Fortunately, she never had an occasion to use it. In fact, the only time she ever pressed it was when she bumped it with her knee by accident. The two officers must have covered the two-hundred-foot hallway located in the back of the stamping plant in ten seconds flat. They arrived winded and with a refrained look of disappointment to find it was a false alarm. She felt bad for inconveniencing them, but she was happy to know they were there.

The fact that Mr. Chadwick was here meant these two had some explaining to do, and fortunately Rich was handling that. Despite her direct nature and sometimes quick temper, Naomi didn't love this sort of confrontation.

"Oh, good, Miss Archer is here. Now you two clowns can explain to her how you abducted an employee who, for all we know, was just visiting the post office. You could have blown the whole investigation!"

The older security officer cleared his throat to speak. "Again, I'm sorry, sir, but the situation changed, and we had to make a decision."

Rich jetted in, "The situation changed, as in you failed to take a couple of simple photos. My teenage daughters could have done it with their iPhones. I should have asked them to do it!"

The older man was at maximum deference without admitting fault. "Well, it's like I said, the streets were crowded—it was rush hour. We observed Mr. Chadwick entering the post office. I followed him in but lost him in the stacks of PO boxes. Also, he exited a door that was roped off and supposed to be sealed for security."

"Because someone embezzling a million dollars is going to be deterred by a retractable stanchion?"

"What do you want from us?" younger man brazenly interjected. "We would have lost him. He had the check, and now we've got him and the check."

The older man shot his young partner a look as though he had casually flipped open the door to a caged tiger that he'd spent the past hour trying to wrangle inside.

Rich's eyes lit up with anger, but fortunately for the younger man, Naomi jumped in. "So you verified he has the check?"

The younger man, realizing the near disaster of his last comment and still keeping one eye on Rich, turned to Naomi and said in his most respectful voice, "Yes, ma'am, he sure does. Look, we didn't mean for it to go down this way, but we did what we thought was right, and now we've got him."

Rich pointed toward the door. "Okay, that's enough, you two. We'll talk later about this."

The two men exited the room and walked toward the elevator banks.

With a hand grabbing the hair on the back of his head,

Rich said, "Well, what do you think we should do now?"

"You've got him here, so any potential damage is already done. We may as well talk to him," said Naomi.

"Okay, let's go."

CHAPTER TEN

Robert Chadwick sat in the same conference room that the lawyers met in earlier, his thinning brown hair fluttering in the draft of the air conditioning vent above him. Robert had a calm look about him, too calm for a man who had just been caught embezzling a small fortune. He sat upright, facing the table with his hands folded neatly in his lap. Perhaps he was a man who believed he could still get away with it; the corners of his mouth were turned ever so slightly skyward, forming a nearly imperceptible smile.

Rich and Naomi walked past the uniformed security guard and entered the room through the glass door. They took seats across the table from Robert.

"Mr. Chadwick, my name is Richard Eisner. I'm the general counsel here at Pennington."

Robert was silent, but he knew who Mr. Eisner was. He was more curious about the beautiful woman sitting next to him.

"I am Naomi Archer from the law firm of Sloan MacIntyre."

Outside counsel, he thought. *Should have guessed it.*

"First off," Naomi continued, "We'd like to make sure you are aware that we do not represent you. We represent the Pennington Corporation, and you are not required to be here. If you stay, it's completely voluntary. Do you understand those two points?"

"I do."

"And do you wish to speak to us?"

"For now, I guess."

Naomi had her answer. She knew that once she started, he was not likely to leave. He'd be looking for any way to avoid the police, and walking out was a surefire bet that the matter would go directly to them. She began with some pedigree information. Simple questions, ones easily answered by his file, but it was important to get him talking truthfully.

"How long have you been an employee at the Pennington Corporation?"

"Fourteen years."

"Has the entirety of that time been spent in the purchasing department?"

"Mostly. I actually started in sales. You know, trying to book large parties, signing up business accounts, that sort of thing."

"So when did you transfer to purchasing?"

"I'd say after about two years. So I guess I've been in purchasing for the last twelve."

Rich wasn't shocked that Robert didn't make it in sales. He had an awkward demeanor about him. Nothing too off-putting, but enough that it would be a liability as a salesman.

Naomi continued asking him about his average workday. Where did he sit in the office, which coworkers did he interact with the most, etc. When she felt that he was speaking freely, she started to probe deeper.

"Mr. Chadwick, how much do you know about the Sunshine Cleaning Supplies Company?"

"I know they provide the downtown Chicago hotels with cleaning supplies."

"And are they a big company? A small one?"

"A small one, I think. Honestly, I'd have thought we'd use a larger distributor given the size of our organization."

Rich responded, "The downtown hotels have done business with Sunshine for over fifty years. The Pennington family is fiercely loyal when it comes to businesses that continue to deliver, as they have."

It was a well-placed comment that highlighted a mom-and-pop shop as one of the victims. It put a face to the crime.

Naomi sensed hesitancy rising up within Robert. Obviously he knew far more about the company than he led on. She could full-court press, but that could potentially end his cooperation. There was another option. Offer him a truth as an olive branch. Give her confidence to him so that he would hopefully give his to her in return.

"Robert, we obviously know about the check."

"Oh, that? I think this is a big misunderstanding. That check isn't what you—"

Naomi held her hand up. "Robert, we know about the check because you had it on you. We also found the invoices—all of them."

Robert started to get nervous. It was no longer just the $2,200 check in his pocket. A minute ago he thought he was going to be fired. Sure, they'd go back and look at Sunshine, but given the recordkeeping, it'd take an army of accountants to uncover the forged invoices. Plus, Sunshine was his smallest account, all told less than $70,000 of the nearly million dollars he had stolen. Surely they'd want the money back rather than demand jail time, and he was willing to pay it.

There was still a chance she was referring to just the Sunshine invoices. "What do you want me to say?"

"We want you to tell us the truth. How much you stole, what companies you submitted fake invoices for—we know of at least three others so far—and also why you did it."

Rich shot a surprised look at Naomi over the last part of the question.

Asking why wasn't just a good tactic to get him talking; Naomi genuinely wanted to know.

Robert's mind raced. *They knew about the others too! How did they possibly find them?* His eyes welled up, and his lip quivered. He put his face in his hands and started sobbing.

The details began pouring out of him. He had no family, no real friends to speak of. He never received so much as a happy hour invitation from his coworkers. The company picnic might have been the most social interaction he'd had outside of work every year, and even then he mostly kept to himself, picking at food and talking shop with those that would speak to him.

Robert had harbored a secret for over five years, the weight of which was crushing his soul. He wasn't a bad person, just a lonely man who thought the money would ease his pain. And he was deserving of it, wasn't he? After nearly fifteen years of loyal service, he was entitled to his share of happiness. But he found out the hard way that money wouldn't fix his problem, and then, like most frauds, it got away from him. It snowballed out of his control until he couldn't stop himself.

He held nothing back. Naomi wrote furiously on her legal pad to keep pace. He kept meticulous records of every transaction, every invoice, every check he cashed. He hadn't even spent much of the money, less than fifty thousand. He just liked checking his accounts, seeing it there, giving him what temporary comfort it provided. Reminding him that although he wanted for many things in his life—most of all companionship—he still exuded a level of control over that money.

Richard was impressed. Naomi had been right on every detail, down to paying off the manager at Mailboxes and More. He laid out how he kept the money in an offshore account in Antigua, how he set them up, the routing numbers, and how he could access them so he could pay the money back, which he offered almost immediately. It was a total victory for Pennington, and Naomi had been the general that delivered it.

It was also Pyrrhic victory. Naomi empathized with the man who sat before her, and in that moment, she felt the sadness that had set off the chain of decisions that had eventually led Robert to this conference room and the crushing guilt he felt now. Surely she had won, but at the cost of a man's spirit who, by all accounts, was a decent human being.

Naomi had hoped over the course of the interview she'd find the answer to another question, but the fifth company, Eclipse, never came up. It wasn't uncommon for a guilty person to hold back details or tell half-truths under questioning. It didn't appear, though, that Robert had done that. In front of her sat a completely broken man searching for redemption through confession. Still, she had to press.

"Robert, thank you so much for your honesty. We will do everything we can to make sure this comes to a fair resolution."

Naomi knew consequences were to follow, but she hoped that with most of the money being returned and the remorse he showed, he would be given a light sentence. A judge would certainly take into account those factors as well as his cooperation. Federal prison would not be kind to a man like Robert. After this was over, she'd try to convince Richard to seek a long probation instead of jail when they brought the case to the attorney general.

Naomi pushed on. "I have to ask. What do you know about Eclipse?"

Robert's head popped up, and he looked at Naomi in awe of her thoroughness.

Rich also shot a glance at Naomi, although his was born of nervousness. Naomi hadn't said anything about a fifth company, but he was sure that she had her reasons. Like a good attorney, he sat silently as his colleague continued.

"It's not quite the same pattern as the other companies that were involved." Naomi used the passive to try to keep Robert from crying again.

"Oh, that one. Yeah, I know about that one, but it's not one of mine." Robert wiped his eyes with a tissue.

Rich couldn't contain himself. "What do you mean, not one of yours?"

"That's one of the other ones—similar to the one I found by accident about six years ago. That's actually how I got the idea. It's different from how I do it, though—it's much more sophisticated. That one employs layers upon layers of shell companies. I tried to follow them once, but I couldn't get anywhere. Technically it's not just Eclipse either. It's a lot of names, and Eclipse is just the most recent one they're using."

"Do you know the names of the others?" Naomi pressed.

"Over the years there were a lot. I don't remember them all. They seemed to change every six months or so. Eclipse, Orbit, Gyre, Compass, probably a half a dozen others. I'm not sure how far back it goes. At least a few years before I started on Sunshine—at least that's how far back I was able to track it, anyways."

"But they are fakes as well, yes?"

"It's a scam, no doubt about it. I think whoever is pulling that one off is some kind of hacker."

Naomi leaned forward. "Why do you think that?"

Robert perked up. For the first time today he felt valued, even needed.

"Well, in my case, I took real invoices, figured out when we were under budget, and just submitted a fake one for the difference. I knew Karen would never think twice about those PO boxes—she typed thousands of those checks a week. Same with the bank in Antigua. They didn't care what the company was called, they just wanted a name and authorized person. See? Nothing fancy about what I did, just a dumb bet that a small discrepancy would go unnoticed."

"Don't sell yourself short, Robert. That bet worked for a long time and would have kept working if Karen hadn't retired."

Robert smiled, and the pace of his speech picked up. "Eclipse, Orbit, whatever you want to call it, that one is partially real. Well, the companies are all fakes. I looked them up. I tried calling, always the same generic voicemail, never a response. I even took a few days off once so I could visit the address in Hinsdale that was listed for one of the early ones."

"And what did you find?"

"Nothing. An empty suite in an out-of-the-way corporate office park. A paper sign on the door was all it was. I never saw an employee. I even sat in my car in the parking lot watching it for two days—two *weekdays*—to see if anyone came or went. Nothing. No doubt about it, those companies are as fake as they come."

"You said they are partially real," Rich pointed out. "What do you mean by that?"

"Yeah, so like I said, the companies are fakes, but the invoices are real. The first time I saw one it was for Gyre for over a million dollars. I thought to myself, 'Gee, that's a funny name, what the heck is that?' So I started digging. First I checked with budgeting, and yep, sure enough, they had a line item for Gyre right there in the computer for the exact amount. 'Okay', I thought, 'so it's a real company.' But I still wanted to know what the heck that company did for a million dollars a month."

"A month?" Rich nearly spit the water he'd just sipped from his glass.

"Oh, yeah, sometimes more. Sometimes it was a few million. That's when I figured if these guys could get away with millions, surely I could get away with much less."

Robert saw a frown come over Naomi's face.

"Which was definitely wrong of me," he backpedaled, trying to regain her good graces. Shifting attention back the larger fraud, he said, "So it was always a lot, but never the same amounts. It went on for a few months, then, poof, nothing. I thought they had stopped. You know, like they had worked the system, made enough to retire, and called it quits. Nope, just when I thought they were done, they'd pop back up, but this time under a different name."

"And the budgets for those? Did you see if those were in the computer too?" asked Naomi.

"Yep, every one of them—like clockwork, there they were. That's why I said he's gotta be some kind of hacker guy. If anyone checks, there's no suspicion, they'll see it right there in the computer. You don't even have to forge a company invoice, because there is no company. You can make it look like whatever you want! It's really quite impressive."

Impressive indeed, Naomi thought.

Robert was right; this was far beyond the level of his scam, which is exactly what she was afraid of. Big numbers, shell companies with rented office space, hacking, or worse—help from someone who has access, someone at the top.

"Okay, thank you, Robert, we are going to step outside for a moment to discuss what you've just told us."

Richard and Naomi exited the conference room past the security guard and walked to Richard's office down the hall.

After closing the door, Richard exclaimed, "This is bad, this could be really bad. I have to notify the board."

"Of course, you should do that immediately. What about Robert?"

Richard saw where this was going. "He stole nine hundred fifty thousand dollars, Naomi."

"Yes, but he hardly spent any of it, and he already committed to giving it back."

"How gracious of him. What exactly do *you* think his punishment should be?"

"Nothing. Let him go."

"What kind of message would that send? Steal from the company, and if you get caught, you just have to give it back? That's a bad precedent to set."

"No, it's not. Only a handful of people even know about it. You fire him and send him on his way. He pays the money back immediately. Hell, it's more than you'd get back for it if you have to litigate. The legal fees alone would eat up most of the money, and that's assuming you could even get a judgment against an Antiguan bank to release it." Naomi could feel the partners at the firm scowling at that business-crushing remark, but it was true. "Mr. Chadwick uncovered what could be a bigger fraud. The last thing you want is to announce that you found a major fraud while uncovering a smaller but still seven-figure one."

She had a point there. Rich was not looking forward to being the messenger on this one. He knew the gruesome fate that often befell messengers. The corporate world was no exception to the tried-and-tested rule of man. Still, he was not too keen on letting the man off scot-free.

"There's one other thing." Naomi pulled the trump card

from her hand. "He helps us with the new fraud—full cooper-ation. If this second fraud is as sophisticated as he purports it to be, his knowledge will prove invaluable at uncovering the perpetrators."

Ever the pragmatist, Richard thought for a moment, "You know, for a cutthroat lawyer, you really do have a bleeding heart, don't you?" He let out a sigh of surrender. "I want every penny, and I want it tomorrow. And he can't hold any details back."

Naomi smiled. "I'll tell him, and we'll get to work imme-diately going through the records."

"I'm serious, Naomi. He has to be one hundred percent truthful from here on out or the deal is off."

"I'll make sure he understands."

"Now, I have to figure out how I'm going to deliver news of this mess to management."

"About that, Rich," Naomi started. "Be careful who you speak to about this."

"Why?"

"Robert thinks it's a hacker, but it could be someone else —an insider, someone with authority. Go as high up as you can; we don't want to tip the bad guys off."

CHAPTER ELEVEN

Cody Evans sat on a plush couch inside a well-decorated waiting area of the Pennington headquarters. A middle-aged reception-ist in a blouse and knee-length skirt sat across from him, typing away on her computer. Cody was tired, and he couldn't get the vision of Melvin Jackson's body falling to the street out of his mind. In fairness, he hadn't slept well since he returned home from his last tour in Iraq over a decade ago.

His eyes grew heavy, and they shut as his mind drifted back there.

Cody was in his midthirties and had short, dark brown hair. He was tall and physically fit with a square jaw. He had gotten lucky with good genes and had been a remarkable ath-lete his whole life. He was raised in an unassuming house on a nondescript block of a working-class neighborhood of Calumet City, on the border of Illinois and Indiana just south of Chicago. He was a solid B student who didn't have many friends. The only thing that may have gotten him noticed was his work as a tight end on the football field, but no colleges came knocking on his front door to recruit him.

Cody's dad had been out of the picture for as long as he could remember, and his mom worked two jobs just to keep the lights on. All in all, it wasn't a bad upbringing, just a hum-ble one. It used to be that someone with average grades and a strong physique could get a job working the steel mills in Gary, but they had packed up and moved overseas years ago. With no other real prospects, Cody did what he thought was the next best thing—he enlisted in the marines.

His mom had instilled in him a sense of service since he was a boy—service to family, to community; service to country seemed like the next logical step. His mother was proud of the decision, but she reacted like any mother would, with restrained tears. She was afraid for her only son, but deep down she also knew that it would be his best shot at a better life. They told themselves that it could one day lead to college, which wasn't a lie, but maybe a misplaced hope. In truth, Cody didn't know where it would lead, but he did know that it was more exciting than moving into a modest apartment and looking for whatever job they afforded to someone with a high school degree.

In the marines he thrived. His athleticism helped, and he was a natural shooter. The reality of shooting was not like in the movies. It's a tough skill to learn, and just like anything else, some get it right away, and others will never get it no matter how many rounds they send down range. For Cody, though, it just made sense. Like a slugger swinging a baseball bat, his weapon was an extension of his body and mind. He was reaching out and hitting targets consistently at four and five hundred yards within the first week of rifle training. As a result, he was quickly singled out to join the Scout Sniper program, and again it was a perfect marriage. He knew how to work in large teams from football, but he never liked it all that much. Cody was a loner by nature, and relying on ten other guys to do their jobs was fine for football but not for when your life depended on it. As a sniper, he was paired up with a spotter, Felix Hernandez, who would come to be the only real friend he had. Felix's buddies called him Nando, so that's what Cody called him too.

So, there they were, Cody the shooter and Nando the spotter, but together they acted as a single unit. They were a two-man smart bomb, a scalpel for operations when you absolutely needed eyes on target and kill confirmations.

They trained, and then they trained some more. Not just shooting but also hand-to-hand combat, survival skills, evade and elude, fast roping into a target area. The duo quickly rose to their rightful spot as top sniper team.

When the planes hit the towers, they knew they were going to be called into action; they just didn't know where. Like millions of eager young men before them, they were ready to go into battle and excited to put their newfound skills to the test.

After a few anxious years waiting, Cody and Felix quickly shipped off to Iraq to be the tip of the spear, and that they were. During the first tour they served mostly as overwatch, covering other marines as they cleared the city streets below. Fallujah was particularly bad—casualties were high, but Cody and Nando did their jobs. Not one of the marines was killed by a threat that they could deal with. Many were killed while they were clearing interiors. Nothing to be done about that; it's dangerous work breaching a defensible position, but Cody and Nando owned those streets.

It was the same story every block. A few guys would come out to fight, and a few well-placed shots put them down. The next brave souls would venture out, more cautious than the first wave. They listened to that misplaced biological urge to move away from a threat. They backed up right into the sweet spot for a sniper. If they're too close, it can get tricky to hit them. Too far and the slightest wind gust could push the bullet wide. But Cody owned anything between five hundred and a thousand yards. So while the insurgents thought they were creeping away from the danger, they were actually moving toward it—right into Cody's wheelhouse. It only took a few more minutes and a few more brave souls to try their luck before the streets would go quiet for good, then it was onto the next block.

There were a few recon missions on some high-value targets, but only twice did they find them, and only once were they cleared to fire. They were told he was a midlevel Iraqi officer in charge of recruitment. Neither Cody nor Felix felt bad about it.

The way they saw it, they were saving lives. Sometimes you must take a life to save a life, and that's exactly what they were doing.

By the end of the second tour, though, it became a job—

one that they still dutifully performed day in and day out—but it wasn't quite the same for them. Lost was the sense of adventure. It no longer felt like a noble crusade to stop those responsible for attacking the United States. They were no longer conquering foreign lands. Instead they felt like occupiers with no sense of when the mission would be over, which was decidedly less glamorous.

Cody's last mission was supposed to be the same as the dozens before it—uneventful. But he had made a name for himself, and a bounty was out on his head.

The hunters had scouted the setting before Cody and Nando even got there. They picked the perfect perch and staged it. One look at it and Cody thought it was a sniper's dream blind.

It was too good to be true. As they lay prone, scouring the empty streets below, Cody heard the whiz of a bullet and felt the spray of blood as it struck Nando. Instinctively, Cody grabbed Nando and rolled, taking cover behind a wall. He did what he could to save Nando, but it was clear he was gone, and so too were the counter snipers disappearing into the fog of war as quickly as they had arrived.

And then so was Cody. He filed his papers and rotated back to the States. No fuss was made to convince him to stay. They all knew he was done. He had contributed more than his fair share, and a piece of him died on that rooftop with Nando. The orders went through, and Cody was honorably discharged shortly after arriving stateside.

He moved back home, worked several different jobs, security mostly—as a bouncer at a bar or sometimes as extra staff for large events in Chicago. When Cody's mom passed from cancer, she left him the house and a modest savings account, neither of which replaced her. They had grown closer after he returned, and her passing was hard on him.

Without the structure of the marines and having lost the only two people he cared about in quick succession, Cody was thrust into a tailspin. Nothing seemed to bring him fulfillment anymore, and he only knew how to do one thing. Fortunately, the man he was about to see found value in it.

As he sat in the office with his eyes shut, his mind raced between images of Nando and Melvin Jackson, unable to purge them from his memory. He felt like he was sinking into murky water devoid of light, unable to breathe.

The receptionist's voice was a hand reaching in to pull him up, if only for a minute. "Mr. Evans, Mr. Whitaker will see you now."

Cody opened his eyes to find her gesturing toward the office of Brendt Whitaker.

CHAPTER TWELVE

Cody stepped through the ten-foot threshold, making sure to close the heavy frosted-glass door behind him. The office of Brendt Whitaker was spacious, and the east-facing windows let in plenty of light. It was impeccably furnished with modern finishes that had a sleek look but with enough classic undertones that it would still be chic ten years from now.

Mr. Whitaker stood at his desk with the phone to his ear and gestured for Cody to sit in one of the plush brown leather seats in front of him. His five-foot-eight slender stature was unimposing, but he carried it in a manner that was authoritative. At fifty-five years old, Brendt had a direct demeanor about him, one that was crafted after years of handling various issues for his employer and a man whose schedule was constantly booked.

"Yes, please call me back when you have the details." He concluded the phone call and set the handset in the cradle on his desk. Turning his attention to Cody, he said, "Cody, I've seen the news, and your assignment has seemed to go off without a hitch. Did you run into any trouble?"

"None, sir," Cody responded. "Everything went to plan."

"Excellent, it seems that we are ready to move to the next phase." Brendt didn't hesitate to speak freely. Cody was a trusted asset who had performed many valuable services for him in the past. Brendt had little reason to doubt Cody's commitment to the overall mission. Of course, if he was wrong, his office was swept for bugs and he employed several high-tech electronic devices capable of scrambling any recording devices.

Brendt continued, "The removal of Mr. Jackson undoubtedly has the sharks circling."

"Yes, sir, the intel you provided all checks out. From my surveillance I can confirm at least four separate factions that will be fighting for control over his territory."

Cody had been stalking Jackson for weeks, gathering information in addition to learning his routine.

"And in your estimation, do you still believe that De-Mario Sherman is next in line?" Brendt asked.

"Yes, absolutely. He is Jackson's closest lieutenant. In fact, I think each group will fall in line and stand behind him. I have audio suggesting a lot of infighting. Particularly between two of the four factions. They do not like each other, but Jackson and the flourishing business seemed to keep them from starting a war. They have the same level of respect for Sherman. He and Jackson seemed to be viewed as a partnership, so I think it's likely it will be business as usual under Sherman."

"Good, then he's your next target." Brendt reached into his pocket for his key ring. He flipped through the keys until he stopped at a small silver one. Using it to open a drawer on the right side of his large oak desk, he produced an eight-by-eleven-inch tan envelope and tossed it on the desk.

Cody reached for it and pulled out the first few files, looking at them briefly. "This is going to be difficult. There's a lot of risk to doing it this way, risk to me, but also a risk it fails."

"Come now, Cody," Brendt retorted. "I have full confidence in your ability to handle this. I'm sure you can see why it's important for this one to look a particular way."

Cody understood it, any detective would look at this hit in one way and one way only—retaliation. He had to admit it was clean. Jackson's death would likely be discovered for what it was, a professional assassination. This would close the loop on the Jackson case, and the commanders who were under a lot of pressure to get their crime numbers down would be happy to chalk it up to a gang-related retaliation. They could stand in front of the press and declare that no innocents were lost in either case. They'd be filed away as unsolved and never given a second thought. Still, this would be dangerous. Cody would have to leave the safety of distance and stealth behind with his rifle.

"What do you say, Cody? Can it be done?"

"Anything can be done," Cody responded, with the marine mentality of "Make do with what you've got."

"Excellent." Brendt let go a half smile. "And about the risk, you are right. Extra compensation is in order." He pulled another envelope from the desk, this one much thicker than the first. It was stuffed with hundred-dollar bills. He placed it on the desk for Cody, who took it without counting it. "We'll need it done quickly."

"Yes, sir, I will need forty-eight hours."

"And what if the target goes to ground in that time?"

"That's exactly what I'm counting on."

CHAPTER THIRTEEN

Naomi sensed Robert's energy level fading. They had worked intensely in the conference room, poring over records for over five hours. Midnight had come and gone like an express train passing an empty station. Working into the late hours took practice. Pacing oneself and keeping focused was a learned skill, and clearly it was new to Robert. She told him he could leave in thirty minutes. He had an early morning appointment tomorrow at the bank to retrieve the funds, and she wanted him well rested. It was likely going to be another stressful time for Robert, and she wouldn't be in attendance to help put him at ease.

Naomi pondered what exactly it was about this man that made him so alone. He was intelligent, well mannered, and reasonably likable. He certainly had his quirks, but didn't everybody? People could do a lot worse in a friend. Despite his crimes, he seemed like a man who would go to great lengths for someone he cared about. Perhaps that was because he didn't have anyone that cared back, a defense mechanism to hold on to any relationship he could muster. Her mind was wandering, and it was clear she was getting tired too. She kept thinking about Robert's future.

What would become of him? she wondered.

On the one hand, he was disgraced and alone. On the other, he got a miraculous second chance at life. She hoped he deserved it; her intuition told her he did. She just hoped he'd make the most of it.

An extreme sense of empathy had been Naomi's gift and her curse. It made her great at her job. Most people see the world in black and white. The heightened political climate had only reinforced the national sentiment that "if you're not with me you're against me." It took a level of comfortable certainty to categorize things so matter-of-factly, but Naomi had seen enough to know that most things weren't so black and white. The sea of life was made up of the unpredictable gray-capped waves that lay between the defined beaches. Her ability to successfully navigate those waters prepared her for any argument.

Empathy came at a cost, though. Her job often took her down the seedy alleys of humanity. Hate, greed, selfishness, vengeance were heaped upon her en masse. Empathy never gave her the choice of what to let in; it was an open door.

But Naomi knew how to control it. Martial arts helped immensely until her hip surgery. Now it was yoga and reading. An hour spent getting lost from the world was wonderfully rejuvenating.

With her own energy levels waning and much more to do tomorrow, she decided it was a good stopping point. No sense in pushing through if she'd just have to pore over the same files again tomorrow because she was too tired to process them fully.

She organized the conference room a bit, stacking piles of documents according to the name of the company under which the invoices were filed. They had already identified six, dating back several years. There was no telling how many more they'd find, but they had an entire conference room at their disposal—a makeshift war room.

Sleeping in war rooms wasn't uncommon, especially when on trial. When she was a junior associate, a team of lawyers in her practice group had rented a one-bedroom apartment outside the midtown courthouse in New York. They were set to defend a man accused of fraud against the US government. The lawyers all stayed in plush corporate housing units, while Naomi was remanded to the tiny bedroom off the living room of the rented apartment to keep costs down. Having the bedroom was nice, but they needed every square foot of space in the cramped apartment, and it became a de facto storage room as well as her living quarters. It wasn't uncommon for someone to poke their head in at an ungodly hour of night and, in an oft failed surreptitious attempt, try to find a box of documents without waking Naomi. With a large conference room and the comfort of her own bed just ten minutes away, the current accommodations were presidential by comparison.

Naomi finished tidying the mountains of accounting records and shut off the light before exiting with Robert. A security officer in the lobby flipped on the orange flashing taxi light, and a bright yellow taxi pulled up to the curb. Robert chivalrously offered it to Naomi, who wished him luck before jumping in.

As the taxi pulled away, she peered out the back window at Robert shrinking in the distance. The streetlights intermittently flooded the interior of the cab as Naomi sank back into her seat and began reflecting on the case. With Robert's help they had made great headway into uncovering all the invoices, but they were no closer to finding out who was behind it. Tomorrow was another day, though, and Naomi knew the answers were sitting in the paper trail. They always were.

CHAPTER FOURTEEN

Cody Evans sat behind the wheel of a silver Toyota Camry parked outside a housing complex. Exposed wires hung from beneath the steering column. Cody had picked up hot-wiring as a skill while working for some less-than-reputable clients. He thought back on those jobs with regret, but as it turned out, criminals also needed security and were in a position to pay for it.

He'd lifted the car from long-term parking at Midway airport. After taking public transportation to the lot, he'd slipped in the back, out of the view of cameras, and waited for the right target—a businessman with a carry-on for luggage. He'd likely get on another flight if his was canceled for any reason, so there was little chance the car would be reported stolen for at least twenty-four hours.

After waiting long enough to feel that the man had made his flight, Cody cautiously made his way over to the Camry. After jimmying the door open, he slid into the driver's seat and fumbled with the wires on the ten-year-old model. Boosting cars wasn't his forte, but after a minute or two, a roar rose as the engine turned over. He pushed the brim of his hat low over his face and drove to the gated exit. Cody inserted the parking ticket, which he found in the cupholder then deposited cash into the machine. It spit out a receipt and lifted the gate, and just like that, Cody had his transportation.

After stopping at a storage unit to retrieve a large blue duffel bag and change his clothes, Cody made his way to the secret apartment of DeMario Sherman. He parked in a spot down the street, leaving enough room in front of him for a quick exit.

During his reconnaissance of Melvin Jackson, he'd followed DeMario to the Marshall Field homes. It took Cody two tries, having lost him the first time, as Demario was very cautious about not being followed. The four-story brown brick building was a low-income building—not public housing, but not far from it. Tenants were supposedly vetted in an effort to stop the building from becoming a magnet for crime like its famous Chicago counterparts—the projects.

It didn't take long for Cody to narrow down DeMario's place to three apartments in the complex. The surveillance equipment provided by Mr. Whitaker proved to be useful in pinpointing it. It was easy to gain access once DeMario left, and the well-placed bugs wouldn't be found. The new devices were sophisticated enough to evade most modern detection systems, so there was little chance of their discovery. Cody was thankful for that, since DeMario was clearly very protective of this property.

It was unassuming in every way, but that was the point of a safe house. Security was minimal. Instead, DeMario was banking on no one ever finding it, and until Cody, no one had.

After Melvin Jackson was killed, DeMario predictably fled here to lay low. He was unlikely to leave anytime soon, but just in case, Cody pulled a receiver from his duffel bag and turned it on. As he expected, the TV was murmuring in the background as DeMario paced the living room.

Cody took a few deep breaths to steady his nerves for the impending action. Dressed in a brown delivery driver shirt and cargo pants, he exited the car and walked to the passenger side. He grabbed a brown mid-length coat and UPS hat from the front seat, putting them on to complete the disguise. Last, he checked around before pulling an AK-47U from the bag. The U variant of the infamous Soviet-made rifle was a shortened version of its more ubiquitous parent and was easy for Cody to conceal in a sling under the right flap of his jacket. He took two extra magazines from the bag and holstered them in the small of his back before grabbing an empty brown box and shutting the Camry door.

It was a risky plan, but Cody was confident that DeMario wouldn't see it coming.

Cody entered the lobby, if you could call it that. The mud-colored tile looked as if it hadn't been updated since the '70s, and the green-and-yellow wallpaper was peeling at the seams. Cody strode toward the elevator, turning his head away from a tenant as she fumbled for her keys at the mailboxes. She didn't seem to notice him as he moved past her quickly and quietly. The rubber soles on his tactical boots insulated the sound so well that his footsteps hardly registered a noise when he stepped on the metal floor of the elevator. Cody pressed the button for three, which failed to light up, but did so on the bank of buttons on the opposite side of the door.

The doors closed, and the elevator lurched into motion as though it hadn't been used in years. The slow mechanics gave Cody time to check his coat once more and make sure his weapon was ready, secured, and, most importantly, hidden under his coat.

After the cab screeched to a stop, the doors gradually parted and Cody stepped off. He held the box firmly in front of him, which helped conceal his midsection. His heart was racing, and he found himself standing in front of DeMario's apartment faster than he anticipated. Cody placed his ear to the door, and upon hearing the TV and the sound of footsteps pacing back and forth, he knocked.

"Delivery," he said forcefully.

The footsteps stopped and the TV went quiet, but no response.

"Delivery," Cody said again.

"Man, I ain't expecting no delivery."

"Well, you got one. You want it or not?" Cody said.

"Leave it by the door."

"No can do, sir. This one requires a signature."

"Like I said, I ain't expecting a delivery."

"I don't know what to tell you. I have a package for unit 316, which is this one."

"Oh, yeah? Whose name is on it?" DeMario asked.

"No name, just this address."

"Well, who's it from?" DeMario started moving closer to the front door.

"I don't have that information either, sir."

"So you have a delivery for me. You don't know who sent it. You don't know who it's going to, but you need a signature? How you supposed to get a signature if you don't know who you even delivering it to?"

Cody sighed. "Look, man, I don't know what you think this is, but it's been a long day. My boss has been on my case because our delivery rate to this building isn't so hot, so can you cut me a break and just sign for the thing so I can go home?"

"First answer me. How you gonna get a signature if you don't know who you delivering to?"

Another sigh. "It doesn't have to be the recipient who signs for it on this type of delivery. It just means I have to see it into the hands of someone—anybody—who's here. It means I can't leave it. If you're worried about signing your name, then make one up. Sign it Michael Jordan, Ryne Sandberg, hell, sign it Jesus, if you want. But can you sign it so I can go home, please?"

Cody paused for a response. "Or don't, I don't care."

"Wait!"

He heard DeMario inch toward the door and saw the light peeking through the peephole go dark. Putting on his best tired and ready-to-go-home face, he stared directly at the peephole, showing his whole face to DeMario. It was a gamble if he didn't bite, but delivery drivers didn't hide from their customers.

Cody heard a thud and could sense the business end of a pistol pressed against the door. After a moment, the security chain rattled into place and the deadbolt clicked. The door opened a crack, and Cody saw two eyes peer out at him.

Before they could get a bead on him, he pushed the package for inspection closer to the crack. When he saw the eyes peer down to inspect the box, Cody struck with a hard front kick inches left of the door knob. The chain gave way instantly and the door flew back, hitting DeMario square in the face.

Cody heard the sound of metal on the floor—and then saw through the wide-open door the pistol that was pointed at him sliding down the hallway. A dazed DeMario, who had landed on his back, flipped onto his side and pawed at the gun as it sailed past him and then came to a rest a few feet out of his reach.

He started crawling toward his weapon, but before he could reach it, Cody unslung the shortened AK from under his coat and took aim at DeMario in one swift motion. He pulled the automatic trigger, unleashing a barrage of bullets upon his victim. The slender DeMario jolted as several rounds hit his torso, then he went instantly limp when the recoil of the gun, pushing the barrel higher, landed a bullet in his skull. Cody let up on the trigger as a smoky haze rose from the barrel, filling the hallway. All told, fifteen rounds found their target, leaving DeMario lying dead in a pool of blood.

Cody turned and walked briskly past the elevator bank to the stairwell. When he hit the ground floor he made his way down a long hallway. He picked up his pace as he heard the sound of doors cautiously opening behind him. He exited through a side door, which put him directly in front of the silver Toyota Camry. He got in, twisted the ignition wires back together, then stopped. He stared out the windshield and saw a perfect vision of DeMario writhing on the floor. Cody shook his head, but he could not shake the image.

He closed his eyes tight as he picked up the faint sound of sirens in the distance. He could hear his own heartbeat thumping in his head. The sound of bullets hitting DeMario, the sirens, and the pumping blood were a symphony of torment crescendoing in his mind. Cody clenched the steering wheel and pulled so hard it nearly came loose.

Then, as quickly as it began, the noise stopped, and there was silence. Only the sirens approaching in the distance remained. Cody looked into his eyes in the review mirror and remained frozen. He wondered what would happen if he just stayed. Finally, when he saw the faint flicker of blue police lights behind him, he put the car in gear and pulled into the sparse street, driving toward the dusk setting in over the Chicago skyline.

CHAPTER FIFTEEN

Across town at the Pennington headquarters, Naomi's words danced around in Richard Eisner's brain. *Go as high up as you can; we don't want to tip the bad guys off.*

He paced around his office, rehearsing the conversation he was about to have. After he was thoroughly convinced that he covered his bases, he walked down the hall to the office of Brendt Whitaker. Technically Whitaker didn't work for Pennington Hotels directly. He was the unofficial chief operations officer—if you could call it that—of all the Pennington family affairs.

This distinction did not stop Mr. Whitaker from being heavily involved in the Pennington Hotel business. Though he never showed up on any SEC filings, no one at Pennington made a decision without his express approval.

Richard Eisner never felt comfortable around Whitaker. It wasn't just Whitaker's clandestine power base that rattled Richard, it was also his demeanor. In all their interactions, Whitaker seemed preoccupied—as if he had five more important places to be than speaking with the lowly general counsel of a multibillion-dollar corporation.

Once, during a rare Friday evening board meeting, Richard made the mistake of assuming no one was paying attention. In fairness, most weren't. The board members and executives all had one foot out the door and were ready to end the work week. Whitaker was furiously thumbing away at his oversized cell phone, seemingly oblivious to the proceedings. When the subject of a recently filed lawsuit came up, Richard, who hadn't yet reviewed it, attempted to punt it until the next board meeting. Richard knew it was nothing, just another frivolous lawsuit in a stack of many others jamming up the American legal system. His mistake was thinking the update on it could wait until the following week. With tired eyes, the room gave a tacit silent approval to wait on it.

That is, until Brendt Whitaker looked up from his phone and said, "And why do you feel the details can wait until next week?"

At the time Richard thought it was a power play, a statement to dress him down. Over time, though, he began to realize that Whitaker was just on another level. He had an inhuman ability to process mountains of information simultaneously. Even the most complex problems seemed to melt away when he involved himself. Like a grand master chess champion, he was able to see ten moves ahead.

Rich was also a high achiever, having graduated top of his class from Stanford law in the '70s. Still, Whitaker intimidated him, and Rich learned from his experiences and made sure he was well prepared for what he was about to discuss with him.

At least they had the Chadwick money back. As he promised, Chadwick returned all but fifty grand, give or take. That would surely soften the blow a bit.

It was past 7:00 p.m. when he walked past the empty desk of Whitaker's secretary, who had already left for the day. Rich stood in front of the heavy glass door and raised to fist to knock, but before he could, a voice boomed from inside the office.

"Enter," Whitaker said.

Rich opened the door and crossed the room to Brendt, who stood scanning files scattered across his desk.

Without looking up he said, "What can I do for you today, Mr. Eisner

"Well, sir, we have an issue that requires your attention."

"What kind of issue?" Brendt asked.

"It's a potentially large one. We've discovered some money is missing."

Brendt finally looked up from his desk, then took a seat. He put his hands together, forming a triangle with his pointer fingers in front of his lips.

"How much money is missing?"

"Just under one million that we know of so far."

A look of relief came over Brendt. "Do you know who took it?"

"Yes, we confronted the employee, Robert Chadwick, and we have most of the money back—a little over nine hundred thousand returned."

"And did you contact the authorities?"

"No, and we don't plan on it either."

"Good. We don't need the scrutiny of outside eyes poring over our books."

"There's more, sir. We didn't contact the authorities because we made a deal with Chadwick. The money and his cooperation for his freedom and a pink slip."

"Cooperation with what, exactly?"

"In tracking down Chadwick's scheme, I believe we have found another one. This one appears to be far bigger. Multiple shell companies, authentic invoices. So far we've found one, Eclipse. We think there are more."

Brendt paused a moment, then walked behind Richard to a glass bar top lined with liquor bottles. He reached for a decanter filled with a Pappy Van Winkle's twenty-three-year aged bourbon and poured three fingers in each of two glasses. He walked to the front of his desk and leaned on it, handing one to Richard as he stood over him.

"Who else knows about this?"

Rich found the question unnerving. "Just me and Robert Chadwick, so far."

"The attorney. The one you work with often; I saw her here yesterday. What does she know?"

"We enlisted Miss Archer to track down the Chadwick scheme, which she did successfully. She knows nothing of this other one—only the name Eclipse, and as of now she believes it's part of the Chadwick scheme."

"That's good. We don't need another attorney meddling in our affairs."

Robert looked up in surprise.

"That is, until we figure out internally the damage," Brendt said, noticing Richard's unease.

"How would you like me to proceed?"

Taking a sip from his glass, he stared at Richard, thinking, then swallowed the $2,300-a-bottle liquor and spoke. "The files, are they at Miss Archer's offices?"

"Some. The Chadwick ones are, but the rest are here in a conference room. I pulled them, and Mr. Chadwick and I were poring through them today."

Richard held back. He wasn't sure who he could trust just yet, and Brendt's questions did little to alleviate his suspicion. In truth, Naomi had been going through the files with Chadwick while Richard sat mostly in observance. In the past twenty-four hours, Naomi had successfully uncovered six different shell companies and nearly $80 million missing, and it appeared to be just the tip of the iceberg. It was a big number to be sure, but spread over the course of seven years and the sophistication of the scheme, it was conceivable that it went unnoticed.

"Keep it under wraps for now. Whatever files you pulled, leave in the conference room, and don't let anyone in there. I will handle this personally. For now, don't discuss this with anyone on your team, and tell Miss Archer she can stop working on whatever she has left," Brendt said.

"What about Robert Chadwick? He's supposed to be here first thing in the morning to continue looking through the records with me."

"His services are no longer needed in the matter. I'll reach out to him personally. I know how to find him."

CHAPTER SIXTEEN

Darkness had set in over the Marshall Field housing complex, making obvious the burned-out lights around the property. The residents who were inside were told to stay there, and those returning from work had been corralled into a small area outside the entrance, which was flanked by several patrolmen. Davis and McCauley stepped off the elevator and made their way through the hallway crowded with cops and crime scene techs toward DeMario Sherman's apartment.

Davis flinched when he saw the violent scene. In his few months in the division, he was no stranger to murder. The bullet-ridden body lying in drying blood, though, was by far the most stomach turning he'd seen yet.

A stocky patrol sergeant, who spoke with a thick Chicago accent, was standing in the doorway and looked up to greet the detectives.

"Detectives, meet DeMario Sherman. He's a slippery son of a bitch. Midlevel dealer that we've had a helluva time trying to lock up."

"Looks like it finally caught up to him," McCauley said, cocking his head to get a better view of the body.

"You know that other homicide you've been working—Jackson? All my coppers say dat guy and dis guy been working together. Every time we stop 'em, though, they're clean. Word on the street is they've been rising up through the ranks—expanding their territory. Way I figure it, dis guy took out his partner to take over solo, and someone loyal to Jackson didn't take too kindly to that. Got some payback."

"Could be. We'll take a look around. I'm not holding my breath, but anyone see anything?"

"You know the drill. Somebody saw something, but no one's coming forward. They're clammed up tighter than a duck's ass."

McCauley gave a nod, then stepped in the door and squatted over the body, looking for anything. The crime scene techs had finished photographing and made way for the detectives to take a look.

"What do you think, Davis?" McCauley asked.

"I have to admit it, the sarge may be right. This guy hires a professional hit on Jackson, makes sure he goes down so he can take over the business. Meanwhile he's holed up here until things quiet down. Somebody gets wind of it that was loyal to Jackson, and blammo, they take him out."

"Yeah, maybe," McCauley said. "It does fit nicely."

He then turned to the tech and said, "What kind of rifle?"

"Not sure what type of rifle, but it looks like 7.62 mm, probably automatic. Fifteen shell casings on the ground starting in the hallway and moving into the apartment. Fifteen rounds in the victim, including two in the head."

"Execution on those?" McCauley asked.

"Doesn't look like it. Looks like all one blast, and those two just found his head. There's an empty box outside—we're thinking they used it as some sort of delivery ruse to gain access. No prints as far as we can tell," the tech said.

"Probably won't find any on the shell casings, but bag 'em anyways to see."

The tech nodded and walked to his briefcase on the opposite side of the room to grab evidence bags.

McCauley closed his eyes and pinched the bridge of the nose, partially to help him think and partially to help push away the nagging headache creeping up on him.

"I know well enough that you don't think this is as open and shut as the sergeant said, but you are always the one quoting Occam's razor."

"Yes, the law of parsimony, the simplest answer is usually the right one. But this case isn't so simple. We have a professional long-range rifle kill, and now this."

"I dunno, an automatic rifle attack? Seems pretty fitting for a payback hit to me," Davis said.

"Normally I'd agree, but how many times you see someone hit one hundred percent of their shots? Bangers aren't usually this accurate," McCauley replied.

"Well, it's close quarters. Makes it easier shooting, but you're right—even this close with an automatic is tough. Guy either got lucky or he had training," Davis said.

"Yeah, and that's just it. Close quarters." McCauley placed his palm over his mouth and stroked the stubble on his cheeks as he thought aloud. "How the hell did they find this guy? This is obviously a safe house for DeMario—limited furniture and a woman's name on the mailbox downstairs. A guy as careful as he supposedly was would know how not to be found. The hitter would hate this place. Forgetting the potential witnesses, there's way too many unknowns. Even if he knew DeMario was holed up in this building, no way he could tail him to this apartment without being made. He'd be better off waiting for him outside. Plus, payback hits that happen this quick are almost always drive-bys and always at known hangouts."

McCauley walked over to the tech's briefcase and grabbed a couple of screwdrivers, tossing one to Davis.

"We have to pull this place apart, and I mean everything. I want this place torn apart, anything that's not nailed down," McCauley said.

"What are we looking for?" the tech asked.

"I don't know yet, but something that's out of place."

The one-bedroom apartment was small, less than a thousand square feet. It was sparse, but it still took nearly an hour and half to search everything. Electronics were opened up, light fixtures were pulled from the ceiling, even the bulbs were unscrewed for inspection. They found nothing suspicious, nothing out of the ordinary. That is, until Davis pried the faceplate off an outlet from the space between the open kitchen and living room.

"Hey, McCauley, what do you make of this?" he asked.

A black cylinder, smaller than a AAA battery was spliced into the outlet's wiring. McCauley had seen a listening device before, but never one as tiny as this or one connected directly to wall power, where the constant hum of electricity would cause interference. A fully functioning light was even plugged in, making the location of the device all the less probable.

Davis carefully unhooked it and placed it in an evidence bag, then handed it to McCauley, who held it up to the light for inspection.

"Well, we can safely say this changes the course of our investigation," McCauley declared.

"How'd you know we'd find a bug?" Davis asked.

"A hunch." McCauley placed the evidence bag containing the device in his coat pocket and said, "Davis, I'm trusting you to finish up here. I need to go see someone about this. I'll call you later."

With that, McCauley left the scene, the possibilities now racing in his mind. It was a break for sure, but if this was as sophisticated a bug as he thought, he just found a whole lot more questions than answers.

CHAPTER SEVENTEEN

McCauley entered a coffee house near the intersection of Milwaukee and North in the Bucktown neighborhood. The shop was a microcosm of the gentrifying neighborhood, and hipsters typing away on their MacBooks filled the tables. His order of a large plain black coffee earned him an eye roll from the barista, who sported a handlebar mustache, but McCauley could care less. He sipped on his drink, deep in thought while tapping his spoon against the wooden countertop he had cozied up to.

He was about to call in a favor, and McCauley was hoping that it would pan out. McCauley considered the man he was about to meet a friend. While he didn't like the idea of holding markers over people, McCauley needed his help on this one.

Two refills later, McCauley checked his watch and made his way to the exit. Across the street was a three-story parking garage with an open top. McCauley marched up the stairs to the roof, where he saw a black Chevy Impala parked with its lights on and engine running.

Stan Butterfield stepped out of the driver's side. He was a tall, six-foot-two and slender. His receding hairline made him look older than McCauley, but in reality they were the same age. He donned an inexpensive black suit, white shirt, and red tie—the de facto uniform for an NSA agent.

McCauley stuck his hand out, and the two men shook. "Thanks for getting back to me so quickly on this one, Stan."

"Well, we owe you one. My boss is very thankful for you walking our agents out the back door of the station."

"No problem, really. No sense in wrecking careers over a

dumb bar fight, particularly since they didn't start it," McCauley replied.

"It's how they finished it that we didn't need in the papers. Those punks got what they had coming to them, but still, arraignments, suspensions—let's just say it was a mess we were glad to avoid."

McCauley looked down at the tan eight-by-eleven-inch envelope that Stan held in his right hand. "That for me?"

"Yes, but first some ground rules. My boss wants it clear that this makes us square."

McCauley nodded in agreement. "What else?"

"This doesn't come back to the NSA at all. We will not get involved in any way in this case, and we will disavow having any connection to this. If you need a warrant, you find other evidence to get it."

"Yeah, yeah, I got it."

"No, I'm serious," Stan retorted. "What I'm about to disclose is highly sensitive."

"Okay, I got it, nothing will get back to you on this. You have my word," McCauley said.

Satisfied with the agreement, Stan began, "The device that you gave me. It's one of ours."

"I knew it. That tech was way beyond anything I'd ever seen before," McCauley said.

"You should see the new ones," Stan said, cracking a smile.

"So what's the NSA doing spying on drug dealers? That's not your jurisdiction."

"I said it was our device. I didn't say we planted it," Stan said. He spotted a look of confusion on McCauley's face and continued. "Six months ago we received upgraded surveillance equipment, like I said, stuff that's even better than this. Protocol states that anything that had a serviceable life we keep, anything that doesn't gets marked for destruction. The device you found should have been destroyed along with batches of other equipment."

"Instead it walked out the door," McCauley said, starting

to put it together.

"That's right. Cameras, bugs, fiber optics, transmitters—most of it made it to disposal. About a dozen items didn't. We investigated, and it didn't take long to figure out who was behind it. One of our technicians with midlevel clearance. He thought he covered his tracks well; he didn't. The guy racked up gambling debts to the wrong people, and he needed the cash. Pretty typical story, really."

"Tell me you know who he sold it to."

"Well, we know who they're not. No foreign connections, no intelligence connections, most likely corporate espionage. That's as far as we got."

"That's it?" McCauley asked in disbelief.

"Security breaches don't reflect well upon you when have the word *security* in your agency name. We recovered half the items, ruled out that a bad actor buying them, so that was it. Inquiries can be a nasty business, and we certainly didn't need one of those given the recent publicity around our operations."

The agency was still reeling from the treasure trove of leaked classified documents outlining a massive domestic surveillance program.

"So you swept it under the rug. What about the corporate espionage angle?"

"That's the FBI's problem, out of our jurisdiction," Stan said coyly, shrugging his shoulders.

"Well, what's in the envelope, then?" McCauley asked, holding out his hand.

Stan handed him the envelope and said, "The company that bought it."

McCauley unsealed the envelope and withdrew a sheet of paper with a single word on it.

"It's just a name. What am I supposed to do with this?"

"You're a detective. So detect," Stan said.

McCauley furrowed his brow at the comment.

"Look, Pat, we owed you one, but that doesn't mean we're in the business of handing out classified intel to local cops. I had to convince my boss to even give you this, and let me tell you, that was no easy task. His idea of returning the favor was Cubs playoff tickets next year, not trading sensitive information."

"Okay, okay, I get it. I was just hoping for more," McCauley said.

"At least this gets you started in the right direction."

"Yeah, I guess I better get back and start detecting," McCauley quipped and started walking toward the exit.

"And Pat, bowling next week, we still on for that, or are you gonna sulk about it? It's league play. Come on Pat," Stan said, yelling so his friend could hear him as he walked away.

Pat turned and threw a half smile. "Yeah, I'll be there, but you get the first round."

McCauley hit the stairwell and started down the stairs, the name bouncing around in his head. It wasn't much, but he hoped Stan was right that it would be enough.

CHAPTER EIGHTEEN

Across the city, Cody Evans sat in the driver's seat of the black Lincoln MKZ. The glow of the interior dash threw a damp light upon face of Robert Chadwick, who sat beside him in the passenger's seat, looking out the window at the passing buildings as they drove. Cody looked the man up and down, trying to make sense of his instructions.

He had never been shy when it came to killing if the person had it coming, but killing for no reason was different. Soldiers sign up for war; they know the risks. Same with drug dealers and murderers. Cody didn't find joy in it, but in his waking hours he could always rationalize it. For Melvin Jackson and DeMario Sherman, the bullets they caught were fired years ago the moment they made the choice to immerse themselves in the violent world of drugs. If selling poison wasn't bad enough, Cody was sure they committed a litany of worse crimes.

But what crimes was Robert Chadwick guilty of? Maybe it was the pleats in his cheap khakis or the fact that he wore them with generic white tennis shoes. You didn't have to be well trained to size this guy up in a heartbeat, and a killer he was not. Cody looked at Robert staring blankly out the window and wondered if the man next to him had even racked up so much as a parking ticket.

Cody didn't like it. Mr. Whitaker was clear that this man needed to disappear. He provided no details, he answered no questions, just gave instructions to eliminate him. Cody shook his head in frustration at his own response. It was obvious to Whitaker that he was uncomfortable with the assignment, and he did not want to lose the man's trust. Whitaker had helped him when Cody was spiraling out of control in the wake of his mother's death. He took him under his wing, gave him a job, gave him purpose again. For that, Cody was forever grateful.

But Cody also swore to defend those that couldn't defend themselves when he joined the marines. If ever there was someone befitting that description, it was Robert Chadwick. The ideals of service to the man who had saved him and service to those in need waged a battle inside Cody. The decision weighed on him, but he needed to make it.

Then, in a blink of an eye, he did, jerking the wheel suddenly to the right and pulling the sedan behind a taxi in front of Union Station. The grand structure sporting limestone facades, Corinthian columns, and dazzling marble floors loomed over the two men sitting in the car.

"I thought we were going to our accounting firm's offices in Oak Brook," Robert said, eyeing the building.

Cody pulled a threaded Beretta M9A3 with a silencer from underneath his coat and spoke. "Robert, look at me."

Robert turned and froze at the sight of the weapon.

"My instructions are to kill you," Cody said

Robert's eyes went wide with terror.

"Don't worry, I'm not going to," Cody continued. "I don't know what you did to earn a death sentence, but I'm not going to carry it out. Instead, you are going to walk into that building and sit down until the ticketing counters open. It's 8:45 p.m., and the first trains leave in about nine hours. You need to be on one of them. Do you understand?"

"What train? To where?" Robert asked, flustered.

"I don't care where you go, so long as you tell no one and you never come back to Chicago. You are going to leave now with what you've got on you. Don't call anyone, don't use your credit cards, don't sell your condo, don't come back for any of your belongings. You need to disappear and convince anyone who comes looking for you that you fell off the face of the Earth, do you understand me?"

"What am I supposed to do for money? How do I even buy the ticket?"

Cody leaned over and pulled one of the thick envelopes that Whitaker had given him from the glove compartment and tossed it onto Robert's lap.

"There's cash in there for the ticket, a change of clothes, and enough to get you set up with an apartment and living expenses for a few months wherever you land."

Robert picked up the envelope and stared at it. "But my whole life is here."

"No, Robert. It *was* here. Whatever you did, it angered someone enough to want you dead. Think of this as the witness protection program. You need to leave and never look back. Don't contact friends, don't contact family, just disappear."

"That part won't be hard. I don't have any friends, and no family left."

Cody's chest twinged at the comment. "Well, then, you're already one step ahead of the game. Look, it's not going to be easy, but it's better than being dead. Do you know how many people in this world secretly pray for the opportunity to escape their lives? You can reinvent yourself, start over, become whoever you want to be. It's a fresh start. I just hope you deserve it."

"Why are you doing this for me?" Robert asked.

"I wish I knew, Robert. I really wish I knew."

Robert paused, then looked at Cody and said, "Thank you. I won't forget it."

Robert stepped from the car and tucked the envelope in his coat pocket. He looked around before walking to the entrance and disappearing through the revolving door. Cody watched him enter, then put the car in gear and pulled away.

Four cars back in a black SUV, a man observed the interaction. As he took a slow drag from his cigarette, the lit end cast an amber glow upon his face—the younger security officer who was tasked with photographing Chadwick at the post office.

He muttered to himself, "What a shame, Cody, what a shame."

He flicked the cigarette out of the window and made his way to the door that Robert Chadwick had just entered. He'd have to be quick with this one. He had one more stop to make tonight.

CHAPTER NINETEEN

It was 7:00 a.m., and McCauley had barely slept. What little time he'd managed to close his eyes wasn't particularly restful. Fueled on coffee and excitement over the name he'd gotten from Stan, McCauley strode into the police station past the desk sergeant and up the stairs to the homicide division. He'd done some checking last night after his meeting with Stan and figured out the company was a front of some sort, but that was it. McCauley was beginning to worry the name would fail to produce a lead, but he was still holding out hope that the department's forensic accountants would have better luck.

Before McCauley could get to his desk, the head of his unit, Lieutenant Perry, flagged him down. McCauley walked into the glass-enclosed office in the middle of the floor. It looked more like a fishbowl than an office, and McCauley wasn't sure if Perry used it so that he could see the detectives or so they could see him. Either way, McCauley didn't love being beckoned to the room for all prying eyes to see. For the most part, McCauley got along with Perry, but he knew the pressure that was heaped upon the lieutenant from the brass. The old-timer was a good detective in his own right before the promotion. He was a no-nonsense cop who had stood by McCauley enough of times to earn his respect. Even McCauley wasn't above walking on eggshells when Perry was in one of his moods.

"Pat, sit down, please," Perry said, gesturing to the chair in front of his desk. "Where's the file on the Melvin Jackson homicide?"

"We haven't completed our investigation. It's still open,"

McCauley responded.

"You've been a detective here a long time, Pat. So I don't have to say what I'm about to say, do I?"

"Lieutenant, I'm not oblivious to the clearance rates. I also know how this looks, but I'm telling you there's more to this case than meets the eye."

"Or maybe you need a break. It happens to even the best detectives. The day-in, day-out grind of this place is enough to drive anyone insane. When was the last time you took a vacation—a year ago?

"Year and a half."

"A year and a half, that's an eternity in this job. Clear the case, then book yourself some vacation time, unplug a little bit."

"I'm telling you, Lieutenant, I'm not going crazy. This case isn't open and shut. Someone just wants it to look that way," McCauley insisted.

Lieutenant Perry placed his hands flat on the desk, then rocked back in his chair. "Okay, Pat. You've got twenty-four hours to investigate the Jackson case. After that, we're marking it closed and that the primary suspect is the now deceased De-Mario Sherman, who shot him over a business dispute. Twenty-four hours after that, if you've got nothing, we're going to mark the Sherman case as unsolved and move on. Even the *Tribune* is reporting that this has retaliation written all over it. I'm inclined to agree, and forty-eight hours from now, unless you bring me something compelling, that's what we're going with."

McCauley debated about disclosing the listening device, but given Stan's directive, he thought better of it. Instead he nodded his head in agreement.

"Good, now that we've settled that, I've got another case for you. There's a lawyer out there. She is here to file a missing persons report."

McCauley peered at the bullpen and saw a beautiful brunette with a worried look on her face talking to a clearly smitten Detective Davis.

"Aw, come on, Lieutenant. Let Davis handle that. I'm telling you this Jackson-Sherman thing is big. Her boyfriend probably just got drunk at the Indiana river boats. He'll make his way back eventually."

"If that's the case, then it should be real easy for you."

"I'm with you on the twenty-four hours, but how am I supposed to close it if I'm stuck tracking down a missing person who probably isn't even missing in the first place?"

"Look at this, McCauley." Perry planted his hand on a stack of files. "This here is my problem stack. These are all the things I have to deal with today. The fact that you have to work these two cases at once, guess where we are going to file that one?"

"We're going to file in the stack marked 'my problem,' sir," McCauley muttered, going through the routine.

"That's right. And according to Lieutenant Perry's handbook for managing detectives, how many fucks do I give about your problems?"

"Zero, sir."

"Good, I'm glad we're on the same page." Perry shifted his hand from the files to the phone. "Sometime in the next few hours this phone is going to ring, and on the other end will be Commander Anderson. He's going to start by cracking a joke about my wife's cooking, which I will pretend to laugh at. Then, the conversation is going to go one of two ways. The first is he's going to say, 'Lieutenant. Thank you so much for putting your best detective on that missing persons case. You know her firm is well connected and contributed a lot to the mayor's campaign, so that was really forward thinking of you to use all the resources available to bring the case to such a timely resolution.' Or, it can go a second way. In *that* scenario, he chews my ass out because my best detective decided, for reasons known only to him, that the two drug dealers who chose to bang it out on our streets are actually part of some much larger conspiracy. And in pursuit of these shadowy figures, he decided to pass this case on to his rookie partner. If that were to happen, well, then, your problem would become my problem. And you don't want it to become my problem. Are we clear?"

"Crystal, sir."

"Good. Get to it, then, Pat. Clock's ticking."

CHAPTER TWENTY

Naomi sat in a chair next to the desk of Detective Anthony Davis. When she couldn't reach Robert Chadwick, she got nervous and rushed out of her apartment, forgetting her suit coat. The white silken blouse she was wearing teased her slender but athletic physique underneath it. Davis forced himself to stare at his computer screen but found his eyes wandering back every few minutes.

McCauley dashed out of Lieutenant Perry's fishbowl and walked over to his desk, which sat opposite of Davis so they could speak face-to-face. He pulled his roller chair around the desks so that Naomi wouldn't have to move, then thrust his hand out for a handshake.

Davis made the introduction. "Naomi Archer, this is my partner, Detective McCauley."

"It's nice to meet you, Naomi. We'll do everything we can do to find your friend," McCauley said.

"Well, he's not my friend. I suppose you could call him a work colleague," Naomi corrected.

Davis chimed in, "Robert Chadwick, male, forty-four years old, Caucasian, brown hair, balding, five eight, two hundred to two hundred and twenty-five pounds. He works in the accounts receivable division of the Pennington Corporation—"

"The hotel chain?" McCauley interjected.

Naomi nodded.

"My lieutenant said you work at a big firm downtown. I have to ask, Miss Archer, how do you fit into all of this?" McCauley asked.

"Well, like I was telling your partner, I—my firm, that is —represents the Pennington Corporation. They reached out to us for help on an internal matter. Mr. Chadwick was integral in helping us to resolve it."

McCauley could feel a headache coming on from the back of his neck. He liked lawyers well enough, but he hated trying to get a straight answer out of them.

"Okay...so how long has Robert been missing?" McCauley asked.

"Well, the last I saw him, he was walking out of the Pennington offices at about eight o'clock yesterday morning."

"So what makes you think he's missing, exactly?" McCauley checked his watch. "We're looking at just under twenty-four hours since you last saw him, not a whole lot of time to be missing. He have any enemies, vices—drugs, drinking, gambling... women? Any reason at all he might run off?"

"He's as straitlaced as they come."

"Eh, don't be too sure. Sometimes the uptight ones are the wild ones when you get a few drinks in them. You never know."

"I'm sure it's not that," Naomi rebutted. "A few days ago he may have had a reason to run off, but now, he's got every reason to stay."

"Explain that. I'm a detective, Miss Archer. I'm here to help you, but even that's a little cryptic for me. What are we talking here, a little hanky-panky? I'm not judging. I'm just asking."

Naomi rolled her eyes in frustration. "No. I mean, no. It's nothing like that. I told you, our relationship was strictly professional, he was helping us with an—"

"Internal investigation, yes, I got it," McCauley said.

"Look, I'm bound by attorney-client privilege. I can't disclose all the details of what we were working on other than what I've told you," Naomi said.

"I get it, so I'll talk, and you listen. You wink if I'm getting warm. On or about three days ago, you catch Robert Chadwick stealing some money from the company. In an effort to keep it under wraps, not spook the shareholders, because we all know they can be fickle, you make a deal with Robert to pay the money back in exchange for his freedom."

Naomi's eyes widened. She'd hardly hinted at that, certainly nothing close to a breach of privilege, and still Detective McCauley nailed it.

He continued, "I'll take it by that look that I got it. Look, it seems to me that the most likely scenario is that he got cold feet and took off with the money. If you want, I know a detective in larceny, good man, he can get you squared away. He can open a case and put an APB out on your man. We can have him in custody before you know it."

"No, that's not it. He paid back the money already. The deal was done, so he had no reason to run."

"So what exactly were you investigating, then?" McCauley asked, leaning in toward Naomi.

"In looking for Robert, we stumbled on something bigger —much bigger. As part of our agreement, Robert had to help us track it down. So you see, all the more reason for him to cooperate."

"Forgive me, Miss Archer, but why are you here? I mean, I get it, Robert may be missing, he may have skipped town. He could have just as easily looked for forgiveness in the bottom of a bottle somewhere. But why are *you* here? He's not your employee. Why didn't you contact someone at Pennington when you couldn't reach him?"

"That's exactly what I did. I called Richard Eisner, general counsel for Pennington. I can't get ahold of him either."

McCauley wrote down Richard's name and title on a small notepad, licked his finger, ripped off the page, and handed it to Davis. "Run him, please."

Davis started keying the information on his computer as McCauley turned back toward Naomi.

"You may be right about Robert," Naomi continued, "I didn't peg him as one to run. Even if I misjudged him, Richard being out of contact means there's something wrong. He keeps his phone glued to his hand. He's not responding to texts, and his number goes straight to voicemail."

Davis elbowed McCauley and gestured with his chin toward his computer monitor. McCauley stood up and leaned over Davis's shoulder to get a better look.

"What is it?" Naomi asked?

"Does Richard live at 1045 North State Street, unit 32D?" McCauley asked.

"I don't know about the unit number, but yes, he lives in that building," Naomi responded.

McCauley's face went somber. "I'm sorry to tell you this, Miss Archer, but Richard was found dead this morning. They pulled his body out of Lake Michigan at four a.m. The initial report here looks like he was running on the lakefront around Chicago Avenue, slipped, hit his head, and rolled into the water. It looks like he drowned."

Naomi's eyes welled up with tears. Richard may have been a client and a colleague, but he was also her friend. The legal world can be rough, particularly on women, but Richard was a kind man and went out of his way to take Naomi under his wing, particularly when she was a young associate. Her sorrow turned to anger, anger that she'd never see her friend again, anger that the stubborn detective across from her wouldn't take her seriously.

"How about now, detective? Now do you believe me that there's more to this than it looks?" Naomi said sharply.

"I'm truly sorry, Miss Archer, I still don't know that it means anything. It looks like just an accident. Did he run there often?" McCauley was unconvinced, but he was showing far more deference than he was moments ago.

"Of course he did. Everyone who lives in River North runs there. I'm telling you it's not a coincidence," Naomi insisted.

"I'm just not sure that it adds up to kidnapping or murder."

"Well, what about this, then?" Naomi pulled her phone from her purse and opened her email. She thumbed through the app, then slammed the phone down on the desk in front of

McCauley and Davis. From 08212017@freemail.net:

I'm afraid I didn't go high enough. Be careful who you talk to.

-R

"And you think the R is Richard?" McCauley asked.

"Of course it's him. Who else do you think it's from?"

"Okay, Miss Archer, give us a moment."

McCauley pulled Davis off to the side, and they quietly chatted while Naomi dabbed her eyes with a tissue.

"What do you think?" Davis asked.

"What do I think? I think it's nothing, wild goose chase. People fall in the lake all the time around that bend just south of Oak Street Beach. No guardrails, right on the water. It's reasonable to conclude that while this Eisner was running in the wee hours of morning, he slipped and fell in. Chadwick might be in the wind. Maybe he tried to contact Eisner, and when he couldn't get through, he spooked and figured they burned him. It might be connected, but I don't see foul play here."

"And what about the email?" Davis asked.

"Again, what's there? A one-line email from a random address—"

"Jesus, you really are a stubborn son of a bitch, aren't you," Naomi yelled across the room at them.

"Look, I know you're upset, but there's no—"

"It's not random."

The detectives looked back at Naomi in surprise.

"I could hear you, you know. Next time you may want to talk softer. The email address is not random, and if you had let me finish, I would have told you as much."

"Okay, so if it's not random, what is it, then?" McCauley asked, walking back over to the desk.

"It's a date. August 21st, 2017," Naomi said.

"That's three weeks from now. Is something supposed to happen on that date?" McCauley asked.

"You really don't read the news, do you?" Naomi said.

"I read the sports page. I get enough news at work, so humor me, what's so special about August 21st?"

Davis spoke up. "It's the Great American Eclipse. It's the first total eclipse in a hundred years over the US. People are traveling from all over the country to go see it."

"Okay, so I still don't get it. How do we get from an astronomy buff who sends an email to Richard Eisner?"

"The name of the shell company we turned up in our investigation—it's named Eclipse," Naomi said.

McCauley's heart stopped when he heard the words. He had to make sure he wasn't crazy. He reached into the breast pocket of his coat and pulled from it the now folded sheet of paper that Stan Butterfield had given him the night before. He opened it up and looked at a single word sitting by itself in the center of the page.

ECLIPSE

CHAPTER TWENTY-ONE

Cody lay on his back in his neatly made bed. His eyes were shut, but restful sleep always managed to escape him. A good night was a few uninterrupted hours of dreamless bliss, but most of the time his mind raced. He saw a doctor for it once who prescribed a sleeping aid. It worked, but he hated the foggy effect that the pills had on him. When he found his waking hours becoming a haze, he swore them off by flushing the contents of the pill bottle down the toilet. In Iraq he had managed weeks at a time of sleep deprivation. He felt it was better to suck it up and deal with it than to dull his mind with drugs.

A small beam of light broke through the crack in the curtains and bounced off the bare white wall above Cody's bed, illuminating the rest of the room with hints of daybreak. A faint buzz began permeating Cody's dreams until he finally opened his eyes. He turned to see his cell phone rattling around the top of his nightstand. Cody picked it up, then sat up on the edge of the bed, planting his feet firmly on the floor. He didn't recognize the number, but any incoming calls on this line were considered important. He tapped the touch screen to answer the call.

"Hello," he said, his voice betraying his recent slumber.

"Cody. Did I wake you?" a man on the other end asked.

"No." Cody cleared his throat. "I'm awake. Who is this?"

"Mr. Whitaker wants to see you. I'm coming over to pick you up. Can you be ready in ten minutes?"

"That won't be a problem."

"Great, I'm in a black Lincoln MKC. I'll be in front when you come down."

Cody acknowledged the information and ended the call. He made his way toward the bathroom to get ready.

On the other end of the call, the younger Pennington security officer, Tony Russo, was satisfied. It had been a long night for him disposing of both Chadwick and Eisner, but this would wrap things up nicely and put him in the good graces of Whitaker.

He didn't underestimate Cody, although he had to admit the circumstances couldn't have worked out better. Cody had just woken up and was probably wondering about the request to see Whitaker on such short notice. He'd be playing defense instead of assessing his situation, and that's just where Tony wanted him.

○

Tony was already parked out front of the six-story mid-rise apartment building when he made the call. It only took Cody eight minutes to freshen up, change, and make his way downstairs.

Cody spotted the SUV as he exited the lobby doors and made his way toward it. As he opened the door and took his place in the passenger's seat, Tony Russo stuck his hand out to introduce himself.

"Hi, Cody, I'm Tony," he said with a big, disarming smile—a trick learned from his Italian grandfather.

Cody shook his hand. "Haven't seen you before."

"Yeah, I'm new to the organization. Mr. Whitaker hired me a few months back."

"Oh, yeah? How do you like it?" Cody asked, feigning interest in small talk.

"To be honest, it's not the most exciting work. I mostly do this sort of thing. Drive people around, deliver a package from point A to point B, that sort of thing."

"Every job has its mundane parts."

"Oh, don't get me wrong, I'm not complaining. It's a good gig, it pays well, and I'm thankful to have it. Just a far cry from kicking down doors in Iraq."

"What branch did you serve in?"

"Marines, buddy, just like you." Russo pulled up his sleeve to reveal a tattoo on his forearm of a blue diamond with a red number one in the middle—the insignia for the First Marine Division.

Cody nodded in approval. "How'd you know I was a marine?"

"Come on, man!" Russo slapped Cody on his left bicep with the back of his hand. "*The* Cody Evans? Every marine in the world knows who you are. You're a legend, man!"

"I'm no legend. I just did my job, like everyone else."

"Hey, you're talking to a fellow marine here. Save that humility shit for the civilians. When they told me to come pick you up, I thought, no way it's him—the actual Cody Fuckin' Evans. I can't tell you how happy I was when I saw you walk out that front door. I mean, what an honor for me to be in the same car."

"How many tours did you do?" Cody asked.

"Two and a half. Would have done more, but I took an AK round off a ricochet. Can you fucking believe it? I spend damn near three years in country, dodging bullets, RPGs, and IEDs. Then one day, out of the blue, some hajji scores a lucky shot from four hundred yards out. I don't think he was even aiming at me. There I was, standing by my Humvee, and I see a cloud of dust pop up thirty yards in front of me. Damn thing clipped a rock and skipped right into my ankle."

"Some guys would give their right ankle for a wound like

that," Cody joked.

"Not me, brother. The docs are a bunch of dumbasses. I mean, don't get me wrong, they did right by me, taking out all the fragments and saving my foot. But when it was time to clear me for active duty, you know what they said?"

"What's that?"

"Not fit for service. Look at me. I've got no limp, and I run five miles a day—on a bad day."

"So why'd they bounce you, then?"

"The weight. See, the bullet clipped my Achilles, along with a bunch of other stuff. They did what they could, but according to them, if I throw my rucksack on, it could rupture again. Like I said, I can march, I can run, hell, I can even jump—though I'm not supposed to. I just can't put on a hundred pounds of gear and hoof it any meaningful distance without it potentially giving way. So that was it. Just another marine cut down in the prime of his career."

"Sorry to hear it. You still could have stayed. They offer you another job?"

"Yeah, they said I could train recruits at Camp Pendleton." Russo raised his hands to make air quotes. "Use my skills to help mold the next generation of marines. It even came with a promotion."

"But you said no."

"You're damn right I did. I'm an operator, not a babysitter. I need to be out in the field kicking down doors, not showing a bunch of recruits how to blow their noses."

"I hear that. At least you made it out alive. Other guys weren't so lucky."

"Yeah, there's that. Plus, now I've got this new job, three hots and a cot, and I get to ride around in this slick SUV—which, by the way, has air conditioning—so it could be wor—"

Russo slammed on the brakes as a bicycle messenger blew through a red light. The SUV screeched to a stop, and Russo threw his hands up in anger at the messenger, who flipped his middle finger back in return.

As Russo gestured at the biker, Cody saw something peeking out of his interior coat pocket that alarmed him—the manila envelope he'd given to Chadwick the night before. It was a thick envelope, and it appeared that Russo had tried to recklessly cram it in the undersized vest pocket. Even more disturbing were the unmistakable drops of blood that had dried on it.

Cody drew only one conclusion. If this kid had killed Chadwick, then Whitaker also knew that Cody had disobeyed his orders by letting him go. If Whitaker knew that, then Cody's was certainly the next name on Russo's list. It all made sense now—the early morning phone call summoning him to an impromptu meeting, the new guy who was an ex-marine himself. It was all designed for Cody to lower his guard.

For a moment Cody wondered if Whitaker had hired this kid as an insurance policy. If he ever needed to take out Cody, who better to have around than a fellow marine. The tattoo on Russo's arm showed he was the real deal, and Cody knew that Whitaker was the type of man who played the long game. Or maybe Russo was to become Cody's replacement.

No time to wonder about that now, Cody thought. Escape and evade just became top priority. His mind began to cycle through his options.

If Tony Russo was half the operator he claimed to be, he'd have his gun stashed to beat Cody in a straight draw. He'd be ready to counter Cody's draw, then he'd use his own pistol to end the fight quickly.

He could try to knock the kid out, but that wasn't a great option either. Cody didn't spot any tail vehicles, but he could sense them out there. They knew the route, so they could be paralleling the SUV instead of following it, making it nearly impossible to spot them. Plus, knocking out Russo could send the car careening out of control. If he failed on the first blow, Cody would be in trouble. If the car crashed, Cody would be in trouble. If they got into a struggle, he had to assume that backup was seconds away, and again Cody would be in trouble. Cody knew his best option was to flee.

Most marines detested the notion of retreat. They tended to equate retreat with cowardice, but not Cody. As a sniper he was used to being alone and outgunned. Evasion was an essential part of his toolkit, and Cody understood the fundamental principle of "live to fight another day." He'd have his moment to deal with Russo, but much better that it take place on Cody's terms.

Cody started compartmentalizing his situation in his mind. *Don't worry about step ten yet, or that sinking feeling of despair will take over. Focus on step one—get your seatbelt off.*

Cody casually unstrapped it, which Russo took notice of immediately.

"Still hard to get used to these things again after all the years riding around in a Humvee. I know it's mental, but we all have our quirks."

"I hear you," Russo said with skepticism in his voice.

Cody jokingly grabbed for the seatbelt again. "Maybe I should reconsider after that close call with the biker."

"No, man, you're all good. I'm a great driver," Russo said, chuckling.

Step two—get out of the car. This part was going to be trickier. The pair was traveling westbound, away from the bustling city center, and entering the more residential Humboldt Park neighborhood. Despite the early hours, downtown would have afforded him cover among the weekday warriors making their way to their offices, but out here the streets were far quieter. The myriad of gangways and alleys would have to be his cover. Now he just needed to pick his spot.

Cody checked the mirrors again for tail cars but saw nothing. He hoped to see one—better to know where it was. With no luck there, he'd have to take his chances.

Russo rambled on about his least favorite MREs—meals ready to eat—that he had the displeasure of sampling while he was on mission back in Iraq.

"Oh, yeah, that one was terrible," Cody said to keep Russo chatting and distracted. His eyes scanned the road ahead and his periphery to his right, looking for the perfect spot to bail.

Then he saw it. A stop sign just ahead, followed by two single-family homes with well-manicured lawns. He could just make out the gangway between the two buildings, which undoubtedly led to the alley in back and hopefully a half dozen other escape routes.

Cody could feel his heart racing as they slowed to a stop at the intersection. He took a deep breath as Russo pressed on the gas pedal to bring the car back up to speed.

Five miles per hour.

Ten miles per hour.

Fifteen miles per hour.

Cody threw open the door and leapt from the SUV, tucking his right arm into his body. Russo was caught totally off guard. Still clutching the wheel with his left hand, he reached to grab Cody by the collar in a futile effort to try and prevent all 220 pounds of him from tumbling out of the car.

Cody's body exited the vehicle just out of Russo's grasp, and Russo had inadvertently slammed on the accelerator as he extended himself reaching for Cody. The powerful V-8 Detroit engine sent the car barreling down the street, but by that time Cody had already cleared it. He landed on his bent knee, then his hip, then his shoulder and rolled—the perfect execution of a controlled parachute fall that the US Army's Airborne Corps had conceived in the days of World War II.

The technique, which effectively dampened the force of the impact, combined with Cody's athleticism allowed him to hit the ground in a roll and pop up into a sprint almost seamlessly. He immediately righted himself in the direction of the gangway. He could hear screeching tires behind him, and out of the corner of his eye he just made out the taillights of the braking Lincoln fifteen yards down the road.

He hoped his head start would be enough to traverse the long walkway between the shotgun-style row homes, which were three times as deep as they were wide. It was a kill box, but if he could make it to the backyard before Russo could get to the front yard, he'd have a pretty good chance of getting out alive.

Cody scooted through the narrow passageway, but not before he heard footsteps and two bullets rip past his head and into the brick facade of the building to his right. The silencer at the end of Russo's Sig P226 muffled the sound of the bullets exiting the barrel. His pistol emitted no noise save for the tapping of the hammer striking the primer on the shell casing.

Cody dug in and pushed his legs to their maximum in an effort to get to the rear of the building. Ahead of him he saw a child's pink bicycle with a white seat and tassels flowing from the matching handlebars.

In full sprint he pushed off his right leg and hurdled the bike in one bound, barely taking anything off his speed.

Ten feet to safety.

Ping ping! Two shots rang out high and wide right again. Russo had made it to the gangway.

Five feet.

Cody drew the 9 mm Beretta from his right hip and immediately pointed it rearward, not even bothering to raise or aim it. His left arm still pumped furiously as he started pulling the trigger.

Bangbangbangbangbangbang.

He unloaded as many rounds as he could in the direction of Russo, who threw himself against the front of the left house for cover. Cody blasted out of the darkened gangway into the wide, sunlit backyard like a rocket bursting out of a storm cloud.

Russo peeked his head down the gangway, then started pushing toward the back, his gun held out in front of him. Cody turned and fired five more rounds at Russo, who dove back for cover.

Going for the gangway was a gamble, but now the kill zone was working to Cody's advantage. Russo waited again, took several deep breaths to psych himself up for action, then made another attempt to traverse the gangway.

Bangbangbangbangbang.

Cody emptied the rest of his magazine toward Russo, who promptly retreated again.

Cody peered down the gangway. Confident that Russo now understood the danger of giving chase via the narrow passage, Cody darted through the backyard for the alley. The only thing separating Cody from freedom now was a four-foot chain-link fence, which he took at speed.

He jumped it by propping his body up on the top bar with his hands and swinging his legs to his left and over, landing on his feet. He knelt against the home's garage for cover while reloading. With his right thumb he pressed the magazine release and let the empty magazine fall to the ground. Simultaneously with his left hand he drew a fresh one from his waistband, inserted it into the Beretta, and depressed the slide release, chambering a round.

Cody got the gun back in action just in time to see a black sedan screaming down the alley at him.

"Shit," Cody muttered to himself at the sign of the chase vehicle.

Cody didn't hesitate. He rose to his feet and fired at the driver. White shatter marks peppered the windshield as Cody's rounds found their mark.

The car screeched to a halt, and two men in dark suits and aviator sunglasses and holding AR-15s exited both sides. They took cover behind the doors and aimed their weapons down the alley at Cody. With no cover of his own, he traversed the alley and barreled his way through a shoddily built, six-foot-high wooden fence into the backyard of a neighboring house on the opposite side of the alley. The fence gave way in one blow as Cody lowered his shoulder and pushed his whole body weight into it, toppling over into the yard.

He heard the sound of the rifles zipping 5.56 mm rounds in his direction, but the garage and the rest of the fencing on the side of the yard successfully obscured Cody from their vision.

The driver moved methodically toward the yard as the man on the passenger side laid down suppressing fire, popping off a round every second.

Cody looked around as he lay flat on his belly in the back-yard. He was totally fenced in, and there was no way he'd have enough momentum from his current position to knock another section of fence down. Going over it would be suicide with the incoming rifle rounds. He looked up at his best option and, without hesitation, popped up onto one knee. Cody fired three shots at the sliding glass rear door to the house. The interior was dark, and Cody felt it was a good sign no one was home.

He started moving in a crouch, then lifted his body to pick up speed. He bounded up the stairs in two strides as the shooters spotted him. The rifle rounds splintered the wood deck around Cody, who covered his face with his jacket and smashed through the weakened glass, which shattered all around him.

Cody shook the glass out of his hair and darted to the front of the empty home. He unlocked and whipped open the door before sprinting up the street. He used the cars for cover as he checked to see if the men followed, but there was no sign of them. The sound of approaching sirens wailing in the distance no doubt gave his pursuers pause.

As the sirens drew closer, Cody slipped down another alley and into an open garage where a late-model Honda Civic was conveniently running. A brown leather briefcase rested on the passenger's seat—no doubt someone leaving for work who ran back into the house at the sound of the gunfire. Finally for Cody, a fortunate turn of events.

He got in the car, pulled out of the garage, and headed south before zigzagging his way back east toward the lake.

CHAPTER TWENTY-TWO

In a doughnut shop down the street from the station, Naomi sat across from McCauley in a booth. Davis waited to order in the counter line, which had swelled with customers stopping in on their way to work. McCauley had suggested getting out of the drab police station in an effort to change the mood. On the way over, Davis let McCauley know with a look that he had been unfairly rough on Naomi, and he was right.

"You know, you're not the first person to call me that," McCauley said, breaking the ice.

"Call you what?"

"A stubborn son of a bitch."

"Well, I was upset, frustrated. I know you are just doing your job. Sorry for saying that."

"Don't be. You're right, I am a stubborn son of a bitch. Probably why no one in the department wants to work with me," McCauley said.

"What about your partner? He seems to like working with you."

"That's just because he hasn't worked with me very long. He's a sharp kid, though, he'll figure it out soon enough."

Naomi cracked a smile at the self-deprecating remark. "I bet it's a quality that makes you a good detective, though. I know it makes me a good lawyer. In fairness, I'm pretty stubborn myself—I'm just not usually on the receiving end of it."

"I guess we traded bedside manner for career aspirations."

"Doesn't exactly help in the relationship department either. So what's your story, you divorced?" Naomi asked.

McCauley let out a laugh. "I guess I deserve that. No, not divorced, although she had a lot of reasons to want one. They say when you marry a cop, you marry the job. I guess I'm just lucky I married the one woman in Chicago who's got more persistence in her little finger than you and me combined. How about you? I don't see a ring, so boyfriend?"

"Here and there. Nothing really seems to ever stick."

"Eh, it'll all work out. Smart, pretty, successful lawyer. You'll find someone, or more likely they'll find you," McCauley said. "Look, I want to apologize for how I treated you back at the station. I'm sorry I didn't believe you. We get a lot of missing persons cases, and damn near all of them turn out to be nothing. That's not an excuse for why I didn't believe you...just a mistake, I guess."

"You don't have to apologize, but thanks."

"And your friend. I'm real sorry that he died. I'm going to do everything I can to figure out what happened, though. That much I promise you."

Davis returned to the booth, drink carrier in hand. "Large black coffee, powdered sugar doughnut," he said, placing them in front of McCauley. "Another large black coffee, and I know you said you weren't hungry, Miss Archer, but I got you an old-fashioned doughnut just in case you change your mind."

"Thanks." Naomi appreciated the gesture.

"Davis," McCauley started, "I want you to go back to the station, call the medical examiner's office, and talk to the ME directly. Tell him we need him to take another look at the Eisner case—a full work-up, but don't tell him why. If he asks, just tell them we need it and not to change the report until I speak to him."

"Understood," said Davis.

"Davis, that last part is important. No one outside of us can know about this yet. Got it?"

"Yeah. I got it. No one will know."

Davis turned and walked out of the door as Naomi tore a piece of the doughnut off and popped it in her mouth.

"Why can't anyone else know about this?" Naomi asked.

"The ME has a form with check boxes at the top. Once says accidental. The check mark by that box may be the only thing keeping you alive right now."

"You really did a one-eighty on this, didn't you? What changed your mind about me? Was it the email?"

"Not exactly," McCauley said. "A few days ago, a midlevel drug dealer was shot and killed. Did you read about it in the papers?"

Naomi shook her head. Gangland shootings were an everyday occurrence. She used to read the *Tribune* recap, but it always seemed the same. So-and-so was shot while sitting in his car, someone else was shot in response, a bystander was the unintended target of another shooting. It was hard to take, so she stopped checking it.

"The dealer was killed with a precision shot from a sniper —not exactly your typical drive-by. Not two days later, his associate is gunned down in the middle of the afternoon at a safe house he was holed up in. It was a grisly scene. This time an automatic weapon was used, and they shot him fifteen times."

"So it's retribution? Or maybe someone clearing the field to take over the business?" Naomi asked, leaning closer with interest.

"My lieutenant, and pretty much every other cop who worked the scene, thinks just that. Second guy, named DeMario Sherman, takes out the first guy, named Melvin Jackson. He knows there's going to be fallout, so he hides out in a little apartment he's got stashed for just such an occasion. Someone loyal to Jackson knew of the place, so he takes out Sherman. Part retribution, but could also be a power grab. Seems like a neat little package, no?"

"But you don't believe that."

"No, I do not."

"Well, isn't this just rich with irony?" Naomi asked.

"Oh, yeah? How so?"

"Thirty minutes ago you said just about anything you could to dismiss my case. Now your boss is doing the same to you. Seems we have more in common than we thought."

"Ha, I guess you're right. All right, now it's my turn to ask the questions. What do you know about Eclipse?" McCauley asked.

"You know I can't tell you."

"Yeah, I know, you're bound by privilege. Look, Naomi— can I call you Naomi?" McCauley asked. After getting a quick nod of approval, he continued, "You have one of two choices. You can stand on your attorney-client privilege and walk away. Go back to your high-paying job and forget all of this. The people behind this, if there are any people or if there is a 'this,' are probably counting on just that."

"What's my other choice?"

"You can put your trust in me to solve it."

"I'm just not sure I can do that," Naomi said.

"I get it, we got off on the wrong foot. So let's start over. I'm Detective Patrick McCauley, and I believe you that your friend may have been murdered. I believe you that Robert Chadwick is missing and that he may have been murdered too. I believe you when you say it's connected to a company that you are investigating and that this somehow is tied to the Pennington Corporation. To show you that I trust you, I'm going to tell you a secret. My friend is an NSA agent. He told me that the listening device I found hidden in an outlet in DeMario Sherman's apartment last night belonged to his agency. He told me that same device was supposed to be decommissioned and destroyed, but instead an employee sold it to pay off a gambling debt. Here's the kicker. The name of the company that bought it is Eclipse."

Naomi gasped.

"That's classified information. I could lose a very good friend by telling you that," McCauley pressed.

"I could lose my career," Naomi rebutted.

"You could also lose your life. If your instincts are right, then you're in danger."

"I know I am. Why do you think I came to the police in the first place?"

"It's not fear. I know fear. I've seen it in a mother terrified that her child is going to get locked up or worse. I've seen fear of death—the look in a person's eyes when they know it's coming no matter how much they bargain or pray for it not to. I see fear every day in this job, and I don't see an ounce of it in you. I think you're doing this because you want to find Robert. I think you can't stop wondering how two dead drug dealers are connected to all of this. But most of all—"

"I want to get the son of a bitch that killed my friend," Naomi said.

"I can help you do that, and we'll toe the line on the privilege issue as much as possible. I'm giving you McCauley privilege," McCauley said.

"What exactly does that mean?" asked Naomi.

"It means I'm getting older, and my recollection sometimes gets hazy. Anything you tell me during the course of this investigation is liable to be forgotten."

Naomi hesitated for a moment, then spoke. "So where do we start?"

A wide grin swept across McCauley's face. "First place any good detective would—Richard's apartment."

CHAPTER TWENTY-THREE

Brendt Whitaker stood looking out the window of his top-floor corner office. It was one of the few offices that still had a marvelous view that hadn't been gobbled up by the sea of high-rise buildings erected over the past fifty years.

He furrowed his brow in thought as he looked down at the thousands of ant-sized people scampering around the city below. The news of Cody letting Chadwick go was a setback—an unfortunate one—but still just a setback.

Whitaker was no stranger to setbacks in his life, having been orphaned at the tender young age of twelve. He grew up in a middle-class family on the South Side of Chicago. His father was a CTA bus driver, and his mother was a teacher at a local Catholic school. His parents were loving and wanted more children, but there were complications during Brendt's birth. The doctors were able to save his mother's life, but Brendt was the last child that she would be able to bear.

That piece of news couldn't stop the love that permeated the household, though, as the three of them were as close as could be. Friday nights were pizza nights. After his father's shift ended, he'd pick up the same pizza combination from the place around the corner—half sausage and garlic (for the boys) and half pepperoni and mushroom for his mother. They would alternate between deep dish or square-cut thin pizza—also a Chicago staple, though less known than its famous thick counterpart.

In the summers they'd often take in a White Sox game at

Comiskey, visit any number of the city's beautiful museums, and go for ice cream. The one constant was that they all did it together.

That is, except the night Brendt's parents were snatched away by a drunk driver. They went out for dinner to celebrate their fifteenth wedding anniversary but never came back. Instead, a police officer and a chaplain came knocking on the door. Brendt cried for a week straight. They considered sending him to live with an aunt on his mom's side in Portland, but she couldn't take him—or, more accurately, wouldn't take him. With no grandparents or next of kin to speak of, they shipped Brendt off to St. Andrew's Home for Boys. The nuns tried to prepare Brendt for the fact that there was not a big adoption market for twelve-year-old boys, an idea with which he decided he could live. Unlike the orphanages in every movie ever made, St. Andrew's was a fine place. The nuns were actually quite nice, as were the accommodations. It had everything a young man could ever want or need, except, of course, a family.

Brendt threw himself into his studies, and it paid off. He became a straight-A student, and he outgrew the classes at St. Andrew's by the time he was sixteen. He begged the nuns to enroll him in some local community college courses, which they did begrudgingly. It wasn't that they minded shuttling him to and from the campus. It was the knowledge that there was no money to send him any further once he graduated. The nuns had learned over the years the importance of managing expectations given their never-ending funding constraints.

When he turned eighteen, Brendt moved into a small studio apartment a few blocks from the orphanage. The University of Chicago accepted him into the undergraduate program and even offered him a small scholarship, but Brendt was still well short of enough money for the first tuition payment. He deferred his acceptance for a year while he worked multiple jobs to save money. He did anything from cleaning toilets to picking up trash on the noisy and polluted highways, but Chicago was an expensive city, and without the free room and board at St.

Andrew's, he found himself not saving enough.

So Brendt tried another way to raise the funds. He may have been short on cash, but he wasn't short on former St. Andrew's acquaintances who knew of ways to get it quickly, which was generally synonymous with illegally. A freckle-faced kid named Mickey Flynn had gotten a job on the bottom rung of an organization that made gobs of money and was run by Jim and John O'Doyle. He got Brendt a meeting with them, and seeing his potential, they hired him on the spot. Earning proved harder for him than it did Mickey, though. He quickly found that no one will approach you to buy drugs if you look like a baby-faced cop. He also wasn't much good at tending bar, selling stolen merchandise, or anything else that involved a lot of people skills. The O'Doyles were nice, though; they looked after him and paid him even when he screwed up. They had been products of St. Andrew's, and looking after Brendt was their way of giving back to the community. But it wasn't all charity. Brendt may have been awkward and bad at damn near everything they asked him to do, but he was smart and loyal—two traits that were highly valued in the underworld.

Just to stash him while they figured out how to use him, the O'Doyles gave him a gig running betting slips between several of their gambling outlets. It was a simple job that involved taking a ledger between different locations in the neighborhood. He'd give the book to the manager behind the counter, who marked the current action and then gave it back to him. Then it was on to the next one. Three times a day he'd shuttle that book between several clubs before returning it to the O'Doyles at their social club, which acted as their unofficial headquarters. The limited interaction with people made it a perfect fit for him.

The first time Brendt walked into a gambling den, though, he was blown away. The room was hot and crowded. Large metal fans were set up to cool the place down, but they only managed to push the thick, hazy fog of lingering cigar smoke that hung at hat level around the room.

A regular named Jarvis clocked Brendt immediately as he

walked in the door and came running over. Jarvis wore a dirty tank top that was probably once white, green shorts, and a floppy tan hat. He looked as though he was down to his last nickel—a place he knew all too well. Brendt took in the room as Jarvis yammered at him about a horse in the next race at Hawthorne. He'd give him the name of the horse if Brendt would post a ten-dollar bet for him. Looking around in wide-eyed awe at the place, Brendt reached into his pocket without saying a word and produced a twenty-dollar bill with two fingers and handed it to Jarvis.

"Hey, that's great, man, ten for you and ten for me," he said. "You're not going to regret this. It's a lock!"

The horse came up lame out of the gates and had to be put down on the track. "A rough break on a sure thing," Jarvis would go on to say, but Brendt didn't care.

On the surface, the place was a dump. A no-frills place to get one's fix for drinking, smoking, and gambling. Maybe a few other vices as well, if you knew whom to ask. The only thing Brendt saw, though, were dollar signs.

It didn't take long for him to see his purpose in the organization. Brendt started spending lots of time at the gambling dens. Over a few short months, he learned the ins and outs of bookmaking. He even started making his own odds and comparing them to that of the O'Doyles' bookmakers.

Brendt loved the idea of it. He looked at every factor as a piece of a giant puzzle. He surmised how a football team's performance in the rain told a subtle story not just about that team but about each team they'd already played, and the teams that those teams played—a butterfly effect of gambling probabilities.

Before long, Brendt was at the O'Doyles' social club, begging them to let him take over one of the gambling locations. They saw his potential but were still wary that he could pick up the business in such a short amount of time. The duo sat in their corner booth and discussed the proposal, which consisted of whispering in each other's ears while Brendt sat silently across from them. After a few minutes of back and forth, they decided to give Brendt a shot at an underperforming club that they were planning to shut down in the Kenwood neighborhood. They gave him three months and a modest budget to turn the place around.

Brendt immediately went to work renovating the club's interior. The main hall was lined with old wooden church pews facing two small televisions—an altar, of sorts, for the gamblers. Brendt ripped out the pews and installed high-top tables in the center of the room and plush red velvet booths around the edges. He replaced the two small TVs with two large projection ones and hung a dozen other televisions throughout the room. Every seat in the house had a view, which was a nice experience for the gambler but simultaneously served as a subliminal reminder that action was just one bet away.

When he replaced the watered-down well liquor with top-shelf brands, he didn't increase the price. It cut into the margins a bit, but at 70 percent, he had plenty of room to spare. Then he hired an army of pretty cocktail waitresses to patrol the floor. He dressed them in revealing black sequined ragtime outfits. They were complete with dangling tassels that danced on their smooth thighs. They offered quick drink service, cigarettes, and a pretty smile.

Within six weeks the clientele dramatically shifted. Gone were the Jarvises, replaced by working, middle-class men. Plumbers, pipe fitters, steel workers, and other skilled tradesmen started coming. Most were union and had the paychecks to prove it. They even got a few professors from the University of Chicago from time to time, the irony of which gave Brendt a certain level of satisfaction.

Soon the place was raking it in. Brent understood the one thing all successful casinos understood. Any bozo can make money being the house, but it takes the right type of customer to make the real money.

Within a year the other clubs all followed suit. They still left a few lower-rent ones in the worst parts of town—Brendt and the O'Doyles weren't ones to turn away customers—but most had become vibrant venues for entertainment.

Even the city's elite began frequenting the establishments. It wasn't uncommon to see aldermen, judges, cops, and even prosecutors lining up to have a drink and take in a game. That's when Brendt started dealing in another type of currency—influence.

He quickly amassed a large list of contacts, rarely resorting to blackmail. It was a dirty business that he quickly learned produced unreliable results. Instead, he became a master at getting what he needed through subtle nudging and by dealing in favors. He found it was much better to have an alderman in your pocket that wanted to be there than one that didn't.

His new "friends" helped pave the way for the O'Doyles to expand even farther into the some of the ritzier neighborhoods.

All told, by the time Brendt was twenty-five, he had built an empire of twenty-three clubs generating just north of $20 million annually. Not bad for an orphaned kid who lacked a college degree and couldn't hold onto even the most menial of jobs.

While Brendt had a grip on the local authorities, he soon found out he was not so powerful when it came to the federal ones. It was a gray, rain-speckled Saturday morning when two FBI agents showed up at his door holding an arrest warrant.

The O'Doyles also lacked the clout to make the charges go away, but they knew someone who could help. Brendt was flabbergasted when he walked out of the FBI's downtown lockup forty-eight hours later with all charges dropped.

A car picked him up and delivered him to the O'Doyles' social club. The driver wasn't one of the O'Doyles' usual goons; rather, he was decidedly more professional-looking. He wore a suit and tie and drove an expensive Lincoln town car, even going so far as to open the door for Brendt.

Now, standing in his office, Brendt closed his eyes and thought back to that day. He remembered it like it was yesterday.

When he entered the club, he saw the O'Doyles sitting in the back with a man in his midforties. He was well dressed in a gray pinstripe suit. It looked good, but Brendt's father had always told him the only way to really tell a man's worth was by his shoes and his watch. The watch was a Rolex, and he couldn't place the shoes, but Brendt estimated by the soft, Italian leather that they probably cost just as much as his impeccably tailored suit.

He waited patiently in the corner until Jim O'Doyle summoned him over to the booth with a wave of his outstretched arm. Brendt walked over, then took a seat across from the three men, his head hung low in shame for having been arrested.

"You pick that head up, boyo," Jim said, speaking also for his brother. He always spoke for both of them, which was good considering his brother seldom uttered a word. They were both second-generation American, but Jim's accent was a strange amalgamation Irish and Chicago. "There's no shame in bein' pinched. It was bound to happen eventually given how well you've been doing, but the important ting is that you did right by keepin' quiet and letting us handle dis."

"I just did what you always told me to do if I ever got picked up by the cops."

The O'Doyles nodded in approval. "Do you know who dis is?" Jim said, gesturing to the well-dressed man next to him.

"I'm afraid I don't, sir," Brendt said with a hint of embarrassment.

"Dis here is Mr. Pennington. Do you know that name?"

"As in Pennington Hotels?"

The man interjected with a charismatic laugh. "Among other things, yes, we have a nice little hotel business."

115

He was being modest. As far as Brendt knew, the Pennington hotel chain was the largest in the world.

The man flashed his impressively straight white teeth at Brendt, stuck out his hand, and said, "I'm Harrison Pennington, and we have a proposal for you, if you are willing to listen."

Brendt knew what that meant. A proposal in his situation sounded nicer than calling it what it was—an ultimatum. With little choice, he shook Pennington's hand and said, "Of course I'll listen. It's a pleasure to meet you, sir."

"I can assure you the pleasure is mine. For the last few years, I have heard the most fabulous stories in the various circles I travel in of a mysterious wunderkind from the South Side. And here we are, the young man who turned"—he paused, parsing his words—"an ancillary gambling business into the foremost sports betting operation in the Midwest."

Pennington looked at the O'Doyles and made a gesture with his eyebrows asking if his last statement was fair.

With a nod of approval, Jim said, "What Mr. Pennington is politely saying is dat you took our shitty bookmaking business and turned it into an money machine. For dat we owe you a debt of gratitude."

"You gave me more chances than I probably deserved, and you've paid me well, so the way I see it, we're square," Brendt said.

"Nonsense," Jim said, holding his sausage fingers up in the air. "Look, you're a good kid. You've made us a lot of money and kept yer nose clean. I wish we had a hundred more guys like you. Which is why I'm sad to see you go."

A look of confusion swept over Brendt's face as Pennington interjected, "The O'Doyles must really like you, Brendt, because they called in a big chit to get you out of this trouble you find yourself in."

"So you're the one that made the charges disappear?"

Pennington nodded.

"But how...why?"

"You don't have to concern yourself with the how. Just

breathe easy knowing that this little matter has been put to bed," Pennington said with a finality in his voice. "As for the why, well, that's a longer story. The O'Doyles and the Penningtons go back a long ways. See, the Penningtons haven't always been in the hotel business."

The O'Doyle brothers chuckled like dear friends reminiscing over a secret.

"In fact, my family started in the dry goods business. My great-grandfather immigrated here in the mid-1800s, hoping to move out west and stake a claim to his very own gold mine. He made it as far as Chicago before he realized there was a lot more gold in selling that dream to others than there was actual gold buried in the California hillsides. This was the last major city before heading west, and he outfitted prospectors, farmsteaders—you name it—with everything they needed for the trip. Eventually he opened up a chain of stores out west, which was the start of the family shipping business. He was moving goods by the ton all over the western half of the United States for his stores. He figured, why not charge people and do the same for them?"

"I never knew that," Brendt said.

"Most people don't. The family sold that business around the outbreak of World War I. It wasn't until just after the war that my grandfather, Henry Pennington, opened his first hotels. He eventually levered the family fortune to expand the hotels into a national chain. For a time the hotels thrived, and it appeared to be a great investment."

"I don't follow. Your hotels are in every major city in the world."

"Ah, yes, but success wasn't a foregone conclusion. The Depression hit us as hard as everyone else. The business was hanging on by a thread when my father turned old enough to work at the company. I guess it was the shipping business in his blood. Perhaps it was the strong survival instinct shared by every member of the Pennington family—save for the few distant cousins who decided it was better to die in some muddy trench halfway across the world fighting someone else's war. Whatever the case, it was my father who saved the business."

"Hey, I take exception to dat," Jim O'Doyle chimed in sarcastically.

"I was getting to that part," Pennington said, looking at him while letting out a hearty laugh. He turned back to Brendt. "As I was saying, it was my father who saved the business—with a tremendous amount of help from the O'Doyle family."

"So you started bootlegging?" Brendt asked.

Jim O'Doyle raised an eyebrow toward Pennington as if to say, *See? Told ya the kid is sharp.*

"In a word? Yes. Although I prefer to think of it as a natural extension to our hospitality business. Like the Pennington supply stores, my father realized that our hotels were the perfect distribution system. Instead of dry goods, though, we shipped alcohol. Just think of it, a hotel in every major U.S. city already receiving daily deliveries. It wasn't hard to add a few cases of alcohol to every truck."

"So what was your family's take in all of this?"

"Our friends the O'Doyles paid us a generous shipping fee to move their product, but we also found a lot of profitable synergy within our hotels. In those days word traveled fast, and it didn't take people long to figure out where one could get a drink. Pretty soon our hotel business was in the black again. Our properties' restaurants and clubs were packed on a nightly basis, and the occupancy rates skyrocketed. What businessman would stay at a dry hotel when he could enjoy his favorite scotch at a Pennington property?"

"So what happened when they repealed Prohibition?"

"By the time the puritans in Washington finally came to their senses, Pennington was already a household name. A lot of the competition couldn't weather the storm, so when the economy turned up, we were in the perfect position to capitalize on it. I think you know the rest. We now have over four thousand locations in one hundred different countries."

"That's a fantastic story, and I congratulate you on your success. Forgive me for asking, but how do I fit into all of this, exactly?"

"Well, Brendt, that's a good question. You see, the Penningtons and the O'Doyles have one thing in common. We have a fierce loyalty to family, and given our history, it's safe to say we're like family. When they told me of your predicament—that the wunderkind had gotten picked up by the FBI—well, I just had to help."

"What's the catch?" Brendt asked. With powerful men there was always a catch. He knew this because he'd sat on the other side of this table more than once with someone in his rolodex of public officials.

"I wouldn't call it so much of a catch as I would an opportunity. I'm going to shoot you straight. The bad news is you're done in the bookmaking business. Even I can't do anything about that," Pennington said.

Brendt's shoulders dropped as if someone had snatched a puppy he'd raised from birth from his hands.

"Don't look so disappointed, son. There's good news in all of this too. Look, let's face facts. You don't belong in this world. You never have. In spite of that, you've built a highly successful business here, but now it's time to move on."

"But it's the only thing I'm good at."

"That's nonsense," Pennington snapped back, like a father quashing his son's self-pity. "A man that can do what you've done, with the hand that you were dealt, is invaluable to any organization."

"So what am I supposed to do now, then?" Brendt asked, already sensing the answer.

"Why, you'll come work for me, of course," Pennington replied.

"At the hotels?"

The three men all laughed in unison.

"No," Pennington said. "Not exactly. You'll work for the family directly. Our affairs have expanded well beyond the hotel chain, so you will be expected to handle a wide range of matters for us."

"I see," Brendt said warily.

"You will be expected to get a college degree. I understand you were once accepted to my alma mater, the University of Chicago. Fortunately for you, I can have that offer reinstated tomorrow, and you can start next quarter. You'll work twenty hours a week for me, where you'll earn your full salary. The rest of the time will be devoted to your studies. How can you say no to that?"

"I can't," Brendt said, accepting his fait accompli. "It's a very generous offer, and I gladly accept."

"Dat's great," Jim O'Doyle said as he beaconed the longtime waiter. "Danny, another round for the table. We're celebratin' tonight!"

John O'Doyle grabbed his brother by the arm to restrain him. Despite Brendt's best efforts to conceal it, John could see the disappointment in his eyes. They told the story of the hometown hero who worked his way up from the minors to become an all-star, only to be traded away for a player to be named later.

Without a hint of his brother's accent, John said, "Look, Brendt, we know this isn't what you wanted to happen. None of us wanted this, but you should know better than anyone that life sometimes throws you curve balls. You've hit every one thrown at you since the night your parents were killed by that drunk. I know it's not fair, but I'm asking—we're asking—you to hit another one."

Brendt nodded affirmatively but didn't say a word. It was the first time he had ever heard John O'Doyle say anything louder than a barely audible whisper.

"Everything Jimmy said about you is spot on. We've gone to great lengths to help you here because you've done so much for us. Now, I've spoken with my brother, and we've decided to go one step further. This," he said, pulling a silver key from his pocket, "is the key to a safe-deposit box. More specifically, it's the key to your safe-deposit box, which is filled with two million in cash that has been graciously funneled through several of

Mr. Pennington's businesses. You know what this means in our world, don't you?"

Brendt did. Money was the universal currency for making amends in the underworld. Every transgression could be forgiven for the right price. Two million dollars was a small amount to walk away from what he had built for the O'Doyles. Brendt also knew it was a lot more expensive to the O'Doyles than a bullet to the head, which is the severance package they would have prepared for most men in his shoes. Between getting the charges dropped, setting him up with a job, and the money, it was as fair deal as he could hope for. Brendt took the key and thanked John.

"Good, now we can toast."

Upon seeing Jimmy finish his speech, Danny the waiter hurried over to the table with a tray full of drinks. He placed a shot of whiskey and a mug of beer in front of each man.

John took the shot and held it in the air as the others followed suit.

"To Brendt, may you have the hindsight to know where you've been, the foresight to know where you are going, and the insight to know when you have gone too far."

The words lingered in Brendt's mind as he stood in his office, still looking out his window. He kicked back the glass of whiskey he poured himself, then held it up in front of him just as he did that day.

"Right back at ya, John."

CHAPTER TWENTY-FOUR

The ride to Richard Eisner's apartment was covered in a heavy quiet. McCauley drove while Naomi sat in the passenger's seat, fighting tears with angry expletives under her breath. McCauley had no doubt that she was a firecracker, but he was sensitive to the toll Eisner's death was taking on her.

When they were a few blocks away, Naomi turned and spoke. "Companies."

"Pardon?" McCauley said, surprised by the break in silence.

"Back at the coffee shop. You said I thought the company that I was investigating was tied to Richard's death and Robert's disappearance. I wasn't investigating a company. I was investigating companies—plural."

"So you think there are multiple actors?"

"It's hard to say. Eclipse was just the first one we found. There are a dozen more that we uncovered dating back over ten years."

"But they're connected?"

"They have to be. Robert and I spent an entire day just looking for them all. Some he remembered, but others we had to find. Since we knew what we were looking for, it made it a lot easier. Once we felt we got them all, we started to run them down. All the cursory checks came back with nothing. They are shell companies registered in countries that take their banking secrecy laws seriously—Antigua, Caymans, Bahrain—you get the idea."

"How close did you get?" McCauley asked.

"I think we must have gotten too close. We had a war room set up so we could pore through those files. We were burning the candle at both ends to try and come up with any sort of lead. Even Richard was helping us with the grunt work. Then suddenly yesterday morning he told Robert and me to take the rest of the day off. I objected, but he wouldn't hear it. That was the last time I saw them."

"Was it unusual for Richard to suggest that?"

"I don't know anymore. It seemed weird to me, but maybe that's just because of everything that's happened," Naomi said.

McCauley pulled the Crown Vic around back of the posh River North high-rise and threw the car in park.

"I think you should stay in the car, Naomi."

"What? Why? Is this because I'm a woman?" she demanded.

"Whoa, whoa. Pump the brakes. It's not like that. They had one place under surveillance, and they could have this one bugged too. If I go in there, I'm just a regular Chicago detective following up on a routine accidental death. If they see you in there, it's a whole different ball game."

"His place isn't bugged," Naomi said definitively.

"How can you be so sure?"

"Richard didn't tell anyone what we had found until yesterday. He was waiting until we had more information first. So whoever he spoke with killed him quick. They wouldn't have had time to bug the place."

"If you're wrong, they'll kill you," McCauley pointed out.

"That's a risk I'm willing to take." Naomi folded her arms across her chest, signaling the end of the debate.

McCauley thought for a moment. He had to give Naomi credit; she was sharp, and she was probably right. Still, there was a risk, but it was painfully obvious to McCauley that he wouldn't be able to stop her.

"Well, let's go, then," he said, relenting.

The two made their way through the service entrance. The back of the building was a maze of dingy white hallways and tan linoleum tiles. The countless garbage bins, laundry baskets, and movers that made their way through the catacombs left their mark in the form of years' worth of scuffing on the floors and walls. The residents upstairs were oblivious to the underbelly of luxurious city living, which reeked of dried garbage. Naomi pulled the silver handle of a heavy wooden door that opened to a lobby with speckled marble flooring and a rocky indoor fountain with a koi pond at its base. To the right of where they entered sat the doorman behind a wooden desk topped with a counter that matched the floor. They made their way toward the barrel-chested man dressed in a dark suit and blue tie and with a gold name tag that said, "William P." McCauley flashed his credentials.

"Hi, William. I'm Detective McCauley, and this is a consultant for the police department. We need to get into Richard Eisner's apartment—unit 32D."

Apprehensive, William responded, "I'm not allowed to give out the key. Shouldn't you have some sort of warrant?"

"Well, it's not like that, William. He's not in any trouble with us. In fact, I'm sorry to tell you, but he was killed this morning running along the lakefront."

"Oh no. Mr. Eisner? You sure it's the Mr. Eisner that lives here?" William asked in disbelief.

"Yeah, I'm afraid so," McCauley said.

"Was it some kind of robbery? You know, I'm always telling him he's got to be careful when he goes out running. It seems like these days, even in the nice neighborhoods you can't go out without fear of getting robbed by some punks."

"It was nothing like that. Looks like just an accident—he fell and hit his head, and I'm just here for a routine follow-up. You know, to look for people that need to be contacted, that sort of thing."

"Oh, man, that's too bad. I really liked Mr. Eisner. He only moved in a few weeks before Christmas, but he tipped the whole staff well anyways. He wasn't above chatting about sports with the doorman either. Don't get me wrong, the people that live here are nice, but most just wave and walk past, ya know? Not Mr. Eisner, he'd rant for ten minutes about all the different ways the management is wrecking the Bears."

"Everyone we talked to said he was a great guy. It's a real shame," McCauley said. "But hey, since we're talking, you said he goes running a lot. Were you working late last night or early this morning?"

"I work the day shift. Seven a.m. to seven p.m., six days a week."

"And how about those cameras there," McCauley said, pointing to the security system behind the desk. "Did they record last night?"

"Those? Those work twenty-four seven. You want me to pull up the footage?"

"Do me a favor. Let me pop up to his apartment, check off the boxes for my file. Can you take a look between eight o'clock last night and four o'clock this morning? See if you can find him coming or going. It'll help to nail down the timeline of his movements for the report."

"You got it." William unlocked a drawer behind him and ran his fingers along the slots until he found what he was looking for. He turned back around and slapped a key on the counter. "Make sure you don't walk off with it. I'm sure I'll have to use it again given the circumstances."

"Thanks, William, see you back here in a few."

Naomi and McCauley walked past the desk and stepped onto a waiting elevator.

"You do that often?" she asked after the doors closed.

"Do what?"

"He's right. We need a warrant to get in here, or at least a family member, something more than what we've got," Naomi said.

"You know, contrary to the cynical legal world you live in, there are a lot of people that see helping the police as their civic duty."

"I didn't mean it like that. I just meant that William shouldn't have let us up, but he did. You have a good bedside manner when you try."

"Thanks for the compliment. We'll work on your bedside manner next," McCauley said, cracking a smile at Naomi.

A man's voice rang out over the elevator speaker, reminding McCauley of a CTA train: "Thirty-second floor."

As they approached Richard's unit, McCauley held his hand out, indicating for Naomi to hang back. He drew his .45-caliber 1911 pistol from underneath his coat and a small flashlight off a pouch attached to his belt. He knelt down and placed his ear on Richard's door, listening a moment for sound. When he heard nothing, he used the flashlight to inspect the deadbolt. Satisfied, he inserted the key and pushed the door open while remaining in the hallway.

"Chicago Police Department. Anyone home, come to the front door with your hands raised."

Silence.

Louder now: "Chicago Police Department. Anyone home, walk slowly to my voice with your hands raised."

Silence again. McCauley entered the foyer walking sideways, crossing one foot over the other. He kept his pistol at the low ready, then pivoted when he got to the kitchen, which opened to the living area of the small one-bedroom apartment. After clearing it, he scanned the rest of the living area and checked behind a couch near the wall adjacent to the window, which looked out to marvelous easterly facing city views. Naomi peeked her head in from the hallway and saw McCauley disappear into the bedroom. Less than a minute later, he re-emerged, holstering his pistol. He saw Naomi and waved her in, then handed her a set of latex gloves.

"Put these on, and try not to touch anything without me. We have to preserve it if it's a crime scene."

Naomi debated telling McCauley the futility of that. A first-year lawyer could have anything they found thrown out in a heartbeat. But she bit her tongue and instead wondered aloud, "Why does it smell like bleach in here?"

"He wasn't a germaphobe, was he?"

"I don't think so," Naomi said, shaking her head. "He was neat, not crazy."

McCauley knelt down by the front door and pointed at the floor with his pen.

"There's some discoloration here, could be bleach. Have you ever been here before?" McCauley asked. "And before you jump down my throat at the question, I'm only asking you if anything—like this spot, for example—looks out of place?"

"No, like I said, I've never been here. I went to his house in Lake Forest for a dinner party once before he got divorced. His wife and kids still live there. Who's going to tell them?"

"The detective that caught the case will make the notification. For now we have to let him do that so we can keep up appearances that it was an accident. Was it bitter?"

Naomi looked at him curiously.

"The divorce. Did his wife have any reason to want him dead?" McCauley asked.

"No, nothing like that. I got the impression it was pretty amicable. No affairs, no drag-down fights. Just a man who worked too much and grew apart from his wife. It happens to a lot of lawyers."

"It happens to a lot of cops too," McCauley commiserated.

McCauley photographed the spot on the wooden entryway floor with his phone. It didn't take long to search the kitchen or the sparsely furnished living room. Off to the side of the bedroom, in a nook, Richard kept a small home office. A newer-looking desk took up most of the space, and a file cabinet took the rest. The top of the desk was bare except for a few wires stretching from the back, its ends laying in the middle of the flat surface.

"Well, his laptop is gone," McCauley declared.

"So are his files," Naomi said, having opened the file cabinet drawers.

"Maybe he stashed them somewhere."

"I don't think so." Naomi pointed to the edge of the cabinet. "Look, the lock is broken."

McCauley thought for a moment.

"Is that what you were looking for out in the hallway?" Naomi asked.

"Yeah. I was checking for scratches, tool marks, any signs of forced entry."

"And?"

"Nothing, it was clean," McCauley said. "Let's check the rest of this desk."

They opened the rest of the drawers only to find them empty like the file cabinet.

"This is crazy. Somebody cleaned everything out," said Naomi, throwing her hands in the air.

McCauley stood in front of the desk and pulled the center drawer out. He reached underneath toward the back and grit his teeth as he fiddled with a lever on the track. He felt it catch, then pulled the drawer up and set it upside down on the desk.

"They didn't clean out everything," he said.

A note was taped to the bottom that read:

Junkyard Wolverine—Kingsbury 223

"Well, that really clears things up," McCauley said. "I don't suppose this means anything to you?"

"A little. I'm the junkyard wolverine."

McCauley raised an eyebrow.

"You know, like, junkyard dog?" Naomi continued. "A while back an older woman slipped on a spill in the bar of one of the Pennington properties. She broke her ankle and was suing for a seven-figure payout. She played the victim well, but she had a history of suing companies for stuff like this. The judge barred us from bringing up her past lawsuits, fearing it'd be too prejudicial, so I did the only thing I could think of."

"You went after her on the stand?"

"You bet I did. It was a gamble. If she didn't break, we would have looked like the bad guys for going after an old woman, but it was worth the shot. I eviscerated her. By the end of it she copped to causing the spill. She didn't admit to slipping on purpose, but it was enough to get the case dismissed. The whole legal team went to Joe's Stone Crab after that to celebrate in typical legal fashion. Rich was three martinis deep when he started saying how happy he was they had a Wolverine on the team."

"Why a wolverine?"

"I went to Michigan. 'What's fiercer than a junkyard dog?' he'd say. 'A junkyard wolverine!' It became sort of a running joke between us."

"So you're the junkyard wolverine, but what does 'Kingsbury 223' mean?"

"That I don't know. Could be anything."

"There's a Kingsbury Street on the North Side. Runs from River North up to Armitage in Lincoln Park. You know, there's that industrial area up there where that steel mill finally went out. Isn't there a junkyard up there, right on Kingsbury?" McCauley asked.

"Yeah, I think you're right. It's behind all that upscale retail on Clybourn. I always thought how funny it is to have that industrial strip right in the heart of one of the nicest areas in the city. That property has to be worth a fortune."

"Do you think he wanted you to check out that junkyard?"

"I think whatever Richard was worried about was enough to go to these lengths. Burner emails, cryptic messages, real spy-craft-type stuff. If you're asking my opinion on whether or not we should check out that junkyard? I say we've got nothing to lose," said Naomi.

"All right, let's hit it."

When the doorman, William, saw McCauley and Naomi exit the elevator banks, he stood up and punched a few keys on the security system.

"Anything on those tapes?" McCauley asked, sliding the apartment key across the front desk.

"Yeah, it's strange, though. He comes in at 11:13 p.m. last night, then nothing," William said.

"You didn't see him leaving?"

"No. He never comes out."

"What about the back, you have cameras out there?"

"The service entrance? No, we don't have cameras back there, but I doubt he'd go out that way."

"Why do you say that?"

"You came through there, you saw what it looks like—what it smells like. I've worked here almost ten years, and the only time I've seen a resident use the service entrance is when the lobby was closed to put in these tiles, which cost more than I make in a week," William said, pointing to the marble floor. "It was only closed a few days, but I fielded complaints for a month after that." William shifted to a whine. "'William, why couldn't they do it in sections so we don't have to use the back door? William, why can't they just clear a path for us with some construction paper?' What was I to do, I'm just the doorman. I just said, 'Yes, ma'am, yes, sir, I'll bring it up with the property manager.' Sheesh, you'd think the world had ended, listening to all that belly aching."

"You're sure he didn't leave?"

"Positive. I got him right there on camera walking in with another man. Never comes out. Only five people even left between 11:00 p.m. and 4:00 a.m. this morning. It's an older crowd that lives here, not a lot of night owls."

"He was with another man? Did he sign in? Do you recognize him?"

"Technically guests are always supposed to sign in, but if they come in with a resident, we don't make them."

"Let's see the tapes," McCauley said, pointing toward the security monitor.

"You know, it's 2017. We don't use tapes anymore—it's all digitally stored," William joked.

"Be careful, Will, you're not that much younger than I am."

William had the recording already queued up. The three of them huddled around the monitor, intently watching the timer in the bottom right-hand corner tick up 11:13.10, 11, 12, 13. When it hit 11:13.21, Richard Eisner appeared through the revolving door.

"There, this is when he comes in. And that's Wanda. She works the night shift. She just started a few weeks ago." William pointed at a portly black woman wearing a more feminine version of the suit William wore.

Her head was looking down at the desk as she thumbed through a magazine—a requirement for any graveyard shift. A second man in khaki cargo pants, a black waist-length jacket, and a plain blue baseball cap pulled low over his eyes scampered through the revolving door behind Richard. An empty-looking duffel bag was strapped to his back. Wanda didn't look up from her magazine until the pair was just in front of the desk. By that time the second man had closed the gap between him and Richard. Richard gave a wave and seemed to mouth a greeting to Wanda, who smiled back as the two men passed her desk.

"You sure they're together?" Naomi asked.

"Looks like Wanda sure thought they were," William replied.

"Yeah, it sure does," McCauley said. "You recognize that guy?"

"Could be Mr. Burns in 11A, but hard to say. The hat makes

it hard to see his face. If I had to bet, I'd say it's not him, though. Mr. Burns dresses real nice, and I don't think he'd be caught dead in cargo pants."

"How about Wanda? You said she started a few weeks ago. How many weeks is a few?" McCauley asked.

"Two. I doubt she'll be any help. She could go a whole year on that shift and never see half the residents. Like I said, not a lot of night owls in this building."

"Okay. Let me get her contact info anyways, and a copy of the footage, if you can."

"Already done," William said, placing a CD in a square envelope on the counter in front of McCauley.

"If you think of anything, or you just want someone to trash the Bears with, here's my card," McCauley said, swapping his card for the CD. "Thanks for all your help, William. We appreciate it."

CHAPTER TWENTY-FIVE

On the way to the junkyard, McCauley placed a call to Wanda. Just as William predicted, she wasn't much help. She didn't know the second man, let alone Eisner, who McCauley had to describe to her several times to jog her memory. No matter, though, as McCauley wasn't anticipating much from her.

"How'd you know that note would be taped to the bottom side of Rich's desk drawer?" Naomi asked.

"Tricks of the trade. A lot of people keep things like that there—passwords, safe-deposit keys, cash. Cereal boxes are another good one. All good places to hide valuables if you get burglarized, not good places if you want to hide something from a detective. You'd be surprised where people think to hide things, and how often they come up with the same idea. I guess it's the common wiring in all of us."

"Do you think Richard was killed?" Naomi asked.

"I think we don't have all the information we need yet to make that determination."

"Yeah, I think he was too."

"I didn't say he was for sure."

"No, but I say the same thing to clients when I'm not quite ready to deliver bad news. Everything we saw points to it. An unknown man who nobody recognizes sneaks in behind Richard. The bleach stain on the floor, the fact that there wasn't any footage of Richard leaving. You know as well as I do what happened to him."

"Okay, look, you're right. No bullshit?"

"No bullshit."

McCauley took a breath, then said, "I think that man followed Richard into the building. To Wanda he looked like a guest of Richard. Once he was past her, Rich must have thought he was a resident. They get in the elevator, Rich hits thirty-two, that guy hits a few floors higher. On thirty-two Richard gets off, the man waits a moment, then slips off the elevator behind Richard, who keys his lock. With the door open, the guy forces him inside and hits him over the head in the entryway. From there, I don't know, but we can presume he cleared out Richard's desk, cleaned up, and then took the service elevator and slipped out the back with Richard's body."

"How does he sneak a body out?"

"You heard William—residents don't take the back. It's night, so not even service personnel would be in that area. Plus, Richard's rug was missing."

"What rug?"

"The one that used to be in his living room."

Naomi looked at McCauley inquisitively.

"His coffee table was askew," McCauley said. "He seems like a pretty neat guy, just seemed odd to me. So I checked the floor a little closer. You could see a faint outline of where the rug used to be. It was subtle, but those eastern views get a lot of direct light, so even after only a year, there was some slight fading of the hardwood that was exposed to it, and no fading where presumably the rug was."

"Hmmm."

"Sorry, but you did ask me."

"Don't be sorry, just be honest. You may see details like the rug and you may know humanity's hiding spots, but I'm capable of seeing a lot too."

"I can tell."

"So let's come to an agreement. You need my help as much as I need yours. Particularly if you are worried about utilizing the resources of the CPD. So let's agree to be one hundred percent truthful to each other from here on out. Deal?"

"Deal."

McCauley pulled the car over to the curb in front of the scrap yard. It was a wonder how this sliver of the city still looked as it did. The west side of the street which sat adjacent to north branch of the Chicago river was lined with warehouses, small mills, and this scrapyard. On the opposite side was high-end shopping—Lululemon, Patagonia, and a slew of boutiques that extended beyond the locally known "Shops of Armitage." Staring at the stacks of crushed cars towering over the rusted barbed fencing, McCauley couldn't help but think one side of the street simply froze in time seventy years ago while the rest of the world kept marching on.

"In the spirit of our deal," McCauley started, "I'm not holding out a lot of hope on this. It's a pretty big stretch to think Richard ever came here. I mean, it's a junkyard, what could possibly be in here? We'll go check it out, but I don't think he intended to send us here with that note."

"I agree...I think he intended us to go to the storage unit a half a block back," Naomi said, the corners of her mouth turning slightly upward. "Want to make a bet on what's in unit 223?"

McCauley put his hand on her headrest to help turn his body and peered through the rear window of the Crown Vic. Sure enough, next to the scrapyard a few hundred yards back was a sign that read:

Self-Storage Entrance
Inquire inside for your first month free!

"Well, Naomi, looks like this new policy is already starting to pay dividends."

CHAPTER TWENTY-SIX

Cody maneuvered his way back toward an industrial strip nestled up against the south branch of the Chicago River next to the famed Chinatown district. He pulled the car into the parking lot of Harry's Chicken Hut and parked around back.

He had eaten at Harry's plenty of times, so he knew the location well. The sole proprietor went by Buck, having bought the business from so-and-so, who had in turn bought it from some other so-and-so, who had bought it from Harry. Perhaps there was a time when it served quality chicken, but now the food was shit. It was a marvel of modern cooking that Buck managed to make his chicken both dry and greasy at the same time. The tables all had a slick sheen to them, a product of years of grease soaking through the thick Styrofoam containers in which Buck served his chicken.

Buck proudly displayed his solid C health inspection rating in the front window by affixing a sign next to it in the same bold red letters so that the combined result said, "C...OME ON IN!"

For what it lacked in quality, Harry's Chicken Hut made up for in quantity, which was probably the sole reason it had managed to stay in business all these years. Like clockwork, throngs of workers from the nearby train yard would arrive in steady waves starting at 11:00 in the morning until the final whistle for the day crew at 6:00 p.m.

Buck would dutifully man the counter—usually with a cig-arette in his mouth—and load up the Styrofoam boxes with chicken and heaping spoonfuls of sides until the box began to sag.

The business probably didn't make all that much money—just enough to cover the one-thousand-square-foot two-bed-room bungalow next door that Buck called home.

The fact that it was all cash also meant that Uncle Sam wasn't getting his cut, but Cody suspected it wouldn't have been much anyway.

It was the perfect spot to ditch the car. It was early enough that Buck hadn't opened up the restaurant yet, and there wasn't a security camera within three blocks of this place that could pick up Cody dumping it. Hell, knowing Buck's demeanor, he'd probably wait days before calling someone to have it towed.

Cody shut off the engine, then wiped down the interior to eliminate his fingerprints. He had been careful while driving it and only touched the door, wheel, and gearshift. The whole pro-cess took him less than two minutes. Satisfied he'd left no trace, he exited the vehicle, wiped the exterior driver's-side handle, and closed the door with his jacket over his hand.

Cody slipped through a gap in a rusted-out fence behind the restaurant and started making his way toward a storage con-tainer he kept in the lot of a trucking company a half mile up the road. The trucking company was struggling to keep up with the wave of automation sweeping over the logistics industry, so they were happy to sell Cody a shipping container and store it on their lot for him. They needed the money, and Cody paid a full year in cash up front, so the rate was favorable.

Cody rarely set foot on the lot—once every six months or so to freshen supplies but mostly just to check in on it. The ship-ping container was his contingency plan, and as such he hoped he'd never have to use it. After the events of the day, though, he felt glad to have it.

After weaving his way through the back of several industrial lots, he found himself standing in front of the red-ribbed shipping container. It showed signs of heavy use via rust spots on the sides and chipping paint. When he first purchased it, Cody wondered about all the places it had been in its lifetime, what exotic locales it may have traveled to.

Often when he had trouble sleeping, he imagined himself sitting next to the container on the deck of some large cargo ship, rocking with the waves. As sleep would creep in, he would find himself talking to it. He would ask it how it felt to go where the wind took it—free of responsibility, free of duty, free of guilt. He would always fall asleep before it could answer him.

Cody slapped his hand on the front of the mighty red container and said, "I guess I may just find out the answer to some of those questions."

Cody dug out a small portion of the dirt patch where the container's edge met the ground with a trowel he stashed nearby. When he was satisfied at the size of the opening, he reached his arm in and felt around underneath the container for the key he kept attached to the bottom. When he felt his fingertips run over the cuts in the key, he closed his hand around it.

He unlocked the large silver padlock affixed to the front, then swung one side of the heavy double doors open. After fumbling around in the low light for a moment, Cody found the power switch to a large electric battery pack. He toggled it, and the fluorescent lights above flickered on with a distinct clicking noise as they struggled to wake from their slumber.

Once they settled down and the electrical current coursing through them remained steady, they emitted an audible hum and cast white light throughout the container.

On the left side of the container lay a cot with crisp white sheets and a gray woolen blanket. The bed was well made, and the blanket was pulled tight around the mattress so that not a wrinkle was present.

A footlocker sat at the foot of the bed containing several pairs of neatly folded T-shirts and cargo pants. On the far wall there were several lockers filled to the brim with dried food, water, and first aid supplies. All told, Cody had enough supplies to live out of the container for weeks if needed, but that wouldn't be necessary today. He had his escape route to his new life meticulously planned, and he would be ready to go soon enough.

To the right was a workbench neatly stocked with gun parts and tools. Cody had the parts in labeled Tupperware containers —one for springs, one for barrels, one for cleaning supplies, and one simply marked as "Mixed Parts."

Several guns hung on the wall above the bench. There were two Beretta M9A3s, much like the one he was carrying. He also had a Heckler and Koch MP5 9 mm submachine gun, which hung next to a M40A3 sniper rifle—the same type he had become so proficient with as a marine. He laughed to himself as he remembered when he outfitted his gun wall. It was impressive, but much less so than the ones in spy movies. He recalled one —though the name escaped him—where the hero spy opened a vault storing what had to be dozens of guns.

Why did they have so many varying types of handguns? Cody wondered. *That's just impractical. Different guns meant different parts, different magazines, different ammunition, and different training time.*

Cody's Beretta had been loyal and reliable since his time in Iraq. He saw no reason to change.

If it ain't broke…, he'd thought to himself when deciding what weapons to hang.

Cody walked over to the workbench and opened a deep drawer that was filled with loaded pistol magazines and nearly a thousand rounds of 9 mm ammunition. He replaced the magazine in his gun with a new one and then pulled several more from the drawer, tucking them into the various pockets sewn inside his pants waistline.

Confident he had all he could carry, he made his way to the locker in the back and pulled out one of the first aid kits. He popped open the plastic lid and pulled from the kit a bottle of hydrogen peroxide, some cotton balls, and a bandage. He looked at his face in the mirror hanging on the locker door. Once the adrenaline had worn off, the pain from the cut above his eye started to set in. He turned his head slightly to get a better look at the damage, which wasn't as bad as he thought it would be. It was certainly minimal for having just thrown himself through a plate-glass sliding door.

Cody unscrewed the lid of the peroxide bottle, placed a cotton ball on the top, and held it in place with his thumb as he tipped the bottle upside down. He dabbed the cut, then watched the peroxide bubbles fizz on his skin—a sign it was doing its job. When the solution on the cut went still, he unwrapped the tan bandage and stuck it over the wound.

Practically good as new, he thought.

While inspecting his handiwork, he stopped suddenly, having caught a glimpse of himself looking back in the mirror. As he looked at his reflection, he stared into his own eyes. Then he balled his hand into a fist and smashed the mirror. It shattered at the point of impact, and several pieces fell to the floor.

Cody stared deeply into the cracked mirror and felt a range of emotions—anger, betrayal, sadness. The stalemate between Cody and the fractured visage of himself was broken when he felt a trickle of warmth running down his hand.

"Shit." He'd cut the knuckles on his right hand.

After performing the same procedure on his hand that he had performed on his eye, he sat down on the bed, his elbows resting on his knees and shoulders hunched over as he looked at the ground between his feet.

He wondered how he got here. He knew the string of events that had led him to this container. He broke the rules by letting Chadwick go. Cody knew the rules when he signed up for this type of work. Hell, he used that line as justification for killing someone on more than one occasion. He wasn't even mad at Whitaker for giving the order.

He was far more concerned with how he'd started down this path. He was a friend, a loving son, a decorated soldier. He swore to defend those that couldn't defend themselves. He remembered his oath. How had he gone from protector to hired gun?

For a moment Cody wondered if he had always been a killer. He wondered if he used the marines as an excuse to free himself from the shackles of civilized society so that he could become his true self.

No, that didn't feel right to Cody. If that were true, he wouldn't carry around the crushing sadness permanently affixed to his back.

Whitaker was responsible for this. He had manipulated Cody when he was at his lowest point. Cody thought back to the De-Paul student he'd beaten up at a local bar after his mother died. He wondered what happened to him. Cody wasn't sure, but he had seen enough injuries in his life to know that whatever it was, it wasn't good.

That's when Whitaker appeared, like an apparition manifesting itself out of thin air, and made it all go away. No cops, no jail time. Poof, the whole thing disappeared. Of course, no thanks was required; Whitaker was clear on that. It was merely his way of giving back to someone who had served his country honorably.

That's when the job offer came. At first it was great. Good pay, not much work, but over time, Whitaker asked for more from Cody. Eventually he came for his pound of flesh when he asked Cody to kill for the first time. Killing for money felt very different than killing for country.

Whitaker assured Cody that they were serving the greater good. The men he tasked Cody with killing were drug dealers and murderers—the lowest scum of society. He convinced Cody that in many ways he was still killing for the good of his fellow man, even if the US government wasn't the one giving the orders.

Deep down, Cody desperately wanted to believe that Whitaker abused Cody's sense of loyalty, that he took advantage of Cody's guilt over the incident in the bar. Maybe there was a sliver of truth to that, but Cody decided it was mostly bullshit.

He knew the path he was walking. Like an out-of-body experience, he watched himself walk down the dark road, but he was too weak to stop it. If only he could go back in time. He'd grab hold of his younger self's shoulders and shake for dear life. He'd yell at him to snap out of it and run.

"Enough!" Cody yelled to no one, rising to his feet. The echoes of his yowl reverberated off the steel walls of the container.

Cody walked to one of the lockers in the back and pulled out a large rucksack that was packed tight. He set his go-bag down on the workbench and checked the contents. Inside were clothes, a pair of low-rise boots, energy bars, water, and two zippered blue pouches.

He opened the first to reveal his new life—ID cards, passport, social security card, and a birth certificate all bearing the alias "Raymond Hunt."

He zipped the pouch closed, then reached for the second one. Inside was $50,000 in cash and a small velvety sack containing $750,000 in diamonds, still the best way to smuggle large amounts of money across borders. In New Orleans there was a safe-deposit box containing another $500,000 worth of diamonds.

Cody had also purchased Bitcoin early on. He figured it was good to diversify himself just to be on the safe side. He didn't understand it. He must have read half a dozen articles purporting to explain the ins and outs of the cryptocurrency, but each left him with more questions than answers. To Cody it was no different than a banker pushing numbers across a computer screen, with one key difference—Bitcoin was anonymous and accessible anywhere in the world that had an Internet connection. He only made a modest investment, thinking back to his mom's advice.

"Cody, be careful investing in things you don't understand," she said to him once.

She didn't have much money, but she was a good steward of the little that she had.

Of course, Cody never predicted the heights that Bitcoin mania would reach. He turned his $50,000 into nearly a million. All told, he had amassed a little over two million dollars, more than he would need to live out his life.

His exit route was set. The used car dealership down the road would be opening up soon. Cody would pay cash for a car —nothing fancy—just something inconspicuous that would get him to New Orleans. Once there, he'd pick up the rest of his diamonds, then make his way to the owner of a shipping company who moonlighted as a smuggler. Cody had already paid the man a nonrefundable $25,000 deposit, which represented half the purchase price of his one-way ticket. The other half was to be paid on arrival in Panama.

Cody had purchased a small house in Almirante, an out-of-the-way northern coastal town. The house wasn't much, but it was right on the beach. There, Cody could hide from the authorities, from Whitaker, and, with any luck, from his own demons.

He hoped that the lapping of the waves on the white beaches would be enough to finally help him sleep.

Cody repacked the rucksack and started to zip it closed. As he pulled the zipper halfway up the bag, he paused for a moment. A feeling he couldn't quite place was gnawing at him. He stood there staring at the bag for nearly a minute before he finally let out a sigh and pulled a laptop from one of the pouches.

Cody inserted a prepaid cellular data stick to the USB port on the side and fired up the computer. After a few seconds of startup, the familiar blue Windows desktop took over the screen.

He moved the mouse to the task bar, opened up a browser, and typed in the address for Google. He paused again, staring at the cursor flashing in the search bar that was patiently waiting for him to type something.

Finally he typed in: "Pennington Corporation, Death."

The Google servers worked quickly to return the results. The first was an op-ed piece from the *New York Times* titled "Will Airbnb Be the Death of the Modern Hotel Chain?" Underneath the headline he saw several bolded places were Pennington was mentioned. That wasn't what he was looking for.

Cody clicked the tab labeled "News" at the top of the page, then set the look-back period to twenty-four hours before hitting the enter key.

One article came up from the *Chicago Tribune*. It simply stated:

Person killed while running along lakefront identified as Pennington Corporation General Counsel Richard Eisner. Police have ruled Eisner's death an accident. This story is developing; check back for updates.

Cody's heart sank. Whitaker was cleaning house, and that meant one thing.

"Come on, Cody, you know she's probably dead already," he tried to convince himself. "Just put the computer back and get out of here. You can't deviate from the game plan."

Cody's mind wandered back to the first time he saw Naomi a few years ago. The job seemed simple enough. Plant the surveillance equipment in her office and leave. Gaining access to the Sloan MacIntyre offices was easy enough. With the myriad of deliveries, it wasn't hard to slip in undetected as a courier.

He damn near blew the whole operation, though, when he laid eyes on her. The first thing he noticed was the same thing everyone did, her radiant beauty. He didn't know they made lawyers that beautiful. Cody was so caught off guard that he nearly dropped all his equipment when she passed him in the hall on the way to a meeting. He closed his eyes and remembered how she had flicked a lock of her silky brunette hair out of her face before looking up and giving him a beaming smile that would melt any man's heart.

For the next week he listened to her every word via the bug he'd planted in her office. He soon realized that she was the whole package—beautiful, smart, and, most importantly, compassionate.

He listened to her as she spoke over the phone to one of her clients serving a thirty-year sentence in prison for multiple counts of aggravated assault with a deadly weapon. The court had appointed her to represent the man, who sustained serious injuries as a result of what he alleged was excessive force by several guards at the Department of Corrections. The man was a three-time felon with a third grade education who wouldn't become eligible to see the light of day until he was well into his sixties. Any other hotshot lawyer would have given this guy the bare minimum—a dismissive fifteen-minute phone call followed by an obligatory, "We'll see what we can do for you." But not Naomi. She sat patiently and listened to him for hours as he went on about his rough childhood, having been forced to live on the streets by the time he was ten. She listened to him as he laid out the laundry list of crimes he'd committed over his lifetime, some for which he was never caught. She even listened when he complained about the channel selection on the prison's cable TV system. Cody couldn't understand how she was able to look past this man's misdeeds and see him as a human being, not just another convict. If she could forgive this man enough to help him, what else could she forgive?

He'd kept tabs on the case for months, which was difficult given the lack of news coverage on the little-known matter. That didn't stop him from checking the news outlets regularly. Then one day he saw the update he was looking for buried on the back page of a legal circular.

"Department of Corrections settles with inmate for $50,000."

A settlement! What a coup! he thought. Fifty thousand wasn't much, but Cody remembered Naomi explaining to the man early on that the DOC had never lost a case involving monetary damages as she warned him not to get his hopes too high. She must have really had them shaking to force a settlement from them.

Cody wasn't a fool, though. He didn't have aspirations that the universe would magically push them together in some sort of fairy-tale romance. Those endings existed only in the realm of fiction. Still, he was fascinated by the existence of such an exquisite creature.

And now Whitaker wanted to snuff her out. Cody's heart

twinged with pain.

"Why did you check the news, you idiot? You knew what it was going to say," he cried out to himself.

Cody stood in silence in the middle of the container, his eyes darting back and forth between his go-bag and his pistol sitting on the workbench. He grabbed the straps of the pack and squeezed until his knuckles turned white.

Soon his hands began to tire, and he finally he said aloud, "Fuck it. One more time, Cody."

He placed the go-bag back on the floor and picked up the Beretta. He press-checked the slide to make sure a round was properly chambered, then tucked it in the holster on his right hip. He reached into a drawer on the workbench and grabbed a small box, the contents of which he was saving for a rainy day. He placed the box in the pocket on the right leg of his cargo pants.

Cody walked outside, took one last look at the bag sitting on the floor of the container, and shut the door, locking it behind him.

CHAPTER TWENTY-SEVEN

McCauley trotted out of the medical examiner's office, flipping his car keys around his finger. The ME's new findings gave him a renewed sense of confidence. While Naomi was reviewing the files at the storage lockup, McCauley decided to take a deeper look into Eisner's death. Wisely, Eisner had made copies of what appeared to be all the files that Naomi was working on before she was pulled from the case. At the very least, it was enough to keep her busy for hours, and it would give McCauley time to speak to the ME. After speaking with Davis, the examiner knew why McCauley was there, but he was hesitant to reopen his findings. It took a little cajoling, but McCauley finally convinced him that there seemed to be more to Eisner's death than met the eye. Convincing the ME that someone had staged the body to try to fool him was enough to get him riled up enough to take a second look. What they found was compelling. Upon careful examination of the body, they found a tiny puncture between the toes—most likely from a syringe. It wasn't hard to see how it was overlooked the first time. Embarrassed, the ME widened the scope of the blood work and put a rush order on it. McCauley wasn't sure what they'd find, exactly, but he suspected it would be big.

He popped open the door of his Crown Vic and took a seat behind the wheel. His good mood was instantly shattered by the unmistakable feel of a pistol pressed to the back of his head.

Cody rose up in the back seat and sat directly behind McCauley.

"Easy there, Detective McCauley. Put your hands on the wheel."

McCauley was cool. It wasn't the first time he'd had a gun pointed at him. "So what's this supposed to be?"

"A conversation," Cody answered. "For now."

"Well, if we're going to have a chat, I'd at least like to know who I'm speaking to. You obviously know who I am."

"I'm the man you've been looking for the past few days."

McCauley reacted by turning to get a glimpse of him. "You're the sniper?"

Cody pressed the gun to McCauley's temple. "I said hands on the wheel."

"Okay, okay, they're on the wheel."

"Keep 'em that way."

"So you're the man behind the Jackson and Sherman hits. You here to punch my ticket too?"

"Relax, cowboy," Cody said, smirking at the pearl-gripped guns peeking out of McCauley's jacket. "I think we both know if I wanted you dead, I wouldn't be sitting here."

Feeling a little emboldened by that comment, McCauley asked sarcastically, "So what, then? You came to turn yourself in? You could have just called me, if that's the case."

Cody fired back, "Don't get too comfortable just yet, Detective."

"I'd be more comfortable if you stopped pointing a gun at my head. It might make this conversation a little more civil, don't you think?"

Cody paused for a moment, then lowered the Beretta and decocked the hammer. He set it in his lap, still gripping the butt with his index finger running down the slide. "Now I've got mine, and you've got yours. And you know I can pull this trigger before you even get that relic from your holster. So nothing funny."

McCauley turned his body to look at Cody. He looked fit and ex-military. On paper it should have been exactly how the hit man he'd been chasing for the past forty-eight hours would look, but something about Cody seemed out of place for a stone-cold assassin. There was something behind his eyes that McCauley just couldn't place.

"You called this meeting, so what do you want to talk about?" McCauley asked.

Cody paused. "Do you believe in karma, Detective McCauley?"

"Karma? I don't know about that. I believe in the law, though. I believe that we all answer for what we've done."

"Yeah, me too," Cody said, staring out the window in thought. "I think that in life we get a precious few moments where the battle between the good and evil that rages inside us is played out. I believe we're judged by these moments."

"So what are you saying? Are you seeking judgment for killing those two men?"

Cody laughed. "From you? No. I may face judgment for my choices in life, but it won't be from you, and it certainly won't be over those two pieces of shit."

"Then what's this all about?"

"It's about protecting the flock from the wolves that surround us."

"And how about you, son, are you a wolf?"

"Yes, I am. But sometimes it takes a wolf to fight a wolf."

"Okay, wolf, I want to know why you're sitting in the back seat of my car with a gun."

Cody turned to look at McCauley. "I'm here because an innocent person's life is in danger, and we're the only ones who can do something about it."

"Who's in danger?"

"A lawyer...her name's Naomi Archer."

McCauley's stomach was in the back of his throat, but he didn't show it. "How do you know she's in trouble?"

"My employer is tying up loose ends, and she's a loose end. He's already killed two people. I know because I was ordered to kill one of them."

"Who, Chadwick? Eisner?"

Cody eyes widened. "How do you know about them?"

"I'm a detective. It's my job."

Cody paused, accepting that answer, and then said, "Chadwick. I was told to kill Chadwick."

"So where's his body?"

"I didn't do it. It was clear to me that he didn't deserve it. So I dropped him at the train station, told him to get out of town."

McCauley was relieved that Chadwick was still alive.

"I need to get him back here. I can protect him."

"That's going to be difficult. He's dead."

"How do you know?" McCauley asked

"Because the man who killed him tried to kill me too."

"So is that what this is? Your employer burned you, and now you need my help? Was all that altruistic talk just bullshit?"

"Hey, I could have killed Chadwick. I didn't, though. I couldn't. Plus, I've got money. I know how to disappear, but I can't yet—not while Naomi is in danger. I don't want her death on my conscience too."

"I'll put her into protective custody immediately. She'll be safe."

"No, she won't. Not with the moles in your department. I've got stacks of intel from the CPD's gang unit—how do you think I got those files? The man that wants her dead is too well connected. He will be able to get to her if you bring her in."

"Then what are you offering, exactly?"

"I help you. We secure her, then we take out the guys who are trying to take her out. We blow the whole thing wide open. That's the only way to keep her safe."

"And what's in it for you? Redemption?"

"Something like that. And when it's done, I walk away and find my own corner of the world to live in peace."

"You know I can't let you just walk after all this."

"That dedication to duty is exactly why I came to you."

"How do I know it's not a ruse? Naomi is safe now. How can I trust that you're for real and not just trying to get to her through me?"

A pause. McCauley heard a rattle of steel and saw the Beretta out of the corner of his eye. Cody gripped the barrel and trigger guard, offering the butt of the pistol to McCauley, who reached up and took hold of it.

"Don't get too attached to it, though. I'm going to want it back," said Cody.

"Is handing me this gun supposed to make me think you're for real?" asked McCauley.

"It's a start, isn't it?"

"A start is all it is," said McCauley.

"Look, this isn't my ideal situation, but as you said, I'm burned, and right now you're my best option. Alone it'll be impossible to keep Naomi safe, but together we just may have a chance. So what do you say?" asked Cody.

McCauley thought for a moment, then keyed the ignition. "I can't believe I'm doing this," he grumbled. "Get in the front, at least. This isn't a cab."

CHAPTER TWENTY-EIGHT

Naomi crossed the lobby of her downtown condo building after catching an Uber from the storage lockup. She lived in a chic two-bedroom condo in the heart of River North, just a short walk from the office. It was a high-end building befitting a partner at a law firm, but not overly flashy.

As she passed the mailboxes, her cell phone rang. She pulled it from her purse and looked at the screen to see who was calling.

"McCauley," she answered, still walking toward the elevator banks.

"Naomi, there's a development. Where are you?"

"I just got back to my building. You won't believe what I found." She pressed the call button and an elevator chimed, its doors opening.

"No, don't...they...for...you."

"What? I can't understand you. Look, I'm in an elevator. I'll call you back when I get upstairs." Naomi clicked the button on the side of her phone, ending the call.

"Shit," McCauley cursed.

"What's wrong?" Cody asked.

"She's home."

"How far are we from her place?"

"We're close," McCauley said, keying a switch on the center console that activated the lights and sirens on his police cruiser. He pushed the accelerator to the floorboard, and the engine roared.

Cody put his hand on the roof, bracing himself as the car raced forward. "I just hope we're close enough."

Naomi placed the phone back in her purse, then pressed the button for the seventeenth floor. Just as the elevator doors began to close, a burly man in a dark suit and freshly pressed white button-down shirt stuck his tightly leather gloved hand in, sending the doors bouncing back to the open position.

"Sorry, I'm in a rush," he said of the imposition.

"No problem at all," Naomi responded.

The man looked at the brushed stainless steel button board, then pressed the one for twenty, which promptly lit up in a blue circle.

They rode in silence as Naomi reflected on the new information she had uncovered at the lockup. It was far from a smoking gun, but it was a lead, and that's a lot more than they had a few hours ago.

The elevator dinged as they approached the seventeenth floor. Naomi smiled at the man, then stepped off and turned to the right. She was still so deep in thought as she walked toward her corner unit at the end of the hall that she didn't notice the burly man slip off the elevator behind her just before the doors closed.

The man moved swiftly and silently ten feet behind her, having subbed out dress shoes for ultra-quiet combat boots complete with noise-dampening rubber soles. It was a detail about his appearance that one could notice as out of place with his suit, but it was a necessary tool of the trade.

Thirty feet to her door, the man picked up his speed. He quickly calculated how long it would take her to reach her apartment, and he paced himself to get there a few seconds after her. It would be just enough time for her to open the door and push her in.

Eight feet behind her now. Naomi still hadn't seen him.

Five feet. Naomi slowed as she reached in her purse, searching for her keys.

Three feet. The man pulled a syringe from his pocket and looked down to uncap it.

Boom.

Naomi braced herself on her door with two hands and delivered a powerful back kick to the man, striking him square in the chest. Her reconstructed hips cried out in pain. While the repaired labrums may have prevented her from pulling off the maneuver painlessly, it didn't take any power off her kick. That was still as strong as ever.

The assassin fell backward and hit the floor both stunned and winded. He quickly gathered his senses, and he picked his 240-pound frame off the ground to recommence the attack.

Pop-pop-pop!

The man stopped in his tracks. The burn in his chest came on slowly. He looked down to where a pool of red began to grow on his white shirt. He dabbed at the wound with two fingers, then held the bloody digits up to his face. He looked up to see Naomi in a shooter's stance pointing Glock 43 at him. Wisps of smoke trailed up from the gun barrel.

The pain subsided, and disbelief washed over his face before his knees gave out and he crumpled to the floor. He let out a final breath, and then he was still.

McCauley and Cody were in another elevator in Naomi's building when they heard the shots.

"You hear that?" Cody asked.

McCauley drew his 1911 and flicked off the safety. "I heard it."

"Give me my gun back."

"Not on your life."

"You don't know what's going on up there. You're crazy not to give me my gun."

"Really? Giving a gun to a hit man who threatened to kill me minutes ago is the definition of crazy. Just stay behind me when the doors open."

The pair watched the display intently, then felt the elevator slow as it reached Naomi's floor.

The doors opened with a ding, and McCauley peeked his head out, expecting the worst. Instead he felt a sense of relief as he processed the scene before him.

Cody observed McCauley relax his shoulders. "What is it?" he asked.

"She's okay," McCauley said, turning to project his voice out of the doors. "Naomi, it's McCauley. We're stepping off the elevator. Don't shoot."

A long pause, then he called out again. "Naomi, can you hear me? It's McCauley."

"McCauley," Naomi gasped. "Come quick."

Cody and McCauley stepped off the elevator as it started to buzz at them. As they approached Naomi, Cody took in the scene in front of him. Naomi still stood with her gun at the low ready, and her finger off the trigger. She appeared shocked, but that instinct to make the gun safe that only comes from training still managed to take over.

McCauley slowly took the gun from her hands as she stared wide-eyed at the man on the ground. "He tried to kill me."

"I know. There was no other choice." McCauley put a hand on her shoulder and looked directly into her eyes. "You did good."

"I'll say," Cody blurted from a crouch as he inspected the body. "Three to the chest, one nearly on top of the other. Nice grouping."

Naomi shifted her focus to this cavalier person she had never met. "And who the hell are you?"

Cody dialed it back. "Sorry, I didn't mean it that way. I'm just glad you're alive."

"That's Cody," McCauley interjected. "I'll explain everything when we get someplace safe, but right now we have to get out of here. Go inside and pack a bag. Clothes, toothbrush, cash if you have it."

McCauley's directive cut through the shock. Naomi robotically darted inside and put together some items. McCauley stayed in the hallway and snapped photos of the scene with his phone, particularly the syringe. He'd need them for Naomi when this was all over. It was a long way from the formal processing of a crime scene, but it would have to do.

"You think he was here with anyone else?" McCauley asked, gesturing to the dead assassin.

"Very likely. If he is, they'd be down in front watching the entrance. I don't know what's in that syringe, but whatever it is, they were going to leave her here, make it look like a suicide or an overdose. If there's a back way, I suggest we use it."

Naomi emerged from her apartment with a brown Coach overnight bag. She cautiously stepped past the dead man, taking one last look at his lifeless eyes staring up at her, before the three took the freight elevator down to the ground floor and slipped out the back.

At Montrose Beach, Naomi and Cody sat on top of a picnic table, their feet resting on the bench. In the distance, McCauley paced back and forth, gesturing with his hands and speaking intensely into his cell phone. McCauley had filled Naomi in on the ride over, and now they were waiting for him to plan their next move.

The beach was nearly empty and quiet. The rhythmic sounds of the Lake Michigan waves lapping up over the sandbar soothed Naomi.

She looked down at her trembling hands. "They won't stop shaking."

"That's the adrenaline," Cody said. "It'll pass. Ball your hands up into tight fists, then release them."

"Does it help?"

"Not really, but it feels like you're doing something about it," he said.

Naomi let herself laugh. "You know, my dad encouraged me to get my concealed carry permit. He lives in Michigan, and he pretty much thinks the whole city is a war zone. I tried to tell him that it's not like that, but he wouldn't hear of it, particularly since I walk home late at night sometimes. I got the license and that gun to make him feel better, but I never thought I'd have to use it."

"Just be glad you had it on you. That guy you took down—he was the real deal."

"You knew him?"

"A little. I mostly worked alone, but occasionally I'd cross paths with other guys...like me. He was ex–special forces. Delta,

I think. He was a bona fide psychopath too. That guy wouldn't have thought twice about killing you and then fixing a sandwich for himself in your kitchen."

"Jeez."

Cody chuckled. "You getting the drop on him was probably the last thing he thought would happen when he woke up today. That must have been some kick."

"I suppose," Naomi trailed off, looking out over the water.

"Hey, that guy deserved what he got, and you shouldn't feel bad about it—not for a minute. But you probably will. Do you feel that pain in the pit of your stomach?"

"Yes, I do."

"That's guilt."

"Will that pass too?"

"Honestly?" Cody asked.

"Honestly."

"No. It won't always feel this way, though. It'll get better eventually, but it stays with you. It's like a dull pain in your back that you learn to live with over time."

"And how about you? Do you carry that pain with you?"

"Everywhere I go."

The words hung in the air as they sat in silence, observing the water. McCauley's body language indicated he was still in the throes of an intense conversation.

"Are you sure Robert is dead?" Naomi asked, breaking the silence.

"I'm afraid so."

Naomi nodded acceptance.

"How did he get involved in all this?"

"He stole some money. I found another embezzlement scheme while I was trying to uncover the scheme Robert perpetrated. He was helping me track it down because he had uncovered it too. It's what gave him the idea in the first place."

"I didn't peg him for a thief."

"He stole, but he wasn't a thief," Naomi said.

"Seems like a distinction without a difference to me."

"He was just a lonely man looking to take control of his life. Stealing is how he got it, but stealing didn't define him."

"I suppose we're all looking for control in some form or another," Cody said.

"McCauley thinks you killed him."

"Did he tell you that?" Cody asked, raising an eyebrow.

"No, but I can just tell. I don't think he trusts you."

"And what do you think?"

Naomi looked at Cody. "I don't think you killed him. I'm not sure you're capable of it."

"Ha," Cody laughed. "That's the first time anyone's told me that. You know I'm a mercenary, right? I've killed a lot of people."

"But I don't think you've killed any Roberts or Richards."

"What makes you so sure about that?"

"It's in your eyes. Once, I was appointed by the court to defend this murderer. It was a brutal crime. He slaughtered a family in their own home while they slept. He did it, copped to the whole thing. I was just appointed to handle his plea deal. He had this look, like whatever light may have been behind his eyes had long since gone. I don't see that look in you."

"Well, thanks. It's been a long time since someone looked at me like you do."

"How's that?"

"Like a normal person."

Naomi glanced down at her still hands and shook them out. "Look at that—they stopped."

CHAPTER TWENTY-NINE

Brendt Whitaker stood in his office and listened to the man on the other end of the line. The call was short and direct.

"I understand," he said calmly into the receiver. "Take the team to the room outlined in your contingency plan. I'm sending someone over to assume command."

With that, he hung up the phone. Cody's escape was unfortunate but not entirely unanticipated. Whitaker genuinely liked Cody—he was more to him than just an employee. Ordering the hit was hard, but Whitaker was no stranger to hard decisions. Mostly he wanted Cody off the playing board. If it was a choice between dead or living his life off the map, never to return, he certainly would have preferred the latter.

He knew there was a chance that Cody would escape, and secretly, he wanted him to. He figured it was a win-win ordering the hit. If it went to plan, Cody was out of play. If he managed to escape, he'd certainly flee. Whitaker knew Cody had a contingency plan, but he could never unmask the details of it. He wasn't used to being in the dark on things, but part of him was content with not knowing. If he had been able to uncover the plan, it would have been a mark against the Cody Evans that he knew.

The most recent development, though, was entirely a surprise. He underestimated Cody's attachment to Naomi, a mistake he would not make again. To handle a problem like this, he'd usually tap Cody. Now, with his best piece working against him, he had no choice but to turn to Russo.

Whitaker had high hopes for Russo. He viewed him as a skilled operator with a strong sense of loyalty. What he liked about him most, though, was his ruthlessness. The combination of those qualities was hard to come by, but he had found it in Russo. Sure, he could use some polishing, but that would come with experience and time. For now, Whitaker was content with what Russo was—a blunt instrument. If you needed a surgeon to make careful and calculated incisions, it was Cody. If you needed to lop off a foot in the field, that was Russo's department.

Whitaker looked at Tony Russo's file, which sat splayed out across his desk. He thought back to the fortuitous events that put in motion their meeting.

Ọ

A congressman from Indiana called out of the blue just after 7:00 p.m. Brad Stevens was a four-term incumbent in a tight race with his challenger. He was a staunch Republican and outspoken supporter of the wars in Iraq and Afghanistan. His district was the definition of middle America, with the modestly populated Fort Wayne being the largest city in the area. His views typically resonated with his constituents, but over the years they, like many populations in human history, began to tire of what felt like a never-ending war. It had been over a decade since President Bush stood on the USS *Abraham Lincoln* and declared an end to major combat operations. Support for sending their children to fight halfway across the world with no end in sight was waning among the citizenry.

Just like that, the advantage that had won Stevens so many elections was turning into a liability. His challenger was a young Democrat named James Donald, who offered an exit to the war and a return of manufacturing jobs to the area. Of course he had no real plan to accomplish either, but the message resonated, and the last poll had Donald trailing by just two points.

Whitaker knew from experience what a four-term congressman covets more than anything else in the world—a fifth term. Who could blame him? It was a cushy job that kept him far from the manual labor jobs of his home district and boasted a six-figure salary. The travel perks and pension were icing on the cake. Whitaker had no trouble approaching politicians for favors, but he knew that when they called him for help, it was a whole lot better.

Whitaker listened patiently as Stevens bellowed over the phone. Like an inconsolable child recounting a run-in with another kid on the playground, Stevens hardly paused to take a breath as he described his problem.

"If this gets out, I'm finished in November," Stevens complained. "I'm barely holding on as it is, and this would effectively end my tenure in Congress. Can you believe it, after everything I've done for this country? My undying patriotism and devotion to this job, to my constituents, to my country. How could all that be ruined by something that happened six thousand miles away that I had nothing to do with??"

"So, I understand you have a problem. Take a moment, Congressman Stevens, and then tell me very specifically what it is," Whitaker said.

"Yes, of course, I'm rambling," Stevens said, calming down. "It's this kid. A marine from my home district—from my hometown, no less!"

Topeka, Indiana, is a one-stoplight town where everybody knew everybody. Whitaker could see where this was going. "What did this marine do, exactly?" Whitaker asked.

"He went nuts is what he did!" Stevens was getting animated again. "Wiped out a whole squad of insurgents. Good for him, but the problem is that he took out a whole family of civilians with them! This is a hearts-and-minds war right now, both home and abroad. So you see, when word of this gets out, I'm finished."

"And why did you think to call me, Congressman Stevens?"

"Well, word around the Hill is that you're a man who's good at handling"—Stevens paused for a moment to consider his words—"delicate matters such as this one. For the life of me, I'm not sure what can be done, but I was told by some of my colleagues that if anyone can help, it's you."

"I most certainly can help you, Congressman Stevens. Now, I want you to do one thing for me, and then put this silly matter out of your mind."

"What would you like me to do?" Stevens asked skeptically.

"Well, the boy has a commanding officer. I need his contact information—name and phone number will do. Can you get that for me?"

"Yes, I think I can manage that."

"Just one thing," Whitaker said. "I need the colonel in charge of the young man's regiment. I don't want his lieutenant. I don't want his captain. I don't want his general. I want the colonel."

"Shouldn't we go right to the top with this? I'm sure I can get you the general if I call in the right favors."

"Excellent, then you should have no trouble getting me the colonel. His name and number where I can reach him is all I need."

"Okay, I can get it," Stevens said, a little confused.

"As quick as you can, Congressman Stevens, and then we can put this matter to rest."

"Yes, thank...thank you, Mr. Whitaker."

Stevens was about to hang up the phone when Whitaker interjected, "Oh, and one more thing. If your race is as close as it sounds, you can use all the help you can get. A campaign contribution is in order for a true patriot like yourself. Call my secretary in the morning to arrange the details. We should have everything sorted by then."

"Yes, of course. That's quite generous of you, thank you again. I can't tell you how much your help means to me. I'll call back shortly with the contact information for the—uhh—"

"The colonel," Whitaker helped.

"Yes, the colonel."

With that, the men hung up, and Whitaker's mind began working. He had already played out a dozen scenarios in his head of how to proceed—some more complicated than others. If he played this right, he'd have a new asset for his team and favors owed to him by a congressman and a high-ranking military officer. Not bad for a night's work.

Forty-five minutes later in Baghdad, Colonel Wesley R. Fox stirred from a dreamless slumber to the sound of his phone ringing. He checked the clock—3:55 a.m. He wasn't due to wake up for another fifty minutes, but middle-of-the-night phone calls weren't unusual.

He coughed, clearing his throat, then picked up the phone and spoke. "This is Fox."

"Colonel Fox. My name is Brendt Whitaker, and I'd first like to apologize for the early morning call, but I have an urgent matter to discuss with you."

"Whitaker? What division are you?" Fox asked.

"I'm not in the military, sir. Rather, I'm a special consultant on matters to some friends in Washington."

Great, a bureaucrat, Fox thought. "Well, that's about as clear as mud, but go ahead, Mr. Whitaker, I'm listening."

Whitaker always admired the direct nature of military men. They were much easier to speak to than politicians, who were so caught up in spin it made it difficult to have a straightforward conversation.

"It seems you have a man in your ranks who is in a spot of

trouble. I'm speaking of the young marine that shot up a house and caused some civilian casualties."

"I'm sure you can appreciate that I'm not at liberty to discuss information of that nature to someone that called me out of the blue on my phone at four in the morning," Fox said, cutting off the conversation.

"Of course, I understand that. Please note, though, Colonel Fox, I am calling you on your secured classified line. If you would feel more comfortable, though, I encourage you to reach out to your command and inquire about me, then call me back on this number," Whitaker said confidently.

"Mmmm," Fox grumbled, hanging up the phone.

Hardly three minutes passed before Whitaker's phone rang. Efficiency—yet another quality of the military he appreciated. He waited two rings, then picked it up.

Fox began immediately. "All right, Whitaker, I don't know who you are, and I don't really want to know. You may have friends in high places, but that doesn't mean much to me. You have five minutes to tell me what you want."

"I understand, Colonel, and thank you for your time. The marine that shot up the house—I'm sorry, I'm afraid I don't even know his name." Whitaker paused.

"Corporal Tony Russo," Fox said.

"Corporal Russo, fine. Can you tell me what happened, exactly?"

"It's pretty open and shut. His unit was on patrol in Mosul when they came under fire from both sides of a narrow street. The lead and rear Humvees were disabled with RPGs, effectively pinning the column in a kill box."

"So it was an ambush, then," Whitaker said.

"Yes, and an effective one. Protocol says in an ambush to pick a direction and fight your way out, but that's pretty hard when two of four routes are blocked. The marines exited the Humvees on the orders of the lieutenant on the ground and took cover behind a small wall to return fire. It was poor cover, but it's what they had."

"What happened next?"

"Three more marines were hit with rifle fire coming from a house on their flank. That's when Russo went off. He stormed the house under fire, kicked in the door, and eliminated an entire squad of insurgents. He single-handedly cleared the house room to room with his rifle—and when that ran out, his pistol. He killed over a dozen of the enemy before anyone in his unit even realized where he had gone. He called to them to take cover in the house, where they set up and laid down fire toward the second insurgent location across the street. Those insurgents took several casualties before pulling out."

"He sounds like a hero to me. It also sounds like the civilians were just unfortunate casualties of war. Victims of a soulless fighting force that would use them as human shields, no?"

"That's just it. They survived the firefight. Russo classified them as noncombatants and bypassed them on his first sweep of the house..." Fox hesitated.

"Yes, and then?" Whitaker prodded.

"When the fighting stopped, he went back for them. He accused them of harboring the insurgents, and then he killed them. So you see, he's not a hero, Mr. Whitaker."

"Was he right? Were they aiding the insurgents?"

"I don't know, and now we will never know," Fox said. "At the end of the day, it doesn't matter. We have rules of engagement, and he violated damn near every one of them."

"What does your gut say, though, Colonel Fox?" Whitaker continued to press.

"My gut says they probably were helping the insurgents. My gut says he saved a lot of marines that day, but my gut also says he's unhinged. Look, the hardest part of training a marine is striking a balance between aggression and restraint. It's a delicate line to walk. Before all this, Russo was pretty well respected as being able to toe that line."

"And now?" Whitaker asked.

"Now? Among the rank and file he's a goddamn hero. A mean marine that everyone wants in their unit. But we're fighting a different kind of war, and frankly, guys like him scare me. I know his type. He's the guy you want on your side in a fight until you don't. He may have just crossed that line."

"I see. It's a fascinating story," Whitaker said.

"And now you know what only a handful of people know. So it's my turn to ask the questions. What is your interest in Russo? What exactly do you want?"

"Well, it's not so much what I want, more of how I can help."

"I'm not sure you can help, Whitaker. This is a military matter, and though you may be well connected, you said it yourself. You're not military."

"Don't underestimate me, Colonel Fox, I have many resources at my disposal, and I'd hate to see a distinguished colonel such as yourself—a man in line for his first star—get a black mark on his resume that could derail that. Particularly for something over which he had no direct control."

Silence hung on the line as Fox thought about that. "So what exactly are you proposing?"

Whitaker smiled; he knew he had him. As far as Whitaker could tell, Fox was the consummate military man, but you don't get to the rank of colonel without having even the most modest aspirations of becoming general. Fox knew that fair or not, this incident would slow his rise, if not end it entirely.

"I suggest we handle this matter with the expediency that it deserves. I see a talented marine who saved the lives of countless comrades. A soldier who may or may not have gone over the line, as you say, in the heat of battle. The civilian deaths are a tragedy. A greater tragedy would be to compound it by shipping the young marine off to the brig and derailing the career of a fine commander. As you said, the line between aggression and restraint is difficult to toe. Sure, we could look back at this event and judge Corporal Russo with the benefit of clear eyes—a benefit he did not enjoy."

"Or?" Fox asked.

"Or we could do the right thing—the patriotic thing. We could send Corporal Russo home and close the matter on this whole mess."

"Cover-ups have a nasty habit of coming back to bite at the most inopportune times," Fox said.

"Well, I don't see what you'd be covering up. As far as I can tell, you'd just be signing off on the findings of the investigation."

"The investigation is already complete. I'm expecting the final report on my desk tomorrow," Fox said.

"Oh, well, I've heard differently. I was told by my friends that an MP by the name of Sergeant Wallace has been assigned to the case to give it a once over. From what I hear, he's a first-rate investigator with a pristine record. I think you'll find his report very compelling."

"And what is his report going to say?" Fox asked.

"I couldn't tell you. I don't know Sergeant Wallace, of course. But, if I had to guess, it would say something to the effect that under extreme fire, Corporal Russo bravely entered the house and in defense of his fellow marines eliminated the enemy threat. Sadly, in that firefight several civilian hostages were killed by enemy gunfire. I would also imagine some sort of medal would be in order for Corporal Russo as well." Whitaker had a rare smile on his face.

"Mr. Whitaker, say for a moment I were to agree to all of this. There is a wrinkle."

"What kind of wrinkle?" Whitaker asked, his smile fading.

"Corporal Russo was wounded by enemy gunfire yesterday," Fox stated.

"Is he alive?" Whitaker asked hurriedly.

"Yes. It was some sort of wound to his foot. He may be looking at a few months of rehab, but he should make a full recovery."

A wrinkle? More like a stroke of luck! Whitaker thought. "Leave that to me, Colonel. All you have to do is sign off on the investigation, and I'll take care of the rest."

Whitaker could feel Fox's mind weighing his options on the other end of the line. Any sound tactician would know that he was just presented with a clear path to safety out of an ambush. All he had to do was take it.

"Okay, Mr. Whitaker, I'll look out for the report," Fox finally said.

"Very good, Colonel...or should I say General?" Whitaker always knew how to end a conversation leaving the other side feeling like a winner. "I just need one other thing from you."

"What's that?" Fox asked.

"The name of the doctor treating Russo."

Russo stood outside of Whitaker's office. He was running on zero sleep, and the ebb and flow of adrenaline between the Chadwick, Eisner, and Cody episodes was taking its toll. His waning energy levels allowed for a fleeting hint of fear to enter his mind—fear of the conversation he was about to have.

Whitaker's secretary motioned him into the office.

Russo shook off any outward signs of fatigue and nervousness, then confidently strode into Whitaker's office.

Whitaker stood with his back to Russo, looking out his window. He didn't turn or acknowledge Russo.

An unsettling silence hung thick in the air, until Russo finally broke it. "We had a problem with Evans."

"Yes, I am aware," Whitaker said. "It seems you let Cody slip through your fingers."

A wave of anger passed over Russo. He had specifically instructed his team to stay quiet so that he could tell Whitaker the news himself.

"Don't worry, the other men didn't betray you," Whitaker said, finally turning and observing Russo's reaction. "But perhaps if they did, we wouldn't have our other problem."

"What other problem?" Russo asked with a look of confusion.

"The team assigned to handle Miss Archer spotted two people with striking resemblances to Cody and the CPD detective investigating him enter her building just before our man was shot and killed."

"What? Why didn't they go in and help?"

"They had their orders to stay put. One man down won't come back to us. An entire team? That's a different story. Plus, Baldwin was a solid operator, and he had a good head start on them. According to the ground team, it was very likely that he would have been able to be in and out before they even got to her floor."

"Dammit. I don't know how Cody knew, but he did. He jumped out of the moving car. I didn't anticipate that." Russo said.

"Cody is the best. I told you not to underestimate him," Whitaker goaded Russo.

"He's not the best. He's a coward who sits behind his rifle. I'm the best. He can't do what I can," Russo snapped back.

"And yet he got the better of you and then apparently took out an ex-Delta operator. Cody's skill set extends well beyond his rifle prowess, believe me, I know. If you want to be the best, then you have to beat the best."

"I can do it. He may have gotten the jump on me once, but I assure you it won't happen again."

"I believe you," Whitaker said. "There are still a lot of moves left in this game."

"Let's flush him out. You said he's working with a CPD detective. Let's grab his family, force Cody to play on our terms," Russo said.

"You're tired and not thinking straight. We're not going after the family of a decorated policeman. I have a lot of contacts in the department that would cease to be contacts if I did something like that. Besides, it's unnecessary and beneath us."

"So what do we do, then?" Russo asked.

"We wait. Take the envelope," Whitaker said, gesturing to the file sitting on his desk. "In it you'll find instructions and a key card to a suite at our Michigan Avenue property. Go directly there, don't speak to anyone, don't stop at home. Your team is already there. Once you get there, stay there. Food will be brought to you regularly, but outside of that, no one will disturb you. When I'm ready, I'm going to call, and I need you rested. Is that understood?"

"Yes, I got it." Russo picked up the envelope and walked toward the door.

"And Russo," Whitaker said. "Get yourself ready to face Cody again. You're going to get another shot at him before this is done."

CHAPTER THIRTY

McCauley closed his phone and walked over to Naomi and Cody sitting on a Montrose Beach park bench. The situation was slipping out of his control quickly.

Naomi saw his furrowed brow as he approached. "What's wrong, McCauley?" she asked, laughing at the ridiculous nature of her own question. "I mean, aside from the obvious."

"That was Detective Davis on the phone. It seems you are both burned," McCauley said, scratching his head.

"Burned? Burned how?" Naomi asked.

"You both have warrants out for your arrest."

"Warrants? For what?" Naomi asked.

McCauley was impressed with Naomi. If she was scared, she didn't show it. "You are both wanted for questioning in the death of Richard Eisner and the disappearance of Robert Chadwick."

"Bastards," Naomi said under her breath. "How can they use Eisner and Chadwick against us?"

"It's Whitaker," Cody said. "That man is always two steps ahead. And if you think you've got him dead to rights, it's only because he wants you to think it."

Cody silently wondered if Whitaker knew about his contingency plan. He wondered if there would be a team ready to pounce on him when he returned to the shipping container after all this. He had been careful to conceal its location, but he knew what Whitaker was capable of.

"Apparently Chadwick was sitting on a lot of stolen money—money he was supposed to return," McCauley said.

"But he did return it!" Naomi said. "I saw the money hit the account."

"That's not what Pennington is saying. They are saying he was all set to return the money, but he never made it to the bank. The story they're weaving is that you two are in love and you conspired to steal the money from Chadwick. When Eisner found out, you killed him too."

Cody was angry at himself. It was unfolding in front of him so clearly now. "And now the ex-Delta operator that Naomi killed."

"A security officer of the Pennington Corporation dispatched to check on the status of Naomi and the funds. They're tying that one to you as well," McCauley said.

The gravity of the situation hit Naomi. "Oh, my God."

"Only the three of us know the truth," Cody said expressionlessly. "It means that he can't stop until we're all dead or gone."

"That's the way I see it," McCauley said. "And now he's got every cop in this city looking for you two."

"But what about McCauley? He's not burned—or whatever—right?" Naomi asked.

"No, not yet," Cody said. "I don't know what Whitaker's plan is for McCauley, but assume he has one. He could be trying to get McCauley to turn us over to him directly. A lot of cops in his situation would. Maybe he's leaving him out there so he can lead them to us, where I'm sure he'd have a nice little scenario ready to go." Cody gestured a newspaper headline with his hands. "*Decorated cop fatally wounded by modern-day Bonnie and Clyde manages to return fire and kill both suspects before succumbing to his wounds.* Whatever it is, it doesn't end well for us."

"So what do we do?" asked Naomi.

"I think we have to start thinking about getting you out of the city, Naomi," McCauley said. "Out of the country would be better. Cody, you said you can run—could you take her with you?"

"Yes, I think so," Cody replied.

"You better be sure," McCauley snapped.

"Yes, I can do it. I'd have to rework a few things. We'd have to lay low for seventy-two hours while we wait for some documents, but it can be done."

"Excuse me, boys, I hope you don't mind if I have a little input on my future. I can't just run. I have a life here," Naomi said.

McCauley turned to Naomi. "Naomi, I think we have to face some hard facts here. Whitaker has us behind the eight ball, and it's not looking good. He just set a lot of things in motion that can't be easily stopped. I'm not saying it's forever, but I think getting you out of town is our best option right now."

McCauley looked her in the eye and continued, "I promise you I will work day and night to fix this, whatever it takes. I swear I will do everything in my power to get you back here, or I'll die trying. You have my word."

Naomi spoke with a quiet defiance. "No."

"Naomi, I think McCauley's right. Whitaker is dangerous, and he has the upper hand right now. Sometimes a calculated retreat is in order," Cody said.

"No. I'm not running. If you have an escape plan, Cody, then you can take it. But I'm staying. Whitaker is using the death of my friend against me, and I can't—I won't—let that stand."

"Naomi," Cody said, "he's smart. It's a very tidy narrative he's woven, and it has the benefit of eliciting an emotional reaction from you. When we get stressed or angry, we tend to make mistakes. We *need* to run. Hell, I think it's what he wants. Out of the country with warrants out for our arrest waiting for us if we step foot back on US soil is just as good as us being dead in his book. He won't follow us."

"No."

"Naomi," Cody pleaded. "Please listen to reason. You're not thinking clearly. If we run, we have a chance."

"I've never been as clearheaded as I am at this moment. A mere chance at life on the run is not much of a life," Naomi said.

"The only way for you to stay," McCauley started, "and for us to stand our ground is to blow the whole conspiracy—whatever it is—so wide open that Whitaker will have no moves left to make."

"I found something at the storage locker," Naomi said, staring at her shoes.

"What did you find?" McCauley said, placing a hand on her shoulder.

Naomi lifted her head to reveal a piercing gaze. "A chance to do just that."

"I don't like it," McCauley said. "It's too risky, and we don't even know for sure it will pay off."

"It will," Naomi said. "Whitaker may be smart, he may be a genius, even, but everybody makes mistakes. And I think I found his."

"Naomi, I can get you out of the country. There's a risk, but a lot less risk than the three of us waltzing into city hall. There are cops crawling all over that place from a half a dozen different agencies. Getting past them, when they are specifically looking for us, won't be easy," Cody said.

"They won't be expecting us to show up there, so we'll have the element of surprise on our side. Besides, I told you I'm not running," Naomi reiterated.

"Somehow I knew you'd say that, but I just wanted to give you one more shot at it," Cody said.

McCauley looked at Cody. "If you have a better idea, now is the time."

Cody just shrugged his shoulders.

"Yeah, me neither," McCauley said, turning toward Naomi. "Okay, take us through it. Start from the top this time. We need to get every detail right if this is going to work."

"Okay," Naomi started with renewed vigor. "As I said, I found something in the files Rich left for me at the storage locker on Kingsbury."

"What exactly did you find?" Cody asked.

Naomi pulled a few printouts from her bag. "As I told McCauley earlier, before we met, I was looking into someone embezzling money from the Pennington Corporation. At first I was looking for just Chadwick, but while looking for him, I found a much bigger scheme. Basically Chadwick had found it too, and he copied it—albeit less successfully and on a smaller scale."

"That's Eclipse?" Cody asked.

"Yes, and a half a dozen other shell companies. Eclipse just seems to be the one they've been using the last nine months or so. Did Whitaker ever mention it?" Naomi asked.

Cody shook his head. "No, Whitaker mostly kept me in the dark on the bigger-picture aspects of his affairs, which, in my business, is a good thing. If I didn't need to know it, I didn't want to."

"Okay, well, Eclipse, Compass, Orbit—all of Whitaker's shell companies—effectively did the same thing to funnel the money out of the hotel business. They'd submit invoices from these fake companies for work that was clearly never done. Chadwick forged his invoices—he changed a single number here or there, just small enough that it would be unlikely for anyone to notice. But Whitaker's invoices were real. They were even in the budget, which he obviously had the means to tamper with. The thing they both had in common, though? They both preferred paper checks to electronic transfers. I suspect that was mostly because it was easier to slip through accounting and, ironically, leave a smaller paper trail than an electronic funds transfer. For whatever reason, the paper checks were mailed out to local dummy addresses before being deposited in offshore accounts."

"And you couldn't trace the accounts?" McCauley asked.

"No. They were dead ends. Even if we could get those banks to release the account holder's information to us, the names would probably be fake. Most likely, the accounts where the checks were deposited were just stopovers for the money before it was funneled to who knows how many other secret accounts."

"And what about the addresses? Can we trace those?" Cody asked.

"No, I tried. Just empty offices registered to the shells. Including this one here." Naomi held up a document to Cody and McCauley.

McCauley read aloud, "5414 South University Avenue. What's so special about that one?"

"This, my friends, is the site of a brand new boutique hotel set to open in a few months. Two years ago it was the global headquarters for Compass, LLC."

McCauley and Cody traded glances as Naomi continued.

"I know this address because I worked on the deal a little over a year ago. Pennington purchased a plot of land and gifted a one-hundred-year lease to the University of Chicago, who then turned around and built a small but upscale hotel to be used for visiting professors, lecturers, dignitaries, wealthy alumni, or any number of special guests of the university."

"Can I take a guess at who's going to run it?" McCauley asks.

Naomi smiled. "That's right, Pennington. Pennington really isn't making any money on the deal, the rates are heavily discounted, but there are a lot of tax advantages as a result."

"I don't get it. So they gifted some plot of land—how does that get us closer to finding out what Whitaker is doing with all these companies?" Cody asked. "You said it yourself, you still can't trace the shell corporations."

"That's true," Naomi said, "but I can trace who represented them in these property deals."

McCauley's eyes widened. "The county clerk's office on the fifth floor of city hall will have every deal the real estate attorney participated in on file."

"His name is Byron Wentz," Naomi said.

"If you know him, why can't we just track him down and sweat him for answers? Why take the risk of sneaking into the clerk's office?" Cody asked.

"I don't think we'd get a lot out of him, considering he died a year ago," Naomi said.

"That your handiwork?" McCauley said, shooting a glare at Cody.

"Hey, I told you I don't kill innocent people," Cody fired back.

"Oh, right, you have a code," McCauley said sarcastically.

"I believe Cody when he says he didn't kill Byron," said Naomi.

"What about one of Whitaker's other henchmen?" asked McCauley.

"Hey, I take exception to that. I know you don't hold me in high regard, but I'm not just a hired thug," Cody said.

Not wanting to debate semantics, McCauley put his hands up as if to say, *mea culpa*. "Continue then, Naomi."

"Okay, as I was saying, I don't think Whitaker killed Byron. The man weighed nearly three hundred pounds and was a two-pack-a-day smoker who only smoked when he was drinking, if you catch my drift. The fact that he made it into his sixties was a small miracle on its own."

"Doesn't sound like you miss the guy all that much," Cody said.

"Yeah, well, I didn't work with him very closely, but the little time I did spend with him was enough for one lifetime. He was three times divorced, and based on his innuendos, I could see why. I just steered clear of him. He worked on the deal to secure the property, I handled the rest—the lease, the operating agreement, and I coordinated with our tax department to make sure Pennington got all the right credits."

"Did that seem odd to you that Pennington would hire a guy like that instead of using you?" McCauley asked.

"It wasn't so much unusual as it was frustrating to have to deal with him. Pennington supports lots of local businesses. I figured they had worked with Byron for years and they were just throwing him a bone. He struck me as a one-client type of attorney, but I didn't think much of it beyond that."

"Naomi, you make a potentially compelling case, but it's a lot of filler and not a lot of meat," McCauley said cautiously. "Just because he worked on this deal doesn't mean he worked on any others. You said it yourself, maybe they *were* just throwing him a bone."

"I don't think so," Naomi said.

"What makes you so sure?" McCauley asked.

"Two reasons. The first is he represented both sides of the deal. Pennington *and* Compass."

"And that's unusual?" McCauley raised an eyebrow.

"No, not necessarily, but given everything else, I think it's pretty compelling," Naomi said.

"What's the second reason?" McCauley asked.

"I keep going back to the scope of Whitaker's plan. Whatever he's up to, it's big, like nine figures big. So how do you keep a big conspiracy a secret?"

"Keep it small," Cody said, nodding his head.

"Exactly. Look, conspiracies are hard to keep quiet. They can blow up for any number of reasons—someone gets remorseful, someone cuts a deal, even a simple slipup can unravel them. There's no defending against human nature, so how do you insulate yourself as best you can from it? Cody already said it," Naomi said.

"Keep everyone in the dark, and involve as few people as possible," Cody said, following along.

"Whitaker needed a real estate attorney—that much we know. Who better than a drunk with exactly one source of income? Maybe Byron knew some minor details, maybe not. But I'll bet dollars to donuts that if he worked on this deal, he worked on all the other ones too."

McCauley was impressed. *She would have made one hell of a detective if she had become a cop instead of a lawyer,* he thought to himself. "Okay, say I'm with you that Byron was the front man on all of Whitaker's real estate deals. And say I'm with you that we can successfully sneak into the clerk's office to get a list of them—which I'm not convinced we can do just yet. What good would that list be to us? We still don't know if there's anything to these addresses besides phony invoices."

"You said our only option is to blow the conspiracy so wide open that Whitaker runs out of moves," Naomi said. "I don't know exactly what we are going to find on that list, but every bit of my gut says Whitaker's secrets are buried in that clerk's office. I just know it."

McCauley's gut screamed the same thing, but it was reassuring to hear Naomi say it. "Okay, so now all we have to do is figure out how to sneak into a heavily patrolled municipal building with an APB out on you."

"I think I can help with that," Cody said with a smile.

"Why do you guys even need to go in? I'm the only one who's still clean. I can walk in and out of the building freely," McCauley said.

"And then what? How are you going to get access to one of the computers? Do you even know how to use a computer? No offense, but you've got a ten-year-old flip phone," Cody jibed.

"Oh, yeah? I don't get the impression that computer hacking falls into your skill set, Cody."

"No, but I know my way around sneaking into places well enough that I won't have to hack anything. If I can pull it off, I'll get the three of us in. I'll get Naomi in front of an unlocked computer. She does her thing, quick and quiet, and five minutes later we're walking out the front door. No one's the wiser."

"You can do all that?" McCauley asked skeptically.

"I think he can do it," Naomi said.

"Why?" McCauley asked.

"Because he has to," Naomi said, flashing a smile at Cody.

The smile melted away his defenses, and he couldn't help but smile right back.

"Okay, Cody. It's your show. How do we get in?" McCauley asked.

"I assume there's a security station at the front?"

"Yes."

"Guards with metal detectors and X-ray machines, like at an

airport or courthouse?"

"That's exactly it," McCauley said.

"Who are the guards? CPD? Sheriff's deputies? Or private security?"

"They're Cook County Sheriff's deputies."

"So I guess that rules out you being able to slip us in," Cody said.

McCauley just shrugged.

"Tell me more about the layout," Cody said.

"I don't know, it's just like you said. There's a few guards, an X-ray machine, and a metal detector."

"I need specifics," Cody shot back. "Is the station to the left or the right when you walk in? How many guards? How many metal detectors. Are there multiple lines or one line that splits at the detectors? I need every detail."

"Okay, okay," McCauley said, closing his eyes. He searched his memory hard for the layout. He'd been to city hall dozens of times, but he never thought he'd have to recall the layout for anyone. "When you walk in, there's an information desk directly in front, manned by two people."

"Are they deputies too?" Cody asked.

"No," McCauley said. "They're just employees of the building. The elevators are to the right of them, just past the security station."

"Good. What does the station look like?"

"There are two of them."

"I thought you said there was only one?"

"One station, but it's split into two sections. The station is set up in a corridor that leads to the elevator banks. There is an X-ray machine on the left wall, then directly to the right of it is a metal detector. Then next to that is a table."

"A table? What kind of table? How big is it?" Cody was firing faster now to keep McCauley on his toes. He found that the first memory was generally the most accurate. Memories, in his experience, were fluid, and with enough time, even a good recollection could turn unreliable.

"It's small. It's where you slide your keys and phones across so you don't take them through the metal detector."

"How small exactly?"

"Like an end table. It's probably a foot across and maybe two feet long. Just enough for whoever is going through the metal detector to put their items down on one side and pick them up on the other."

"Okay, then what? You said it's split into two," Cody continued to press.

"Yeah, so there's the X-ray machine and metal detector on the left, and then the table, like I said. To the right of the table is another metal detector, and then to the right of that is another X-ray machine."

"So the right side is a mirror image of the left side, with the little table in between separating them?" Cody asked.

"Yes, that's right," McCauley said, pointing with his hands as he processed his memory of the layout in his mind. "The left side is for building employees. All the building employees have badges that they swipe as they walk up to the metal detectors. The right side is for visitors. There's a desk with a computer in front of it that's manned by a deputy. He checks IDs, then issues temporary badges. Once you get past him, you can go through the metal detector on the right side."

"How many other guards are there?"

"I don't know, Cody," McCauley said, finally opening his eyes. "Enough guards that if they figure out who we are, we aren't getting out of there."

"Come on, McCauley, this is serious. How many guards?"

"I said I don't know. Maybe two for each side, plus the deputy at the desk. Five total? Could be six, I'm not sure."

"Okay, that's good." Cody rubbed his fingers across his cheeks down to his chin in thought.

Naomi and McCauley stood quietly as they saw the gears turn in Cody's mind.

After a few minutes, Naomi broke the silence. "What do you think, Cody?"

He looked up at her and caught sight of her hazel-green eyes. He hadn't until then appreciated how uniquely beautiful they were. At that moment he wished he had more time to scout out the building, but time was a luxury they could ill afford. Whitaker had a substantial head start. They needed to be quick and decisive if they had any hope of getting back in the game. He learned as a marine to work with incomplete intel and on a short clock. This, he hoped, would be no different.

"Well, I've got a crude plan that should give us pretty good odds of success," Cody finally said.

"What kind of odds are we talking about?" McCauley asked.

Cody shrugged. "Fifty-fifty?"

"I generally like to tip the scales a little more in my favor," McCauley said.

"Me too, but our backs are against a wall. Those might be the best odds we see from here on out," Cody said.

"All right, hotshot, let's hear it," McCauley said.

"Okay, but first, we'll need to get a few things," Cody said.

"Like what?" Naomi asked.

"Well, do either of you happen to have a Costco membership?"

Naomi and McCauley shared a look that said everything they were thinking: *Oh brother, this better work.*

CHAPTER THIRTY-ONE

Chicago's city hall is a large stone building designed in the classical revival style, complete with stately columns that span the upper five floors on all sides. Adjacent to the Daley and Thompson Centers, city hall sits on a full city block in the heart of the Loop bounded by Randolph Street, Clark Street, Washington Boulevard, and LaSalle Street. The building's east side, known as the "County Building," houses many offices of Cook County, while the west side houses those belonging to the city.

A light drizzle of nearly frozen rain set in over the city, not an uncommon occurrence for March in Chicago. Nonetheless, the Loop was bustling with men and women scurrying about, unprepared for the rain and armed with the false hope that a light jog would save them from getting wet as they trotted back to their offices from lunch.

McCauley pulled the white cargo van they'd rented from Home Depot into a thirty-minute loading zone in front of the grand building and flicked on the hazards. Naomi and Cody jumped out of the passenger side of the van, dressed in black-and-white checkered pants and white knotted-button coats. Naomi even sported an accordion-style chef's hat that was a bit oversized for her and which was already beginning to hang dangerously close to her eyes. She thought it looked ridiculous, but Cody insisted that the success of their operation would hang on the details. The group gathered at the curb near the back of the van as Cody coached them one more time.

"Remember—" he began but was immediately cut off by Naomi and McCauley repeating his instructions in a drone.

"If you look like you belong, then you belong."

Cody didn't love the eye roll that accompanied the response, but he was happy that the repetition had worked. "Stick to your script as much as you can, but you also have to believe it. We aren't pretending to be bakers—we *are* bakers. If you believe it, then they will believe it. And if you have to deviate from the script—"

Again Naomi and McCauley jumped in simultaneously: "Say as little as possible."

"That's right," Cody said with a smile. "They want to let you in. We are doing a nice thing, they don't want to stop us, they want to help us. Remember that, and we'll cruise right through."

"What do you think?" McCauley started. "Still fifty-fifty?"

"We look good, and you guys know your stuff. Sixty-forty," Cody said.

"I'll take it," Naomi said as a serious look swept across her face. She began to whisper to herself, "I'm a baker, I'm a baker, I'm a baker."

"All right, let's go," McCauley said as he popped open the rear door of the van. He stared at the enormous blue-and-white birthday cake sitting in the back. At nearly five feet long, two feet wide, and half a foot tall, it served three hundred people. "We're going to have a helluva time getting this monstrosity in there."

"That's kind of the point," Cody said, stepping up into the van and around the giant cake. He squatted and got his hands under the edges, then looked at Naomi, who readied her hands on the other side while standing outside the van. "On my count."

"Wait!" Naomi shouted.

"What's wrong?" Cody asked.

"If they catch us, we're looking at life in prison. Any last words of wisdom before we go in there?"

Cody thought for a second, then flashed a smile. "Yeah, whatever you do, don't drop it."

Naomi laughed as if Cody had just released all the tension out of the air.

"One, two, three!"

Naomi and Cody both lifted. With the cargo bay of the van already a few feet off the ground, Naomi didn't have to lift too high. Cody let his arms dangle like an orangutan as he supported his side of the cake with his muscular forearms and duck walked out of the van. As he leapt out of the back, the cake hardly shifted, as if his upper body was frozen in place irrespective of what his legs were doing.

McCauley shut the door, then took up his spot on their right flank as the three carefully made their way to the front door of city hall. With little hope of getting the cake through the revolving main door, they fixed their sights on the swinging door next to it. The trio played their parts immediately. McCauley opened the door emphatically and strolled in before realizing he should probably help the pair struggling with the massive cake behind him.

Realizing the error of his ways, he went back, but instead of walking back through the doorway to hold the door, which swung outward, he instead stood inside protected from the rain and leaned his body forward to prop the door open.

He played it almost too perfectly; the door nearly clipped the cake when he thrust it back open. Naomi's eyes went wide, and McCauley couldn't help but whisper, "Oh, shit" as Cody used his body to deflect the door.

More serious than pretend now, Cody yelled out so the entire lobby could hear, "Sir, could you get the door from the other side, *please*?"

Nearly everyone in the lobby looked over in awe of the curious scene, which consisted of McCauley running frantically through the revolving doors and opening the side door so two bakers could delicately maneuver what appeared to be the largest cake on the planet through it.

Once the cake was across the threshold, McCauley drew more attention to the three by calling out boisterously, "Step aside, please. Cake coming through! Make room, everyone."

The trio passed the information desk at the front as the employees stared and joked at the size of the cake. All eyes were on them—or rather on the cake. No one was looking at the faces of the two bakers carrying it through the lobby, which was the general idea.

They turned the corner at the visitor's desk when McCauley suddenly stopped dead in his tracks.

"What is it?" Cody whispered.

"The deputy who checks in the visitors. I know him," McCauley said, his mind racing. "Should we scrap this? Maybe he'll let us in another way."

"No," Cody said. "It's too late for that. If you think he'd let us in under other circumstances, then that's to our advantage now. Just remember, he wants to let you in. If you know each other, he'll want to let you in even more. Stick to the plan and keep moving."

The deputy looked up from his cell phone and noticed the giant cake thirty feet in front of him.

McCauley stood motionless, his legs locked straight as he started down the hall toward the security station.

"Move, McCauley," Cody said in a firm whisper.

It was enough to rein him back into the moment. As if he didn't miss a beat, McCauley picked up his stride where he left off and marched confidently down the corridor, ushering people out of the way.

Seeing McCauley out in front, the deputy rose from his stool and stepped around his desk. "What the hell is this, Pat? Some kind of practical joke?"

"Hey, Dave! Good to see you. They promoted you to front desk duty, I see," McCauley said with a cheeky grin.

"Yeah? Well, at least it keeps me dry and fed," Deputy Dave said, patting his belly, which extended over his duty belt. "Speaking of which, what's the deal with Mount Cakemore there?"

"That, my friend, is a cake for Doris up in records."

"It says 'Happy Birthday' on it, though," Deputy Dave said, gesturing to the neat red-and-white frosted lettering.

"Yeah, so?" Pat said.

"So Doris's birthday is in July. Everybody knows that," Dave said.

McCauley looked at Cody for help, who shot him a look as if to say, *What do you want me to do about it? Say something...anything.*

"Well, that's true. She celebrates her birthday in July, but her real birthday—her actual...uhh...real birthday is today."

"So if her birthday is in March, why does she celebrate it in July?"

"That's a great question," McCauley said, buying time. In that brief pause he thought of Cody's advice: *Say as little as possible. Let them fill in the gaps.* "Why does Doris do half the crazy stuff she does? Am I right?" McCauley said, laughing as he patted Dave, who looked thoroughly confused, on the shoulder.

"Yeah, I guess you're right. Doris is crazy when it comes to birthdays," Dave said, joining McCauley in laughter.

"Don't you and I know it. You know, I think she's celebrated her forty-eighth birthday four years in a row now. But you didn't hear that from me."

Cody cleared his throat, keeping McCauley on track.

"But that's neither here nor there. Doris did a little favor for me on getting my property tax appeal expedited, so I figured since she likes birthdays so much, what better way to show her my appreciation than with a real birthday celebration."

The bit about the property tax was true; it was McCauley's only connection to the Cook County clerk's office, and though it was thin, they hoped it'd be enough.

"All right, you're good to go through. Let me just get their IDs," Deputy Dave said, gesturing to Cody and Naomi.

"Ummm, okay. I've only got two hands," Cody said, lifting up the cake. "It's in my right front pocket."

McCauley awkwardly fished around Cody's pants for a wallet before pulling his empty hands out. "It's not in there."

"Check the other one, then," Cody said.

At this point a line was beginning to form behind them. The disparity in height between Cody and Naomi was making it genuinely difficult for her to hold the cake steady. Her arms started to burn ever so slightly as the lactic acid began building up in her biceps. Her awkward stance also made it difficult to keep the oversized chef's hat from sinking on her head.

"It's not in there either," McCauley said, putting his hands up. "So where is it?"

"I don't know. Maybe it's in the van, maybe I left it back at the store. I was kind of focused on not dropping this thing, and no one said anything about needing ID."

Deputy Dave pointed to Naomi and said, "All right, how about you? You got ID on you?"

"I can get it from your pocket," McCauley said, reaching toward her pants.

His timing couldn't have been any more perfect. Just as McCauley's fingers penetrated the outer edge of Naomi's pocket, her hat, which she had struggled mightily to keep up, finally gave way and tipped forward, covering her eyes in comical fashion. With her eyes fully covered, she matter-of-factly said to McCauley, "If you so much as *think* about sticking those fingers in my pockets, I'm going to sue you and the city for everything it's worth."

"Don't worry, it's not sexual," McCauley shot back.

On hearing the word *sexual* cross McCauley's lips, a look of panic came over Deputy Dave. It wasn't fear, but rather the kind of look one would give if you were standing in line at the airport, getting ready to board, only to hear your friend make a rather loud joke about how he *didn't* have a bomb.

"I don't care what you think it is. I don't want you rooting around in my pockets. I value my personal space, *man*."

McCauley almost chuckled at the last part; it was a nice touch. "Okay, okay," he said, putting Naomi's hat back into place instead.

"Look, everyone, just take it easy. I can see that thing is

heavy, and the faster we figure this out, the faster you can get in there. Look, just set the cake on the table there, and one of you give me ID. That's good enough for me," said Deputy Dave.

They all simultaneously looked at the small table between the metal detectors that usually held keys and cell phones and then looked at the cake. It didn't take a physicist to realize that there was no way the cake was going to fit.

"Look, Dave, can you just let them through? We'll be in and out, and I'll be with them the whole way."

"Pat, you know that's against protocol," Dave said apologetically.

"I'm a police officer, I'll be with them the whole time, and it's not like they're going to rob the place," McCauley said.

"I don't know, Pat. I could get in a lot of trouble if anyone finds out," Dave said.

Cody could see Dave starting to relent. "Look, guys, I hate to break the news to you, but this is getting heavy, so we either take it upstairs or we take it back to the van. Your choice, but let's get moving before we lose it."

"Please, Dave, just do me this solid. Ten minutes—we'll be in and out," McCauley said.

Dave thought for a moment, then pulled two visitor badges off his desk and pushed them into McCauley's chest. "No dilly-dallying. You guys have made a big enough scene as it is," Dave said, gesturing to the line forming behind them. "Ten minutes, you stay with them the whole time, no exceptions. Got it?"

"Definitely. It'll be like we were never here. Thanks, Dave, I owe you one."

"Don't mention it," Dave said as Naomi and Cody passed through the metal detector with the giant cake.

McCauley followed them, his weapons setting off a buzzer and red light. Just as he passed under it, he turned back. "Hey, Dave, when are you on break next?"

"I got another hour and fifteen minutes, why?" Dave replied, looking at his watch.

"You should come up and have some cake."

The clerk's office looked like one would expect. Two glass swinging doors bore the Cook County seal and the words "Office of the County Clerk" in the same gaudy gold lettering that you'd only find in an old accountant's office or a government building.

The office itself looked nice, but like everything else, it was screaming to be updated, having probably not had a facelift in decades. As soon as you entered, plain black retractable stanchions created a zigzagging spaghetti line that funneled patrons to five teller stations. *Teller* was the appropriate term since the black-and-white speckled marble desk with large wooden privacy screens between the stations gave the office the look of a Savings & Loan bank straight out of the eighties.

To the right of the clerk stations was a locked door marked "Employees Only" that led to the support staff for the office. McCauley explained the layout—like he did the security station—to Cody, who surmised that if they could just get back there, they'd have access to any number of unlocked computers.

McCauley pushed open the door and Naomi and Cody followed, the cake really starting to take its toll on their arms now.

"Haaaaaaappy birthday to you!" McCauley began as the half dozen people impatiently waiting in line for their turn at the one clerk station that was staffed turned to look at them.

"Haaaaaaappy birthday to you!" he continued.

"Happy birthday, dear Doris—" McCauley didn't see her among the few curious back office employees who had poked their heads out from behind the desk.

"Doris Hayes, I'm talking about youuuuuu," McCauley stalled.

Finally the door opened, and a woman that appeared to be in her early fifties stepped through. She wore a white button-down shirt tucked into a herringbone skirt. She had a red cardigan around her shoulders and readers hanging from her neck. She was short, maybe five foot two, but her gray curly hair woven tightly into a bun on top of her head gave her a good extra few inches.

"There she is," McCauley said. "Happy birthday tooooo youuuuuu."

A light golf clap erupted from the line jockeys. The round of applause reeked of societal obligation, as though they were more concerned with just how much this would slow things down for them.

As Doris stepped through the door with a coquettish smile, she adjusted the cardigan draped around her shoulders. "But it's not my birthday."

"Oh, sure," McCauley gave her an exaggerated wink. "When has that ever stopped you from celebrating with cake?"

"Oh, stop, Pat. Really, what's this all for?" she asked, batting her eyes at him.

"It says it right there on the cake. Happy birthday!" McCauley leaned in and whispered to her quietly, "Also, it's a little thanks for helping me on my property tax appeal."

Doris smacked him on the shoulder. "You didn't have to go to all that trouble just for me!"

"Of course I did. Now let's cut this big boy up and eat some cake."

"Big boy is right. That thing must feed two hundred people."

"Three hundred, actually," McCauley corrected.

"Three hundred!" Doris said, slapping her forehead. "You know there are only twenty people that work in this office."

"How many of them are available to work the window?" a man said under his breath, to chuckles from his line mates.

"Sir, we advise against coming during lunchtime for faster service. We'll be with you just as soon as we can." Doris said this as if she had said it a thousand times before.

"Can we come in?" McCauley asked.

"Yeah, this is getting pretty heavy," Naomi said, her hat sliding back down her head.

"Oh, yes, of course, darling, please come back this way." Doris reached for her keys to unlock the door. "I haven't the foggiest idea of where we are going to put this."

"How about the conference room to the right? Does it still have that long table?" McCauley asked.

"Oh, yes, that's perfect, it's just to the right when you walk in," Doris said, holding the door for Naomi and Cody.

The back office was one long hallway in an L shape. The base of the L formed the teller windows and conference room. Just past the conference room, the hallway took a ninety-degree left turn and stretched about fifty feet, ending in a modest kitchen. Along the hallway were employee offices—some private, some shared—and a bathroom.

Naomi and Cody maneuvered the cake into the conference room. It wasn't huge, but it had a long eight-person table, where they set the cake down with room to spare.

McCauley yelled down the hallway, "Everyone, there's cake in the conference room!"

Those that hadn't already wandered to the front to see the commotion emerged from their offices.

Doris playfully smacked McCauley on the hand and said, "They're supposed to be working."

McCauley waved her off. "You said it yourself. It's lunchtime. If you can't take five minutes for a cake break, what can you take five minutes for? Besides, it's all for you."

"Well, if you insist," Doris said, bashfully relenting.

"There's only one catch."

"Isn't there always?" Doris smiled at McCauley.

"Oh, it's nothing bad. We left the plates and forks downstairs in the van. And getting this cake through security downstairs was easier said than done, even for a cop—if you can believe it. Do you have that stuff in the kitchen back there?" McCauley gestured toward the end of the hallway.

"Oh, sure, we've got all that stuff. I'll get it—it'll just be a minute."

"Nonsense. This is *your* celebration. These are the best bakers in Chicago. I'm sure they can manage to find it back there."

McCauley gestured to Naomi and Cody, who began squeezing their way out of the room, which was now lined shoulder to shoulder with the whole office, who was buzzing over the size of the cake.

The pair exited the conference room, then turned the corner toward the kitchen.

"Her office is last on the left," Cody reminded Naomi.

"Got it," Naomi said, increasing her pace to a brisk walk.

Just before reaching the kitchen, they checked behind them to make sure the coast was clear and cut quickly into Doris's open office. Naomi ducked behind her desk as Cody crouched next to the door to stand lookout. She shook the mouse back and forth to bring the darkened screen back to life.

"Shit," Naomi said.

"What is it?"

"A lock screen. She locked it."

"Dammit. Okay, plan B. Let's get to one of the other offices."

"What if they don't have access? What if those computers are locked? What if they come back?"

"We have to chance it," Cody said, peering his head out the doorway.

"Wait, just wait one second."

"We don't have time, Naomi, seconds count right now."

"And I need thirty of them. Just give me that much."

"Okay, thirty seconds. Then we move."

Naomi quietly searched the desk, looking for any hint to the password—a printout, a scrap of paper with a code on it—anything. There was only one drawer under the desk, and there wasn't paper of any kind to be found. Just piles of neatly organized pens, pencils, paper clips, and other assorted office supplies.

"Twenty-five seconds, Naomi. Time to get moving." Cody pointed to his watch.

Then it hit her. "One last thing," she said as she dropped to the ground and lay flat on her back under the desk. That's when she saw it, staring back at her in the face. On the underside of the desk drawer was a Post-it note that read:

Login: Dhayes

Password: July17th:)

"Got it!" Naomi almost shouted. "And look at that, her birthday really is in July."

Cody looked back in surprise. "How'd you know where to look?"

"Trade secrets," Naomi said with the corners of her lips slightly turned upwards. She tapped a few keystrokes and said, "Okay, I'm in, but..."

"But what? We're running out of time, Naomi. McCauley can't stall forever."

"I'm not seeing any database software. I don't see it on her desktop or the start menu."

"Check the recent programs tab," Cody insisted.

"I did that too. It only shows her email and Internet Explorer."

"That's it," Cody said.

"What is?"

"Internet Explorer. It's probably web-based. Open it up, then check her bookmarks."

Naomi double-clicked the venerable blue "e" icon for Explorer and saw the link she was looking for—*Property Records Database.*

"You're right," she said, looking up at Cody. "How'd you know?"

"Trade secrets." He smiled back at her. "Hurry, and keep your ears open for footsteps. I need to run to the kitchen."

"What? Why?"

"To get the plates."

Naomi nodded as Cody darted out the door quickly and silently. The link brought up a simple form with various criteria for searching the records—address, property tax ID, buyer name, seller name, and more. And then Naomi saw it: *attorney ID number.*

"ID number?" She cursed quietly. "What the hell is an ID number?"

She searched her memory for what an attorney ID number was but came up blank. She didn't have one, nor had she ever heard of one. It must be something unique to the property database.

As she was debating what to do next, she froze. She heard McCauley's booming voice echoing down the hallway.

"I'm sure they can find it," he shouted down the hallway at Doris, who was coming to help them find the paper plates and forks.

Naomi was huddled behind the desk, but it was open in the front. All Doris had to do was peek in, and she'd have no trouble spotting the baker crouched in her office.

Naomi's heart beat out of her chest. She quickly scanned the room for a better place to hide but found none. It was just a no-frills, windowless municipal employee's office, and the open desk was the best cover she had. For a moment she thought about darting out of the office, but the growing sound of Doris's quick heel steps, muffled slightly by a thin layer of carpet, told her it was too late for that. Out of options, Naomi clutched her knees, forced her body into a tight little ball on the ground, and squeezed her eyes shut.

Then suddenly the footsteps stopped directly in front of Doris's open office door. Naomi's stomach was in her chest now. It was over. They were finished. There'd be no talking her way out of this. The deputies would race upstairs and arrest Cody and Naomi. They'd probably arrest McCauley too. Breaking into the records office would only make them look more guilty. They'd be convicted and buried in Statesville Correctional Center for the rest of their lives. They took a gamble and lost. More painful to Naomi in that moment, though, was that Whitaker won.

"Oh, good, you found them," Doris said to Cody in the kitchen.

"Yes, ma'am," Cody said, holding up a stack of paper plates high so Doris could see them from where she stood just outside her office. "We just need to wash our hands, and we'll have that cake sliced up for you in a jiff."

"Wonderful. Hurry now, they're practically salivating over that cake in there."

With that, Doris made a 180-degree turn away from her office and started back up the hallway toward the conference room.

Naomi let out a long, slow breath of relief as she clutched her hands into fists to steady them.

Cody came back in with the plates, forks, and a long serrated knife and set them on the desk. The look on his face said it all: *We've got to go…*now.

Naomi silently held up her index finger to him, then turned to the computer screen.

The field marked "attorney ID number" looked back at her mockingly. *I've never heard of an attorney ID. What the fuck could that be?* she thought.

Then she saw it—a small link next to the field that said "attorney ID lookup." She clicked the link and was directed to another form, this time prompting her for a first and last name.

Yes! Her slender fingers moved quickly over the keyboard. "Wentz, Byron." She clicked submit, and the computer instantly revealed a number: 187377.

"One eight seven, three seven seven," Naomi said to herself. "One eight seven, three seven seven."

She hit the back button, bringing her to the main search form, where she entered Byron's ID number. She hit submit again, but this time the results took longer. The Explorer icon spun and spun and spun as the servers searched over the millions upon millions of entries of every property transaction for the last hundred years. One by one, the server looked at every transaction for any entry that matched attorney ID number 187377.

Naomi was getting impatient; she considered stopping the

search and trying again. It had only been twenty seconds, but it felt like an eternity. The fact that Cody was getting visibly antsy didn't help either. Naomi moved the mouse on top of the "X" to stop the process, but just before she clicked it, the query finished. The screen populated with a few hundred entries—all for attorney 187377, all within the past ten or so years.

Naomi pulled the prepaid phone they had bought at Costco along with the cake and disguises and snapped a photo of the screen. She quickly closed the browser and hit CTRL+ALT+DEL, then selected the option to lock the computer.

She walked around the desk and said to Cody, who was peering out the door down the hallway, "I've got it. Let's go."

"Wait," he said sharply. Naomi froze in her tracks.

They were so close! We have the list, can we just get one break? Naomi wanted to yell. Instead she whispered to Cody, "What is it?"

"Grab the plates," he said, smiling at her.

CHAPTER THIRTY-TWO

After slicing nearly thirty pieces of cake for the waiting employees, McCauley faked an urgent call, said his good-byes to Doris, and then escorted Cody and Naomi to the elevators. McCauley gave Deputy Dave a thanks and a handshake as they dropped off the visitor badges back at the security station.

In and out in under fifteen minutes. *Who knew it could be that easy,* he thought. Either that or Cody really was that good. The trio piled into the van still parked in the loading zone with its hazards on. Naomi sat in the middle, examining her phone, with McCauley to her left in the driver's seat and Cody to her right in the passenger's seat. She pinched her fingers and swiped away at the device as she zoomed around the photo of the list of ten-plus years of Byron Wentz's real estate transactions.

"So?" McCauley asked. "What do you see?"

Naomi didn't respond, too focused on the screen to process what McCauley had asked.

Cody placed a hand on her shoulder. "Naomi."

She turned and looked at him with her beautiful green eyes, but she couldn't hide the worry behind them. "I don't...I don't know."

"That's okay," Cody said, squeezing her shoulder now. "The hard part is over. Just take your time."

"I was sure I'd see something on here. An address, a name, something. Oh, my God, what if there's nothing here?"

"There's something on that list, Naomi," McCauley said.

"Your gut was right. Ask me how I know."

"You don't know that, McCauley," she replied.

"Ask me, Naomi."

"How do you know?"

"Because you're smart. You're a helluva lot smarter than most of the detectives I've worked with, maybe all of them. Plus, after you laid it out, my gut said the exact same thing."

"But what if your gut is wrong too?" Naomi asked.

"When it's screaming at me like this—it rarely is."

"Or that cake got you hungry," Cody quipped.

They all let out a laugh.

"Look, I've worked enough cases to know how this goes. Contrary to what every TV show says, the evidence never jumps out at you—especially when the perpetrators have gone to great lengths to conceal it. But believe me, it's there."

"So how do we find it?" Naomi asked.

"First things first. We need a break, a few minutes to clear our heads. After that, we need to get the proper tools to analyze that list. Scanning it on your phone in a van won't get us anywhere."

"Yes, I could use a laptop. We can drop pins on all these addresses—maybe the pattern will reveal something."

"Now you're thinking like a detective, Naomi," McCauley said. "Except I've got something better than a laptop."

"Oh, yeah? What's that?" she asked.

"Kinko's. It's still a detective's best friend."

CHAPTER THIRTY-THREE

McCauley pulled the van over to the curb and parked three blocks from his house in Beverly just after 6:00 p.m. Darkness was setting in, and the rain picked up from a drizzle to a light spray. Nestled on the south edge of the city, Beverly was a working-class neighborhood made up largely of municipal workers —particularly cops and firefighters. It was a close-knit community, and the smaller bungalows afforded the residents the perk of being one of the last places in the city where one could still have a proper lawn.

McCauley, Naomi, and Cody weaved through the meticulously maintained yards and alleys, careful to stay off the roads as much as possible in case anyone was watching. They all agreed that McCauley's involvement had not yet been discovered, and a call to McCauley's partner, Anthony Davis, confirmed as much. Still, Cody was wary of Whitaker and insisted they take every precaution.

Naomi approached the back door with her coat draped over her head and her bag slung around her shoulder. Cody followed closely behind holding a box of supplies, and McCauley brought up the rear holding a large tube under his coat to shield it from the rain.

Before Naomi could knock, Emily McCauley opened the interior door and unlatched the small white screen door. Naomi, with her view partially concealed by her coat and the darkening skies, was almost taken aback to find Emily standing in front of her with an apron on and an oven mitt over her right hand.

Like McCauley, she looked young, much younger than her fifty years. She dressed well—even in an apron—and her flowing, golden-blond hair was well kept. If she dyed it, no one could tell. In fact, the only feature that betrayed her age was a single crow's foot nestled up against her left eye.

"Mrs. McCauley, I'm sorry, I didn't see you there. We're friends of your husband," Naomi said, pointing to McCauley as he trudged through the wet grass.

"Well, don't just stand there, darling, come in out of the rain before you catch a cold."

Naomi shook her coat and wiped her feet on the mat before walking through the door, which led to a modest kitchen. Cody did the same, and then finally McCauley, who was less cautious with his shoes.

Naomi flipped her coat down and stepped into the light as Cody set his box of supplies on the kitchen table.

"You two," Emily burst out. "I should have known it involved you two when he didn't call. He works long hours, but Pat always calls."

Naomi and Cody looked at each other, confused.

"Well, don't you know? You're all over the news. Not just local either—you made the 5:30 national news programs too."

"We didn't do it. Well, not all of it," Naomi said, thinking of the man she shot.

"Well, it's a good thing you came in the back, because as a police officer's wife, I know from experience that the 'I didn't do it' defense rarely holds up in court. Half our neighbors got called in on their day off just to look for you two."

"I guess it's bigger than we thought," Cody said.

"You can say that again. I just hope whatever you two are into, you don't drag my husband down with you. He's an honest cop and a good man."

"We know, ma'am—" Naomi started.

"Don't ma'am me, I'm not your mother. You can just call me Emily."

"Emily, we're sorry to have to be here, but as you can imagine, we don't have a lot of options. Detective McCauley is the only one outside of us that knows the truth, and without him, I don't know what we'd do."

"Emily, take it easy on them," McCauley jumped in, having kicked off his shoes and hung his coat on the coatrack near the door. "They really are innocent."

"Of *most* of it, according to Miss Archer," Emily said, gesturing to Naomi.

"Of all of it," McCauley said. "I can explain everything."

"Actually, it's better we don't," Cody said. "Look, I'm sure you share everything, but in this case, for Emily's safety, it's better that she doesn't know what's going on."

"I am perfectly capable of taking care of myself, Cody."

"Yes, that's very clear to me, especially given you remembered our names from the news."

"Like I said, I can take care of myself," Emily said.

"With all due respect, Mrs. McCauley—" Cody began.

"I told you it's Emily," she fired back.

"Yes, sorry, Emily. The people that are after us are dangerous, and you just opened the door to two wanted fugitives."

Cody looked at McCauley for backup on this point, but he merely flashed a wide grin and gestured back at his wife. Cody turned back to Emily, but this time he was staring down the barrel of a Smith & Wesson 686 revolver loaded with hollow-point .357 magnum rounds. She had concealed it under the oven mitt, which was now lying on the floor.

"You were saying, Cody?"

"Clearly, I was mistaken," he said, putting his hands up and sniffing the air. "You're not cooking anything, are you? I should have noticed. The apron was a nice touch."

"If the news is accurate on your background, then you of all people should know that the devil is in the details," Emily said, de-cocking the revolver and placing it in her apron pocket. "And just in case six rounds wasn't enough, I've got the street sweeper here." Emily casually opened the pantry door to reveal a Remington 870 shotgun hanging from it. It was no doubt loaded, and attached to it was a sling that doubled as a bandoleer with an additional twenty shells.

"I see you have an affinity for the classics," said Cody.

"I like the semiautos enough, but even the good ones still require a lot of maintenance. I could bury this revolver in the backyard, dig it up a year from now, and it'll still shoot as good as the day it left the factory. Same goes for the shotgun."

"You've really got a keeper here," Cody said, smiling at McCauley. He couldn't hide it—he was impressed.

"That's why I married her." McCauley walked over and planted a big kiss on Emily's lips.

"Please just tell me you know what you are doing," she whispered to him.

"I'm not sure that I do," he whispered back.

"Then tell me you're being safe."

"As safe as can be."

"You're lying, but I trust you." Emily turned to Cody. "You're in the military, right?"

"I was, but now I'm...I don't know...something else," Cody said.

"I don't care about any of that. You took an oath once to defend this country, yes?"

"I did."

"I want you to take the same oath to defend my husband."

"I don't know what's going to happen, things—"

"Promise me you'll watch after him," Emily said with ferocity in her eyes. "I'm fifty-one years old, and I plan on being on this earth a lot longer. I'm not spending that time alone, you understand me? So you promise me."

"Okay," Cody said. "I promise."

Satisfied at his sincerity, Emily said, "Okay, good. I'll get some towels for you, and there's leftover pot roast in the fridge I can warm up. Knowing my husband, I'm sure none of you have had anything to eat since your morning coffee."

"Thanks, Em," McCauley said. "We're going to set up in the

basement."

With that, McCauley opened a door off the kitchen to reveal a drab green-painted staircase leading down to the small, cool basement. He flipped on a light switch at the top of the stairs, which set the lights flickering for a moment before fully turning on as the trio descended the stairs. It was clear to Naomi and Cody that this was McCauley's home office. Against one wall was a large bulletin board on wheels with photos and documents tacked to it. Across from it sat a metal desk with papers scattered across the top.

Cody walked to the bulletin board and looked at two gruesome photos—one of Melvin Jackson, his eyes wide open, staring at the camera. The other was of DeMario Sherman's bullet-ridden body, his limbs a tangled, bloody mess.

McCauley observed Cody staring at the macabre photos. Only hours ago, Cody had told McCauley he had no love lost for these two. Maybe that was the truth, maybe he was able to justify their murders by reminding himself of their evils. They sold addictive and deadly poison to their community. Surely they were responsible for dozens of overdoses over the years. At the very least, they bore some responsibility for destroying hundreds or even thousands of other lives. McCauley had to admit, the world was a better place without them.

But he'd sworn to uphold the law. He didn't know what would happen when all of this was over, but he knew Cody would have to answer. But the look on Cody's face said it all— that he already was answering for his actions. McCauley knew from experience that this type of pain was not easily shed, and for a moment he felt sympathy for Cody.

McCauley walked over to the board and searched for something reassuring to say, but all that came out was, "I guess we can close the books on these two."

Cody just nodded.

Naomi helped McCauley pull down the rest of the case files in silence. When they had cleared the board, she shifted topics. "Are you sure this is the best way to flush out this list?"

"Trust me," he said. "Sometimes the old techniques are the best."

"Okay," she said, "where do we start?"

Within minutes McCauley had expertly arranged the bulletin board with an oversized map of Chicago, the list of addresses freshly printed from the shot Naomi had taken with her phone, and the only photo of Brendt Whitaker they had been able to find on the Internet. McCauley knew the photo served no investigative purpose, but he hoped it would keep Naomi and Cody focused in case they got stuck. He insisted on it, knowing it would be a not-so-subtle reminder of the man trying so hard to destroy them.

"So what now?" Naomi asked.

"We do exactly what you said. We start dropping pins on these addresses. He might have been an attorney for a long time, but according to the list, Byron Wentz didn't cut his teeth as a real estate specialist until later life. The list of the few hundred properties that you so expertly pulled from Doris's computer only goes back eleven years."

"That's true, but he was busy. There must be over two hundred and fifty properties on it."

"We've got time. It's not like we have every cop and mercenary in the city looking for us," Cody said sarcastically.

"Not helpful, Cody, but you know what would be?" McCauley asked.

"What's that?"

"If you take the yellows and start pinning," McCauley said as he handed over a box of pushpins. "Anything over ten years old gets a yellow tag. Seven to ten years gets blue. We'll call four to seven years ago green, and anything two to four years purple. Anything within the last year we'll flag as red."

"You know, I have a small cache of arms hidden in the city, including a well-oiled rifle. Whitaker rarely leaves his offices at Pennington, but he has to eventually. I can end this tomorrow if we get lucky."

"If he's really two steps ahead of us, then he'll be expecting that. Besides, that won't solve the problem of the murder charges against you."

"I can live with that."

"But Naomi can't. This might be her only shot at getting her life back, so start marking the map," McCauley said.

"Okay, but just know the rifle option is in your back pocket if you need it."

McCauley and Cody took turns calling addresses off the map as Naomi searched for them using the Google Maps app on the burner phone. She'd give them general guidance of direction or neighborhood as they searched for the exact spot and dropped the pushpin on it. They started slow at first, but McCauley knew the city well, having worked in a number of different districts over the years. In addition, the numbering of Chicago's addresses in a grid helped speed things up. The 0-0 block is famously State and Madison. Addresses fan out from there in all directions. If you went north twenty blocks, you could expect the address to be 2000 North. The same for south, west, and east, although the east addresses ended quickly at the lakefront.

After a few minutes Cody even found a rhythm, and soon he wasn't asking Naomi for directions except for the most obscure streets. Still, with the sheer number of addresses, it took them nearly ninety minutes to locate and mark each one on the map. Finally, when they had crossed the last address off the list, the trio sat back and looked at it as they picked at the leftover pot roast Emily had prepared for them. The design on the map staring back at them was as plain as day—a ring that wrapped around the Loop forming concentric circles. It was dotted and disconnected, but the pattern was clear.

"So it's a big circle," Cody said, stating the obvious.

"That's got to mean something," Naomi said. "Does it mean anything to you, Cody?"

"Not really."

"How can that be, Cody," McCauley jabbed. "You worked for Whitaker for the past decade. How can it mean nothing to you?"

"Hey, don't jump down my throat. I told you I was insulated from his plans. Unless it was an operational detail, he didn't share, and I didn't ask."

"Well, what kind of operations are we talking about here? Killing more drug dealers?" McCauley asked with a twinge of regret as soon as he said it.

"Hey, I'm here, I'm risking my life for Naomi, just the same as you. Even more than you, McCauley. You can still go back to your life after this. I don't have that option anymore."

"Some life," McCauley muttered.

Cody lunged at McCauley and grabbed him. "I told you I'm not some psycho. I never killed anyone that didn't have it coming. When you sign up to be a criminal, you assume a certain level of risk. One of those risks is that one day you may find yourself staring down the barrel of a gun."

"Easy, fellas," Naomi said, pushing her body between Cody and McCauley. "We're all tired. We're all on edge. He didn't mean anything by it, Cody."

Cody's nostrils were still flaring as he clutched the lapels of McCauley's sport coat. Naomi put her hands on his cheeks and turned his face to hers.

"Cody," she said softly. "I believe you. And I will forever be grateful that you came back for me. I don't know why you did, but I'm glad that you're here. I couldn't do this without you."

Cody's anger instantly subsided. He couldn't help it. Something in her eyes, which were partially blocked by a single lock of her hair, made him feel like a person again. Although he had never experienced love, in that moment he knew what it felt like. He wanted desperately to kiss her, but he restrained himself. Maybe when it was all over, he'd find a way to tell her how he felt about her. For now, though, those feelings were best left unsaid, at least until they were out of danger. Cody released his grip on McCauley and took a step back.

"Thank you, Cody," Naomi said. "And I think you have something to say, McCauley, don't you?"

Like a child scorned by a teacher, McCauley begrudgingly spoke. "She's right. I'm tired. I haven't slept much in the last forty-eight hours. I'm...well, I'm glad you're here too."

"Okay, thanks," Cody said. "I shouldn't have grabbed you. I'm not exactly running on full sleep either."

"No, I deserved it, we're all good," McCauley said, the apologies now freely flowing.

"Good, I was worried for a second that I'd have to finish this out on my own," Naomi said. "Now, if we can figure out what Cody was doing for Whitaker, maybe we can figure out what Whitaker was up to. There must be something on that board that looks familiar, Cody."

"The addresses don't mean anything to me, but the areas do," Cody said.

"Give me an example," Naomi said.

Cody studied the board for a minute, then pointed to a blue pushpin at Eighteenth and Ashland in the city's Pilsen neighborhood. "Here. About ten years ago we ran an op around here. It was one of my first."

"And what did you do? Were you...targeting...drug dealers? Do you remember anything about it?" Naomi asked.

"Of course I remember everything. That time we targeted the Ortiz brothers."

"*You* took out the Ortiz brothers?" McCauley asked in shock.

"I didn't pull the trigger or anything, but I may have set a few things in motion."

"I don't get it. Who are the Ortiz brothers? Are they drug dealers too?" Naomi asked.

"On the contrary, those guys weren't organized enough to compete in the drug business. They fenced stolen goods, ran a few chop shops, but their biggest business was funding violent robberies throughout the city for a percentage of the score. That is, until one of their lieutenants, a guy named Mateo Lopez, took them out. I never had enough to bring charges against him, but I was convinced he was the trigger man. I guess he wasn't."

"No, you were right. He did it," Cody said.

"So what was your involvement, then?" McCauley asked.

"I merely told Lopez about the deal the Ortizes struck with the FBI to become confidential informants."

"They turned snitch?"

"Oh, no way. They hated anyone affiliated with law enforcement. Technically it was a bluff by the FBI to try to secure some high-level street assets, but the Ortizes didn't go for it."

"So if they didn't take the bait, how did you get Lopez to go after them?" McCauley asked.

"I showed him the immunity agreement and photographs of them walking into the Chicago FBI field office. Those immunity agreements are books, and he only got through a quarter of it before he was in a rage. He definitely didn't see the blank signature pages at the back."

"Let me guess, you got the immunity agreement from Whitaker," McCauley said.

"I told you, he's well connected. It was the real deal too, which was important, because I would have had no idea how to fake something like that."

"This makes no sense," Naomi said. "If Whitaker is some sort of vigilante, then why did he kill Eisner? Why did he try to kill me? Chadwick may fit the motive since he stole, but we certainly don't fit it."

"I don't think he's a vigilante, Naomi," Cody said.

"Well, he apparently has you running all over town snuffing out street crime," she replied.

"Not very effectively, though," McCauley blurted out.

"What do you mean?" Naomi asked. "Doesn't taking out high-level crime bosses drive crime down?"

McCauley thought for a moment, then snapped his fingers. "That's it! Cody, show me another one."

Cody studied the board and pointed to Division and Damen
—the northwest corner of Ukrainian Village. "Here, Anatoly
Carencko."

"The head of the Carencko crime family?"

"He's dead too?" Naomi asked.

"Nope, but he's in jail for the next hundred and twenty years.
Good old-fashioned wire fraud, twenty years per count," McCauley said. The quickening pace of his speech injected a new level
of excitement back into the room.

"How did you—" Naomi started.

"It's illegal for the FBI to plant warrantless wiretaps."

"But not for you," Naomi said.

"No, that's probably illegal too, but I'll defer to you as my
attorney on that one. However, if the FBI receives a package of
incriminating evidence from someone inside the organization
with a letter asking to cut a deal, that's a different story."

"So you found someone on the inside to cut a deal with the
FBI?"

"Well, he didn't exactly know about it, but by the time the
feds knocked on his door, they had plenty of evidence against
him too. It was simple math for him—testify as the voluntary
informant and receive immunity or go down with Carencko. It
didn't take a genius to figure out which he was going to choose."

"What else?" McCauley asked.

"Here," Cody said, pointing at Armitage and Sheffield.

"Didn't think there was much organized crime in the heart
of Lincoln Park," Naomi said, referring to the wealthy neighborhood.

"Nope, there we set up a crew, mostly neighborhood kids, to
spray graffiti, snatch purses from diners at outdoor patios, a few
smash-and-grabs at cell phone stores. That sort of thing."

"That makes no sense. All the other ops you mentioned were
going after criminals, and on this one you were encouraging
them?"

"Of course," McCauley said. "It makes perfect sense."

"I'm still lost," Naomi said.

"Think about it for a second, Naomi," McCauley started. "You said that taking out these crime bosses should drive crime down. Long term, that may be true, but what happens in the short run?"

"Oh, my God. A turf war," she said.

"Exactly. The sad truth of policing is that we can't stop people from committing crimes. We can slow it down, we can contain it, we can punish those that do it, but from a police standpoint, it's hard for us to wipe it out entirely. There will always be someone that needs a loan, or a fix, or want to throw money on a football game. There will always be an armored truck or a bank to rob. It always plays out the same. When the big guys go down, stability goes out the window. Take the organization out of organized crime, and you just have pure crime. It's mayhem for the next year or two. We doubled the officer count in Pilsen for six months after the Ortiz brothers were killed. I bet it was the same for Ukrainian Village when Carencko got swept up by the FBI. And what happens to property values when crime rates go up?"

"They plummet," Naomi said.

"That's right," McCauley said. "He was driving up crime, which drove *down* property values so he could snatch them up at a discount. Like the saying goes, 'When there's blood on the streets, buy property.'"

"It tracks. Some of the other ops fit that narrative," Cody said.

"That's great, McCauley!" Naomi exclaimed, smiling and grabbing McCauley's hands and shaking them euphorically. "So what's he going to do with all the property?"

"I haven't the foggiest idea," McCauley said, shaking her hands back excitedly.

"Then why are we still smiling?" she asked, still holding his hands.

"Because the bulletin board works!"

Just past midnight, Naomi was curled up in the basement on a worn brown couch that had seen its fair share of catnaps. She tucked her body under a white afghan that Emily had knitted ages ago. Cody sat in the corner with his legs sticking out and crossed in front of him. He too had his eyes shut and his arms folded across his chest—a little sleeping trick he learned as a marine. After the epiphany about Whitaker driving down property values, McCauley insisted they get what sleep they could. They were making progress, but it was clear they all needed rest. McCauley couldn't sleep, though, and instead sat at his metal desk, staring at the oversized map with the pushpins.

He stroked his chin deep in thought. Perhaps if he managed a few hours of sleep himself, the answer would come to him. The pattern was clear, and the ring of properties was vaguely familiar to him, but he just couldn't place it.

Naomi's eyes opened, and after a moment of getting her bearings, she sat up and stretched her arms above her head, letting out a little murmur as she torqued her shoulders.

Quietly, so as not to wake up Cody, she threw the blanket off and whispered to McCauley, "You were supposed to sleep too."

"Couldn't sleep," McCauley muttered.

"Well, then, did staring at the map give you any ideas?"

"Maybe. It looks like something to me, but what, I just don't know."

Naomi turned to look at the board and crooked her head in thought. "Could it have anything to do with building hotels?"

"I don't think so. There are way too many properties, and they are too close together." McCauley pointed to the map.

The pushpins were clustered in a five- or six-block radius, then a fifteen- or twenty-block gap leading to another cluster.

Those clusters were what clearly formed the ring around the city stretching from Fullerton to the north, Damen to the west, Garfield to the south, and Michigan Avenue to the east.

"What about gas or sewer lines?"

"I don't know much about those, but I think they run all over the city. I don't know how the ring would fit into those, or for what purpose."

"I'd say it looks like a canal almost, but the city could never afford to build such a massive one, and it doesn't stretch all the way to the lake," Naomi said. "It could be something like that —maybe Whitaker just couldn't drive down the lakefront property values enough, or he hasn't tried yet."

"Yeah," McCauley said, touching his lips in thought. "How much did you say he embezzled?"

"One hundred and fifty million dollars that we found. Could've been more—it probably was."

"The list has the purchase price on all the properties, though, doesn't it?"

"Yeah, I totaled it earlier. One hundred and thirty-two million and change."

"So if someone has that kind of money, they can afford to buy lakefront property," McCauley said.

"I know, I know. I'm just throwing ideas out there," Naomi said.

"No, look, you're on to something," McCauley said, walking up to the board. "What do all the properties have in common?"

"Nothing as far as I can tell," Naomi said.

"Focus on the clusters. What do you notice about their locations?" McCauley asked.

"None of them are in highly desirable areas, or at least not as desirable as the areas around them."

"Why?"

"Whitaker may have a lot of money, but maybe he wanted more bang for his buck, which he's definitely getting by buying these clusters rather than their more expensive neighbors."

"No, I mean, why aren't they as desirable as the areas around them?"

"They're too far from the El. All of these clusters are smack dab in the middle of the spokes of the train system. Living in these areas could be double or triple the commute time of living closer to one of the train lines. Like this cluster near Fullerton and Ashland," Naomi said, pointing to a group of pushpins on the north end. "If you want to get to the Loop from here, you have a twenty- or twenty-five-minute walk to the Fullerton stop at Sheffield and then a thirty-minute train ride. Or you can wait for the Fullerton bus, which is so slow. Sometimes those east-west buses take as long as it does to walk, although in the snow that may be worth it. Or you could skip the train entirely and take the Ashland bus south, but you'd still have to walk or transfer to another bus when you got downtown. During rush hour? Forget it—you'd be commuting for over an hour."

"But if you live just a mile or two in either direction..."

"It's a huge difference. The train is fast, but you have to get to it first."

"You're a genius, Naomi!" McCauley shouted.

Cody snorted awake and jumped to his feet.

"What's going on?" he asked, clearly still trying to get his bearings.

"Naomi might have just cracked the case."

"What did you figure out?" Cody asked.

Naomi just shrugged her shoulders and looked at McCauley, who was rooting around in a file cabinet off to the side of his desk.

"What are you looking for, McCauley?" Naomi asked.

"I need to find something."

"Well, that's obvious, but what?" Cody asked.

"When I closed my first case, Emily saved the article from the *Chicago Tribune*. It became sort of a tradition that she'd save the articles of the cases I solved. My whole career as a detective is summarized in the *Tribune* articles in these drawers."

"Okay, so what case are you looking for?" Cody asked.

"A very special one...here!" McCauley held up a full-page

spread: *Leaders of Multi-State Car Theft Ring Arrested.*

"What do car thieves have to do with Whitaker?"

"It's not the thieves I'm interested in. It's the ad on the back of it. Look," McCauley said, unfolding the newspaper.

There it was. A full-page color ad of a map with a circle on it that was nearly an exact match to theirs. At the top read: *Announcement for Public Meeting and Feedback on Chicago Transit Authority's Proposed Expansion to 'El' Called the 'Circle Line.'*

"Oh, my God, that's it, McCauley!" Naomi exclaimed. "He's amassing property for the Circle Line."

"I hate to slow you guys down," Cody said, "but what exactly is this Circle Line?"

McCauley explained, "Every five years, like clockwork, some politician—be it an alderman or even the mayor—floats this proposal. For years they've discussed building a massive line that runs in a larger circle around the city. Look here," McCauley said, pointing to map. "The El is a good train system. It's reliable, it's fast, but it was built a hundred years ago when Chicago was still growing. It's a hub-and-spoke system that travels from the edges of the city in all directions and culminates in the Loop downtown. It's great if you live near a line, but if you don't, it doesn't do you much good."

"So?"

"Naomi said it. The Circle Line would cut commute times in half—maybe more—for dozens of neighborhoods that don't have easy access to the train."

"Okay, so what's the catch? If it's such a good idea, why haven't they built it yet?" Cody asked.

"At this point, it's just too hard. The city is too developed and has too much debt already. I mean, theoretically they could afford it, but the property would cost billions, and then building it would cost billions more. So it never gets any serious traction. Mostly now it's just a political tool to drum up some votes from underrepresented neighborhoods. Then as soon as the elections are over, the plans go right back in the archives."

"But a powerful man with all the right connections could get it built, couldn't he, Cody?" Naomi asked.

"Whitaker could," Cody said. "He might have to call in a lot of favors, but he's so well connected—especially in this city—that he's fully capable of getting it built."

"And if you had an inside track on the most massive public works project that the Midwest has ever seen, how would you capitalize on it?" McCauley asked, leading Cody to the answer.

"Buy up the property around it," Cody said.

"That's right. The second that the project is announced, the value of his real estate holdings will quadruple. Hell, in some areas, it may be more—if they could even keep the most prime locations for their hotels and make money off that too. There will be dozens of new locations that would now be perfect for a hotel with quick access downtown."

"And construction too," Naomi added.

"How do you mean?" McCauley asked.

"Over the last five years, the Pennington holding company has acquired a dozen construction companies. I figured it was just good synergy given all the property they develop, but as you said, there will be billions in construction contracts up for grabs. Anyone want to bet *against* Whitaker getting the bulk of those? Between the property holdings and the contracts, the final windfall would be in the billions."

Cody just looked at the board. He scanned the pushpins and what they meant to him. "All this. All this for a train?"

"Not just a train, Cody," Naomi said, putting her hand on his shoulder. "The largest property scam in history."

"It still makes me feel empty. I rationalized the last ten years of my life by saying it was for some level of greater good. And now..."

"We know you're a good person, Cody, and there's still time to turn this around," Naomi said. "Everything you're feeling now, we need to use it to take down Whitaker."

"I suppose that's all I can do now," Cody said.

"We'll do it together," Naomi said, grabbing a hand each from Cody and McCauley.

Cody gripped her hand tightly. "So now that we know what he's up to, what's next? Go to the papers?"

"I think it's too early for that," McCauley said. "We need to have airtight proof before they'll consider running something this big."

"I hate to say this, but every time we get closer to exposing Whitaker's plans, it feels like he moves farther away," Cody said.

"Maybe, maybe not," said Naomi.

"Whatcha thinking?" McCauley asked.

"It's an idea, really. I've handled a variety of investigations—nothing of this magnitude—but they almost always unravel the same way," said Naomi.

"Which is?" Cody asked.

"Follow the money. It's the back door to tracking down crooks."

"How do you mean?" Cody asked.

"Look, the best criminals are good at what they do. As is often the case, if they weren't criminals, they would probably be pretty good business people. But there is one constant across all criminal endeavors, be it drugs, corporate embezzlement, gambling, cooking the books."

"The money," McCauley said.

"That's right, the money. A criminal enterprise is hard to run, but it's much harder to turn the ill-gotten gains into dollars that can be freely used."

"You're right," McCauley said. "It's how they got Capone. They could never get him on bootlegging, robbery, gambling, or any of the dozens of murders he ordered. But they had no trouble nailing him for failing to pay his taxes."

"Exactly. And at the height of the war on drugs in the eighties, Congress enacted a slew of new banking laws to report unusual deposits. Someone figured out that you don't have to get the drugs if you can get the money."

"So you're saying that Whitaker has to launder the money somehow?" Cody asked.

"No, he's done that already. The money he stole from Pennington is gone. He made sure of that with all the different shell companies and offshore bank accounts. If he wanted to run, he could have taken that money and fallen off the map, never to be seen again. Bye bye, bon voyage, vaya con Dios."

"But he's not going to run," Cody said.

"That's right," said Naomi. "We know what he's planning to do with it. He's already bought the property, effectively locking it back up here in the States. If he ever wants to sell those, he'll need to find a way to legitimize it."

"So how does one legitimize a bunch of properties bought with stolen money?" Cody asked.

McCauley put his hands up. "Don't look at me. I'm out of my depth when it comes to this stuff. This is Naomi's area of expertise."

"Again, this is a bit of a reach for even me. So I'm not entirely sure," Naomi said.

"Think like him, Naomi," McCauley said. "If you were in his shoes, how would *you* get the money back?"

"Well." Naomi pressed her index finger to her lips. "He's already done the hard part. He got the money out of Pennington and managed to funnel it to untraceable shell companies. There's no way the city is going to buy property from a bunch of untraceable shell companies. He may have a lot of contacts, but someone is going to throw up some red flags if he starts doing that."

"So what can he do?" McCauley asked.

"To put it simply, he's going to need a real company—perhaps some kind of trust. I'm not sure, exactly, but it will have to be able to pass thorough scrutiny. As we said, the government is very good at tracking money, so I don't think he can fake it. I think he has to create a real company, with all the bells and whistles. Articles of incorporation, a *real* headquarters, company officers, and tax forms."

"And so what happens when he makes this company?" Cody asked.

"I think he already has," Naomi said, walking back to the

board now. She held her hands up to the map and said, "What do you see? Or rather, what don't you see on the board?"

"I mean, there are plenty of gaps in the clusters," Cody said.

"Yeah, but that seems on purpose. I don't know much about eminent domain laws, but if this isn't enough property to allow the city to buy the rest, I don't know what is. No, I'm talking about the clusters themselves. What's missing?"

McCauley stared at the yellow, blue, green, and purple push-pins on the map. "The red ones."

"That's right," Naomi said. "Did he stop buying property in the last year?"

"I don't know, Naomi. The list only covered the properties that Byron Wentz worked on. You said he died a year ago, and without the name of the new attorney, we can't expect to have any from the last year," said Cody.

"I assumed Byron Wentz died of natural causes, but what if I was wrong? If Whitaker is going to create a legitimate entity, who's the one person that would know enough to be a liability?"

"Wentz," McCauley agreed.

"Look, there's going to be a paper trail at the new entity. There's no getting around that. It will be there, but it will be hiding in plain sight. No one will ever be able to put all the pieces together; it's far too complicated. Unless—" Naomi said.

"Unless they know what to look for," Cody interjected. "If Whitaker took out his trusted real estate attorney that can only mean one thing—he's in the endgame."

"Yes," said Naomi. "And there is one company that we know of that doesn't own any property as far as we can tell."

"Eclipse," McCauley said.

"Bingo," said Naomi. "I think he's consolidating all his holdings into Eclipse."

"It's thin," McCauley said.

"Paper thin," replied Naomi. "But my gut was right once. I think it's right again."

"So how do we track down Eclipse? How do we find this paper trail hiding in plain sight?"

"If Whitaker is truly in the final stages, then he'll need ready access to all of it. So, where does any company keep copies of records that they need?" Naomi said.

"At their headquarters," McCauley said. "If it exists as you say."

"If I'm right, then the mere existence of that headquarters goes a long way to proving my theory."

"But you know where Eclipse is, right? Didn't you find a bunch of embezzled checks made out to them?" McCauley asked.

"No, just one, actually—delivered to a PO box that has since been closed. All the big-dollar ones were to the other companies. In comparison, the half a million dollars made out to Eclipse was just a drop in the bucket."

"I don't get it. Why would he risk exposing Eclipse like that?" Cody asked.

"Well, he's starting a big new company that will be buying hundreds of properties. Since it's a real company, he won't be able to avoid all the fees associated with that. My guess is that he just needed a little start-up cash. It had worked dozens of times before that. There wasn't much risk of exposure. Really, without a perfect storm of seemingly random events, it never would have been found. A lonely man sees the scam. One day he tries it himself, and it works. A longtime check processor retires, and her replacement notices a discrepancy."

"Don't forget a brilliant attorney who was able to uncover it," Cody said.

Naomi blushed. "I was well trained. But you see my point—it was a pretty fortuitous chain of events that led us to this. So it's not crazy that he tried to slip one last check through."

"So, we find the HQ for Eclipse, and we find our evidence?" Cody asked, polling the room.

"I doubt we can just Internet search them," McCauley said.

"You mean Google them? It's a verb now, ya know," said Cody.

"What?"

"Never mind," said Cody.

"Okay. I can tap the CPD's resources to track it down. It should be easy enough," McCauley said.

"I wouldn't do that," said Cody. "That could tip him off. I've told you he has lots of contacts in the department. If that search gets back to Whitaker, he could move the evidence."

"Cody's right. Whitaker may have taken just enough steps to conceal the location for now. We don't know for sure that the CPD can find it. Plus, we can't risk him finding out that we're on to him. Right now he thinks we are on the run, and that's to our advantage," said Naomi.

"Okay, but I don't know that we have any other options," said McCauley.

"We have one," Naomi said. "We'll get him like they got Capone. Eclipse will list the address for their headquarters on their federal tax form. They're required to."

"It's federal. I don't have access to that," McCauley said.

"I don't want to offend the oath you took as a police officer, but do you know of anybody that might be able to hack their way in?" Cody asked.

"I don't know if you've picked up on it, but I'm more of a street crime kind of guy. Computers aren't exactly my specialty, and I don't really cross paths with anyone that's capable of hacking the Internal Reven—" McCauley paused.

"What?" Naomi asked.

A wide smile spread across McCauley's face. "Actually, I do know one guy."

CHAPTER THIRTY-FOUR

McCauley backed the white cargo van into a darkened parking space on the top floor of a parking garage in Bucktown. It was the same garage where he had met his friend and NSA agent, Stan Butterfield, only twenty-four hours ago. He put the car in park and shut off the engine. The van was bulky, but they figured it was less conspicuous than his detective's cruiser, and since they had paid cash in advance for a three-day rental, it would be hard to track. Home Depot took a credit card as a precaution, but they wouldn't run it unless it was late or damaged.

McCauley leaned back in his seat and let out a sigh. The progress they had made gave him a second wind, but he wasn't sure just how long it would last.

"Okay, now listen up." McCauley turned to Naomi and Cody sitting next to him. "You two stay in the van and stay out of sight. I can tell from the phone call that Stan is in a real mood about all of this, and we desperately need his help to get that address."

"You're sure he can get it? I know it's the NSA, but can he really hack the IRS?" Naomi asked.

"Oh, yeah. To be fair, he's not the computer whiz that will do the hacking himself, but he can definitely get in there. The real question is whether or not he did it, and more importantly, will he give the results to us."

"He's your friend, though, right?" Cody asked.

"Yeah, we've known each other a long time. Still, this is a

big ask, and he's not the type to hand it over freely. Just getting the name of Eclipse was like pulling teeth, and that's when they owed me a big favor. This time, I don't have anything to trade but my charming personality. That's why you guys stay out of sight and let me handle it."

"What if he doesn't give it up? Do you have a plan B?" Cody asked.

"No, I'm kind of putting all our eggs in the plan A basket," said McCauley.

"Well, if things don't go as expected, then leave plan B to me," Cody said.

"And what is plan B?" asked McCauley.

"Plan A is we stay out of your way and let you work. Plan B is you stay out of my way and let me work. And another thing, I need my gun back."

"No fucking way. This is a friend of mine, not some lowlife. There is no scenario where you get to shoot him," McCauley said.

"First off, in my experience, NSA guys *are* lowlifes. Second, I'm not going to shoot him. The gun isn't part of plan B."

"Okay, hotshot, what's it for, then?" asked McCauley.

"It's not to shoot him, but it *is* for insurance. Look, it's safe to say your friend is armed, yes?"

"He most certainly is."

"Okay, is it also safe to say that he—of all people—knows that we're wanted?"

"Yeah, so?"

"So the way that this goes south is that he's agitated with your request and *he* pulls *his* gun on me. You have my word I'm not going to shoot him. It's just for insurance so he doesn't shoot *me*. Okay?"

McCauley took a moment to think through the various scenarios of the meet and then spoke. "If I give you this gun back, I need to know with one hundred percent certainty that you aren't going to put one in his knee, or something equally insane."

"Well, as tempting as it would be to see an NSA goon squirm, and it would be very effective at getting him to talk..." Cody said.

"Hey, I'm serious," said McCauley.

"Take it easy, I'm only kidding. You have my word. I'm not going to shoot him. Besides, plan A's going to work, right?"

"Mmmm," McCauley grumbled. He tapped his hands on the steering wheel, trying to talk himself out of what he had just decided to do, but instead he reached under his sport coat to the small of his back and retrieved Cody's Beretta M9A3. He flipped it in his hand until he was holding the barrel and trigger guard, then extended the butt of the pistol to Cody, just as Cody had done earlier.

Cody grabbed the butt of the gun and started pulling, but McCauley held on tight and said, "Don't make me regret this, Cody."

"After everything that's happened? When are you going to trust me?" Cody asked, still holding the butt of the pistol.

"I'll trust you when you're dead," McCauley said, relinquishing the firearm to Cody.

"Well, if you don't start soon, that's just where we may end up."

"Look alive, boys. I think Stan just arrived," said Naomi, pointing to a black Chevy Impala driving up the ramp. The lights flooded the van only briefly as it turned the corner and backed into a spot on the other side of the deck. McCauley flashed his brights twice at the driver, who flashed his brights back in response.

"Okay, remember, stay low and out of sight. He doesn't know you are here, so let's keep it that way. I don't want this going to shit because you didn't keep your head down. Got it?"

Naomi and Cody nodded in unison and then slinked down low on the bench seat, their eyes just barely above the dash line so they could see.

McCauley exited the van and crossed the parking deck toward the Impala. As he approached, Stan Butterfield exited the car, dressed in his usual drab suit and red tie. This time around, though, he donned a dark trench coat that looked a half size too big. The coat hung open, and the ends of the belt used to cinch it hung low around his knees. As McCauley neared him, he could see his suit was wrinkled and his tie hung loosely around his neck. Gray stubble wrapped his chin, and his eyes were visibly red.

"Jeez, Stan, I thought I looked bad, but you look like shit," McCauley said.

"Not today, Pat. I'm in no mood. You're lucky I even agreed to meet you here," Stan barked back.

"Which I really appreciate. I wouldn't have asked for the information unless it was urgent."

"About that. You're not getting any more information from us."

"What? Why not?"

"Oh, let me see. First, we're the NSA. We're not in the habit of breaking into other federal agencies to steal data," Stan said.

"But you *did* get into the IRS, and you *do* have the address I asked for," McCauley said.

"Did you hear what I just said?" Stan asked angrily.

"Yes, I heard exactly what you just said. You said you're not in the *habit* of breaking into other agencies. That means that you're not above it."

"So we're going to argue semantics now? Just because I said 'habit' doesn't mean we hacked the IRS."

"Actually, Stan, that's exactly what it means. I've been a detective a long time. I know what to listen for, and I know what sidestepping the truth sounds like. To someone else maybe that wouldn't have registered anything, but to me it means that you have hacked other agencies before—probably only in extreme circumstances. I know your boss is nervous about the equipment that went missing, so I think this qualifies as an extreme circumstance in his book. Tell me I'm wrong."

Stan sized up McCauley's confidence level in that claim and replied, "Even if we did breach the IRS, it would have only been because of the hornet's nest that *you* stirred up. So what makes you think we'd give you that address now? We're in damage control, Pat, and God only knows what you'd do with that intel."

"How much do you know?" McCauley asked.

"Some. Also a helluva lot less than we'll know twenty-four hours from now. The whole field office has been called in on this. We are working around the clock."

"You don't need to do that. I can spell it out for you," McCauley said.

"In exchange for the address?"

"And maybe some help. We're talking about a major conspiracy, American lives at risk. You have a duty to help," McCauley said.

"Don't lecture me about duty, Pat. This was supposed to be about some drug dealer. Whatever you did got that Cody Evans running all over the city killing people," said Stan.

McCauley raised his eyebrows in surprise.

"Oh, you didn't think we knew about him?" asked Stan. "He's the one link to Eclipse we do know of right now. My boss flipped his shit when he saw his face come across the wires. Hell, he's all over the news. You turned that kid into a major liability for us."

"So what are you going to do?"

"I'll tell you what we're going to do. We're going to plug this leak before it gets any worse. We're going to find Evans before anyone else does and pick him up. You know what we're capable of, Pat. So you know I'm serious when I say that."

"Then what are you going to do? Kill him?" McCauley asked angrily.

"We don't need to kill him, Pat. We're going to pick him up and charge him with a bevy of terror-related crimes so we can detain him indefinitely. It's only a matter of time before we get everything we need to know out of him, so you see, Pat, you have nothing to trade. You're not getting that address."

At that moment Cody stepped out of the shadows behind Stan Butterfield, holding the Beretta in his right hand. Cody wrapped his left bicep around Stan's throat, putting pressure on his Adam's apple as he pressed the gun to his temple. A look of shock washed over Stan's face.

"What the hell are you doing, Cody?" McCauley shouted.

"Plan A didn't sound like it was going so well, so we're moving on to plan B," said Cody.

"Evans?" Butterfield gasped, trying to turn and look at the face of his captor.

"In the flesh. Would you look at that, Stan? You found me just like you said. I bet you'll get a medal for this. It's your choice if it's posthumously," said Cody.

McCauley put his hands up at chest level, trying to calm Cody down. "Cody, don't shoot him. I told you he's my friend."

"Not for long," Stan said indignantly.

"I guess you're not friends anymore, so does that mean I can shoot him now?" Cody said, tightening his arm around Stan's throat, causing him to cough.

"We said no shooting, Cody," said McCauley.

"I told you that NSA guys are lowlifes. You heard him, McCauley. His boss wants to violate my constitutional rights by throwing me in a hole somewhere for the rest of my life, and for what? So that he can keep his hundred-and-twenty-five-thousand-dollar-a-year job? Putting a bullet in Stan here seems like justice to me."

"I know what he said, but you don't have to shoot him, so just let him go and we'll talk this out. All we have to do is explain the situation to him," McCauley said.

"You hear that, Stan? McCauley's a good friend. You shouldn't be so quick to dismiss him," said Cody.

"Go to hell," Stan shot back in a low wheeze.

"Only one of us is going there tonight, and I'm pretty sure it's you, Stan. Unless, of course, you want to give us that address."

"You're not...getting...anything from me," said Stan. He was struggling to breathe, but Cody was squeezing him just enough to keep him restrained while reminding him that any tighter would mean the end for Stan Butterfield.

"Okay, listen up, Stan, because it's time to get down to business. If I had my way, you'd be in the trunk of that car already with a bullet in your head. I'd have your credentials, building access code, and your severed right thumb in this." With the gun still in his right hand, Cody pulled a rolled-up ziplock bag from his coat. He held it in front of Stan's face as he clutched the top, then flipped it downward. In one motion, the bag unrolled, revealing a layer of ice at the bottom. Stan's eyes went wide as Cody continued. "So you see, Stan, I don't actually need you alive to get that address, I just need your identity. Now, I was planning to cut the thumb off *after* you were dead, but given what you just said about me, I'm rethinking the order."

"You're crazy. Who the fuck do you think you are?" Stan gasped.

"I'm someone with absolutely nothing to lose. Best-case scenario? I am running for the rest of my life, looking over my shoulder. Worst case? I'm dead," Cody said, then paused for a moment. "No, strike that. Worst case is I'm buried in some shitty NSA-run terror prison somewhere for the rest of my life. Middle case is I'm dead."

"If that's the case, why don't you just run?" Stan asked.

"Great question, Stan. I'm glad you're starting to participate. I could run, God knows I've thought about it. But you see her?" Cody pointed toward the van at Naomi.

Naomi saw Cody point and stepped out of the van. There was no point hiding anymore given the circumstances.

Stan Butterfield's vision was blurring, but he could just make out enough of Naomi's face to recognize her. "Your girlfriend?"

"That's very flattering, but she's not my girlfriend. She's the lawyer that uncovered this whole plot, and while I may have the luxury of running, she doesn't. You know, Stan, you and I aren't that dissimilar. We've both done bad things in our lives. We've justified our actions by saying that we are doing it for a cause that we believe in—that the greater good would outweigh the bad. But not Naomi. She is an innocent. She is pure, she is righteous, and she sees the good in others. She already made her choice. She chose to stay and fight, despite the risk of death or jail. Most people confronted with that choice would run. I know because *I* wanted to run. But not Naomi—she truly is one of a kind. And now because of her decision, she's facing an insurmountable enemy hell-bent on her destruction. So we need to protect her. If ever you believed in the oath you took when you joined the NSA, then you'll give me that address."

Stan said nothing, but Cody could feel the gears in his mind turning. Cody could sense he was close to giving it up. *Just one more nudge*, he thought.

Cody held the ziplock bag back up in front of Stan's face and said, "Or we'll just get that thumb."

"1405 West Cortland Street," Stan said.

"See? That wasn't so hard, was it? Now I want to apologize in advance for this," Cody said.

"For what?" Stan asked nervously.

"You're going to wake up with a headache."

Cody tightened his arm around Stan's throat, cutting off his air supply. Stan futilely slapped at Cody's powerful biceps, but having already been deprived of air, his arms were weak. It only took a few seconds before Stan let out a gurgle and passed out. Cody set him gently on the ground and started rooting around his belt.

"Jesus, Cody!" McCauley said furiously. "You said you weren't going to use that gun."

"No, I said I wasn't going to shoot him," said Cody.

"What if the gun went off?"

"What if the gun went off? Please, McCauley, I'm not an amateur. I know how to exercise proper trigger control."

"Well, what if he struggled and you fought? There's a million ways that could have gone bad," McCauley said, throwing his hands in the air.

"I told you I'm not an amateur, and besides, it's pretty hard to shoot someone with an empty gun."

Cody took a set of handcuffs off of Stan's belt, then stood up, pulling the slide back on the Beretta and locking it into place. Nothing came out, showing there really wasn't a round in the chamber. He held it up to McCauley's face for him to see. McCauley looked through the chamber out of the bottom of the gun where the magazine would be. Empty.

"I still don't like it," McCauley said. "He's never going to forgive me for this."

"Take him to Gibson's for a steak. I'm sure he'll get over it," said Cody.

"I think I'm going to owe him a little more than a steak and a jumbo slice of carrot cake to smooth this over."

"Frankly, McCauley, I don't really care. The only thing that matters is making sure Naomi is safe. We needed that address, and now we've got it, and no one got hurt. So stop complaining."

"You call that not hurt?" asked McCauley as he pointed at Stan's unconscious body.

"He'll be fine. Thirty minutes from now he'll wake up, and ten minutes later it'll be like nothing happened."

"Yeah, well, speaking of which. Thirty minutes doesn't give us a lot of time to search that property, and when he wakes up, he's going to be pissed. You better believe they are going to descend on that place, especially now that they know we're going there."

"That's what the handcuffs are for. We'll lock him to the steering wheel. By 9:00 a.m. this garage will be packed, someone will find him, and that should give Naomi plenty of time to find the files. Speaking of which..." said Cody.

Naomi approached them and looked at Stan Butterfield lying on the pavement. "Cody, you didn't—"

"No, he's just unconscious, he'll be fine," said Cody. "Plan A wasn't going so great."

"I guess not," said Naomi. "What did plan B get us?"

"Plan B proved to be much more fruitful," said Cody with a smile. "According to the IRS, the global headquarters for Eclipse is located at 1405 West Cortland Street."

"About that," McCauley said, "that address seems familiar to me. It's over on the west side of Lincoln Park in that industrial strip, not far from Eisner's storage locker. Not exactly the kind of spot you'd pick for a multibillion-dollar property manager, if that's what Whitaker's going for."

Naomi was tapping furiously away at her phone. "You're right. It comes up as Fine Brothers Steel."

"Oh no," McCauley said, rubbing his furrowed brow. "They moved that steel mill to the South Side a few years ago."

"So?" Cody asked.

"So it's an old steel mill. There are half a dozen buildings over twenty acres of land. It could take us days to find the documents, if they are even there."

"The files are there," said Naomi.

"Well, I don't know about you, Pat, but I like her optimism," said Cody.

"It's Detective McCauley. I'm still mad at you."

"Yes, but you still need my help, and given it's coming up on 4:00 a.m., we should really get moving. Now, do you want to help me load Stan into his car?"

"You were strong enough to choke him out, so I think you can handle it," McCauley said. "I'll pull the van around."

"Suit yourself," said Cody. "Let's get moving."

CHAPTER THIRTY-FIVE

Whitaker lay on the couch in his office with his eyes shut. He was no stranger to sleeping in his office, and with Cody still lurking around, he decided it was not the time to chance leaving. As he lay with his forearm draped over his eyes, the computer emitted an audible alarm, and a screen popped up. Whitaker lifted his arm and opened one eye as he awoke from his slumber.

Ding, ding, ding—the alarm was soft but constant.

He rose from the couch, locked his fingers together, and then cracked his knuckles. He meandered around his desk to the front of his computer monitors, then wiped the sleep from his eyes. The computer was alerting him that his state-of-the-art security system at 1405 West Cortland Street had been tripped. He slowly scanned over a dozen camera angles until he saw a white van rolling through the open front gate. The gate itself didn't trigger the alarm, but the seismic detectors he buried under it, designed to pick up any surface vibrations, did.

He watched curiously as the van pulled into the main lot, made a wide circle, then came to a stop. Three figures emerged, and Brendt's eyes widened.

"It can't be," he said as he used his mouse to pan and zoom the camera in an effort to get a better look at the figures in the frame. "How could they possibly have found it?"

He worked the mouse furiously in an effort to see their faces, but it was no use. It was too dark for the camera to pick up any detail. He tapped the keyboard to cycle through the different cameras until he finally stopped on one. They were facing it, but it was still much too far away to make out their faces. He pushed the scroll wheel forward on his mouse, and slowly the camera began to zoom in. As it did, he used the keyboard to keep their bodies at the center of the frame. Finally after a few seconds, the camera was tight around their heads and shoulders. He saw the unmistakable visages of Naomi Archer, Detective McCauley, and Cody Evans.

He slammed his fist on the desk and shouted, "Impossible!"

Without hesitation, Whitaker picked up the phone and hit a button.

"Russo here."

"Russo, it's Whitaker. It's time to move. I need you to assemble your men and pick me up immediately."

"No problem, we are already set to move out as you instructed. Where are we going?"

"We're going to take out Cody," Whitaker said, "and finish this once and for all."

Whitaker could practically hear Russo smiling at the other end of line. "Yes, sir. What's the address?"

"1405 West Cortland. I'll be in front of the office waiting for you. How fast can you get us there?"

"We're already moving to the vehicles. I can pick you up and have us there in thirty minutes."

"Make it twenty-five," Whitaker said before hanging up the phone.

CHAPTER THIRTY-SIX

Standing in the main parking lot of what was the Fine Bros. Steel Mill, Naomi couldn't help but feel nervous. McCauley was right about the size of the property, and with six buildings that she could see, it could take all day to properly search them. She kept reminding herself of what she told the others in McCauley's basement, though—that the evidence would be hiding in plain sight. Although nothing appeared to been rehabbed yet, that didn't mean there wasn't a small office somewhere on the premises.

"Maybe we should split up," McCauley said. "We can at least cover more ground that way."

"I don't think that's a good idea, McCauley," said Cody. "What if we run into security?"

"You said you disabled the system on the gate," said McCauley.

"I did, but someone could still be on site. It's too dangerous to split up."

"We only have a couple hours before this place is crawling with NSA agents, and you know what that means."

"It's a risk we have to take," said Cody.

"I think Cody is right," said Naomi. "The paperwork we're looking for won't be hidden. It'll be obvious when we find it, and we don't have to go through it all right now. Once we locate it, you can call in the cavalry."

"How sure are you that these files are here?"

"The fact that this place exists makes me feel pretty damn sure that they're here," she said.

"All right, we stay together. I have a bad feeling about this, though."

"It's been twenty-four hours since I've had a good feeling about anything, and we made it this far," said Naomi.

"Good point."

"So, should we start with building one?" Cody asked.

"It's as good a place as any to start," McCauley said. "Who knows, maybe this time we'll catch a break, and the office will be right in front."

The trio walked up to the front door of a large mixed-use-looking building. In fairness, they all seemed to have that look. Building four was the only one that had a very clear manufacturing look to it, but there still could have been an office in the back. As they approached the door, Cody put his hand out for Naomi and McCauley to hang back. He carefully ran his fingers along the frame of the door, then peered into the darkened window.

"I don't see an alarm," he said. "I think we're clear to go in."

Using his elbow, he quickly struck the glass of one of the squared windowpanes.

"I usually try the doorknob first," McCauley said.

"They're not leaving it unlocked," Cody said, trying the knob.

To his surprise he was able to turn it, and he pushed the door open. McCauley slowly trotted through the door while maintaining eye contact with Cody as he passed by.

"All right, so they left one unlocked," Cody said.

Naomi followed McCauley in, and Cody took up the rear. McCauley took the flashlight off his belt. It was small, but at over 1,200 lumens, it was powerful and cast a bright beam across a swath of the empty space.

"At least this one won't take long to search."

Though it was empty, they were thorough and took the better part of fifteen minutes to inspect all the rooms off the main floor as they made their way to the back of the building. Satisfied with the search, they returned to the entrance. They walked out the door, then took a right toward building two, which seemed to be some sort of storage facility or warehouse. The front sported a large double door and had a small set of railroad tracks that terminated at it—likely once used for shuttling the heavy steel around the property. To the right of the loading dock was a small door similar to the one at the first building.

"Are you sure you don't want to smash it, McCauley?" Cody asked, patting his elbow. "It's a great stress reducer."

"You should try a squeeze ball, you're less likely to get hurt —" McCauley started.

"Shut up," Cody said suddenly.

"Hey, I was just joking, no need to get testy."

"Shhhh." Cody put his index finger up to his mouth. "Do you hear that?"

"Hear what?" Naomi asked.

"Cars," Cody said.

Just then two large black SUVs exploded through the main gate, and their headlights flooded the entrance to building two. In a flash, Naomi, McCauley, and Cody were enveloped in light.

"Shit," Cody said. "It's them. We have to move."

"Where?" McCauley asked.

Cody looked around. The next building was over a hundred yards away, and they'd never make it. Cody quickly calculated the odds of covering the distance before the security team could exit their vehicles to engage them, and it didn't look good. They would have to make their stand in building two. McCauley tried the doorknob, but it didn't budge.

"Forget smashing the window. Kick it in, McCauley," he yelled.

Without hesitation, McCauley delivered a powerful front kick to the space just below the knob, sending the dilapidated door flying open and nearly separating it from its hinges. Cody drew his Beretta and waved Naomi and McCauley through just in time to see two carloads of heavily armed mercenaries exit the vehicles and run in their direction. He sized up the team as best he could, then dashed inside.

"Keep moving to the rear of the building," he said. "It's our only chance to get out of here alive."

CHAPTER THIRTY-SEVEN

Whitaker entered the warehouse flanked by Russo and the group of mercenaries covered head to toe in black tactical gear and carrying AR-15 assault rifles. He pulled a nickel-plated semiautomatic handgun from his coat and held it to his side.

"Spread out. Find them," Whitaker said to Russo.

Russo nodded a look at the mercenaries, who cautiously fanned out, covering as much of the warehouse floor as they could.

"Cody," Whitaker yelled loudly, his voice reverberating off the walls. "I know you're in here, Cody."

Near the back, Naomi, Cody, and McCauley quietly weaved their way through the maze of stacked crates, taking cover at the sound of Whitaker's voice shattering the silence.

"Why'd you do it, Cody? Why did you betray me? After everything I did for you? Do you remember when I found you working as a bouncer in that dingy bar? Do you remember that kid you tuned up? Why? Because he made some disparaging remarks about the war? You just kept punching him. For a minute I thought you had killed him. He still walks with a limp. Did you know that?"

Crouched behind a large wooden crate in the back, Naomi saw a mix of regret and anger sweep over Cody's face.

"They wanted to lock you up for that. Not me, though. You see, society doesn't value a man like you, Cody, but I do. Sure, they may want you if they need you for a fight. They'll send you halfway around the world, call you a patriot, put a gun in your hand. They'll have you kill, but for what? For your country? For honor? It's all lies. You know who you killed for over there? Some politician looking to line his pockets with a war but who's to chickenshit to fight it himself. I know it, Cody, because I own a lot of them."

Cody hung his head low, staring at the floor. Naomi put her hand on his chin, and he brought his eyes up to meet hers.

"Don't listen to him, Cody. Deep down, you're a good person."

"And when they're done with you," Whitaker continued, "when they've used you up, what are you supposed to do then? Get a nine-to-five in an office somewhere? Have people walk by your desk and say, 'Thank you for your service,' so they can feel like they did their good deed for the day? That's no life. Society doesn't want you for what you are. They don't see your value… but I do."

The mercenaries moved up through the rows of crates, inching their way along the sides before quickly turning the corner—muzzles pointed at what lay behind them. They were silent and efficient. Slow is smooth, smooth is fast. Whitaker trailed one row behind the wave of men methodically making their way through the warehouse.

"I saw the rage in your eyes as you cocked your fist and delivered blow after blow to that little punk. That's the moment I knew what you are—a warrior…a lion. Lions have to be free. Free to hunt, free to kill, free to be lions. I couldn't watch the cruelty of them trying to cage you, Cody. That's why I made the whole thing go away. That's why I bought off the kid. That's why I bought off the cops. That's why I took you in and gave you a job. I gave you more than that, though, didn't I, Cody?"

The mercenaries pushed forward. Slow is smooth, smooth is fast. Eight hundred feet left to cover.

"I knew that if I could take your skill, your raw power, and focus it, then we could do such great things. I'm talking about something bigger than us, Cody. The hub of the most modern transportation system the world has ever known, and you're standing on it! Picture it, a million people a day passing through here on their way to work, to the movies, to spend a day at the lakefront. I'm talking about express buses, water taxis, regional trains, and the crown jewel that ties it all together—the Circle Line."

Slow is smooth, smooth is fast. Seven hundred feet.

"An express train encircling the city and connecting the outer spokes of the El. A loop around the Loop. A perfect Eclipse!"

"Of course," Naomi whispered to herself.

"East meets west, north meets south. No more invisible walls to divide this city. No more invisible walls trapping people in ghettos. No more food deserts. The riches of this city will finally be available to everyone—not just those in the right zip code. Economics is our weapon to beat back the gangs who have spread like a plague throughout this city. Parents will be free of the fear that their children might get killed by a stray bullet when they send them off to play at the park. No more drugs drowning entire communities. We will create a new Chicago, one that our children can be proud of. I'm talking about a legacy!"

Slow is smooth, smooth is fast. Six hundred feet.

"All of it made possible by you, Cody. The politicians of this city couldn't do it. For the last forty years they've waxed poetic about the benefits of the Circle Line. But when it came time to displace residents in the name of progress, they all backed down. All they want is to stay fat and rich. They thought it better to slowly bleed their constituents dry than to make a hard choice, but one that will make real, meaningful change. They're all spineless!"

Slow is smooth, smooth is fast. Five hundred feet.

"But not us, Cody. Not you. The gang wars you manufactured throughout this city over the years drove down the property values. You are Andy Warhol with a rifle. You knew how to start them, and just when they showed signs of waning, you knew how to stoke them. Just a nudge here or there to keep the wars raging on. Even with our wealth, we never could have been able to buy up all that land. It was your artistry that allowed us to do it."

Slow is smooth, smooth is fast. Four hundred feet.

"This last war that you set off is the pièce de résistance —Hyde Park. Can you imagine my surprise when Obama was elected president? I have to admit, the fact that he still kept his home there was a bit of a roadblock. No matter, though. Rome wasn't built in a day. In just a few months, the war you started will take its toll. The property that we will acquire will put us past the point of no return. Once we have it, the citizenry, the politicians, the courts—they will all be powerless to stop us, powerless to stop progress."

"And what's the cost of your legacy, Brendt?" Cody yelled.

One of the mercs started moving quickly toward the sound of his voice until Russo whistled and pointed at him to get back in formation. They had them; it was only a matter of time now. No sense in taking the bait of an ambush.

"What are you doing?" McCauley whispered. "You're giving away our position."

"They have us cornered, but I've got a plan. Just stay quiet and let me work," Cody said.

"Cost?" Brendt continued. "You're starting to sound like the politicians. Don't tell me you care what happens to gang-bangers and drug pushers. This is war, Cody, and they are the enemy."

"Was Robert Chadwick an enemy too?" Cody yelled back.

"Chadwick? He was no innocent; he was a thief. Just ask Miss Archer there, that man stole nearly a million dollars. Don't you shed a single tear for him."

Slow is smooth, smooth is fast. Three hundred feet.

"Maybe he was a thief, and maybe he deserved to die. But Eisner didn't, and neither did Naomi."

"Oh, it's Naomi now? Glad to see you are getting along so well. Well, shit, I felt bad about Eisner. I always thought he was kind of a rube, but not a bad guy on the whole. You know what they say, though, you have to crack a few eggs to make an omelet. I was more upset over having to kill Miss Archer. But the second Eisner said he discovered Eclipse on his own, I knew it was a lie. We covered our tracks well. Miss Archer was the only one smart enough to uncover them. It's a real shame too. I had plans to offer her Eisner's job. Like you, Cody, I saw great potential in her. And wouldn't you say I was right? She found this place, didn't she? No doubt she accurately deduced that the only paper trail would be stored in our corporate files. How about it, Miss Archer? Little too sharp for your own good this time, weren't you? Wrong building, though. You should have picked one building over."

Naomi squeezed her hand into a fist and clenched her teeth.

"Lawyers are replaceable, Cody," Whitaker continued. "You are not."

"And what about the money? You say everything you did was for the city, for your legacy, but you stand to make a fortune off the Circle Line," Cody yelled back.

"Someone is going to get rich off of this. If not us, then who? Politicians and their friends? No, Cody, we earned that money. They don't deserve to be rewarded for something they should have done years ago. Not when you and I have done all the work and handed it to them on a silver platter."

"Is that what we are calling it now? Work?"

"It *is* work. Change is always hard work. We started this together, Cody, and there's still a path forward for you here. It doesn't have to end badly for you. Asking you to kill Chadwick was wrong, I see that now. After tonight, I will never ask you to pull the trigger again if you don't want to, but I need to know you're still with me. Just this once, I need you to take that pistol in your hand, point it at Miss Archer and the detective, and shoot them. Do this one thing for me, and we wipe the slate clean. We can still finish this thing. Together."

Whitaker paused for a moment, listening for a response.

Slow is smooth, smooth is fast. Two hundred feet.

"Cody? Did you hear me, son?"

Pop-pop!

Two quick shots rang out. The bullets ripped across the warehouse floor, striking one of the mercs above his right eye and sending his body crashing to the floor. Whitaker ducked at the sound, then looked over to his left to see the lifeless man lying awkwardly on his side, his equipment and arms intertwined in a tangled mess.

"That's disappointing, my boy."

"Yeah, well, I guess you have your answer," Cody yelled back.

The men had halted and took cover from the shots as Russo looked to Whitaker for instruction.

"Okay, Russo, you're up," he said.

An ear-to-ear grin came over Russo's face. "*Co-dy.* I told Mr. Whitaker you wouldn't go for it. I told him you'd gone soft. Well, now you get to deal with me."

Russo grabbed a merc by the vest and whispered to him, "The shots came from behind that large crate near the back wall. Tell your men to fan out, hold their positions, and keep him pinned down. You are with me. We're going to make our way from crate to crate around the right side to flank him."

The man pinched the radio wrapped around his neck and whispered the instructions to the team. They acknowledged with a thumbs-up and started taking up their positions, keeping their rifles trained at the crate that Naomi, McCauley, and Cody were crouched behind.

"Deal with you, eh? Well, if it's anything like your man there, it should be just a walk in the park," Cody yelled.

"Now might be a good time to key us in on your plan, Cody," Naomi said.

"Right now they are fixing and flanking us," Cody said.

"We're not special forces, Cody, what the hell does that mean?" McCauley asked.

"It means that we're in trouble. I make four men remaining of a five-man tactical team, plus Russo and Whitaker. Right now the bulk of that tac team is taking positions to keep us pinned—that's called the fire team. Then, a two- or three-man assault team is going to make their way around one of these sides to flank us while we are pinned down."

"Which side?" Naomi asked.

"Our left, their right. The right side is too exposed—there's not enough cover for them to move safely," Cody said, pointing to a twenty-five-by-twenty-five-yard open swath of warehouse floor to the right of the crate. "But they can move on the left side using the crates as cover. They will be exposed as they move between them, but they will be counting on the fire team to keep our heads down with covering fire."

"What happens when the assault team makes it all the way around to our left side," McCauley asked.

"Well, Detective, first they'll kill us, then they'll build their stupid fucking train on our graves."

"Cody," Naomi said, pulling him to focus. "Just tell us what to do."

"At our eleven o'clock there's a wide gap that they are going to have to cross. When we hear the assault team move, I'll pop out right and draw the attention of the fire team. They will be looking high, so it should be easy. Detective McCauley, you peek out low and left and unload on the assault team as they move. Hit them if you can, but we could be taking fire, so that's not necessarily the main goal."

"What is, then?" asked McCauley

"Your priority is to slow them down, make them think twice about crossing that gap between the crates. How many rounds you got for that thing?" Cody asked, pointing to McCauley's 1911.

"Eight rounds in, two spares, twenty-four all together."

"Well, don't be afraid to use them. Unload your magazine at them. You have to slow them and buy us time. Got it?"

"Got it."

McCauley crept to the left of the crate and Cody to the

right.

"Go on my call, Detective."

Cody closed his eyes and focused his breathing, bringing his internal clock to a crawl. Finally he heard the sound of footsteps across the concrete floor. "Now!"

Cody jumped up and fired his Beretta at the mercs, who instantly shot back. McCauley popped out low and left to see Russo and the team leader trying to bridge the gap between crates on their left side, just as Cody said they would. McCauley opened up on them. As soon as he started shooting, they dove back for cover, realizing they had been made.

Pop-pop-pop! Pop-pop! Pop! The shots slowed from a flurry to a trickle, like a bag of popcorn during its final seconds in the microwave.

When it was done, one merc on the fire team was hit. He released his grip on his rifle, letting it dangle from the sling around his chest. He clutched his throat and gasped, but he was taking in deep gulps of blood instead of air. After a few seconds he dropped to his knees, then his face, and then the gurgling went quiet.

"That kept them there for now, but I'm not sure how long we can keep this up," McCauley said, returning to cover while loading a fresh magazine.

Cody slumped back down behind the crate in pain. A red circle slowly expanded across his shirt like a paper towel over a coffee spill. Naomi, realizing Cody had been hit, ripped his shirt open to find a wound on the right side of his torso. He grunted as she pressed her hands against his chest, trying to stem the flow of blood.

"Oh, shit," McCauley said. "Is it bad?"

"Well, it's not good," Cody barbed back.

Meanwhile Russo shot an angry look at the team leader after nearly getting his head blown off. "I said to keep them pinned down. Your guys shoot first, *then* we move, not the other way around. You think your team can handle that?"

"We got it," the team lead replied, keying his radio.

"That's reassuring, because from where I'm sitting, it doesn't look like you've got it," Russo said. Resetting the diversion, he turned his attention back to Cody.

"Hey, bud. How you doing over there? Are you hit? It sounds like you're hit. Stings like a bitch, doesn't it?"

"I've had worse hangovers," Cody responded. "How about your man over there? Is he okay? Why don't we ask him, see what he says?"

"I hate to break up this reunion," McCauley whispered. "But at what point of this plan do we get the hell out of here?"

"Not we," Cody said. "You."

"What? No, Cody. We're getting out of here together," Naomi said.

"We're in a bad spot, Naomi They have us trapped, but I can buy you a chance. You see those blue barrels over there?" Cody pointed across the swath of open warehouse to a wall of blue industrial drums. "Look above them. Do you see what's behind them?"

"An exit!" McCauley said, just making out the top edge of a door.

"Your ticket out of here. A twenty-five-yard flat run between living and dying."

"That's why you wanted me to unload my magazine."

"Yes. This time the assaulters will be so focused on crossing that gap that they won't be even thinking about you making a break for it. When they move, I'll shoot everything I've got at the fire team."

"No, Cody," Naomi insisted. "You can survive this wound. We can still save you."

"Naomi," he said, squeezing her red-stained hand on his chest. The blood seeped through their fingers. "You already have."

"Cody—" Naomi started.

"It's a bad wound, Naomi," Cody said, coughing as a trickle of blood ran from his lip. "I'm not going to make it. But you are. You're going to get those files, and then you're going to get your life back."

"Naomi," McCauley said, placing a hand on her shoulder. "He's right. It's the only way."

"I know, goddammit," she said, wiping her eyes. "It doesn't mean I have to like it."

"Good, at least we're in agreement," Cody said. "Now help me up."

McCauley and Naomi pulled Cody to one knee, and McCauley handed him his loaded 1911 and remaining magazine.

"Sixteen rounds left, it's not much," he said.

"It'll be enough," Cody replied. He grabbed McCauley's hand and wrapped it around a black cylinder. "Take this. It just may save your life."

McCauley opened his fingers, stared at the object for a moment, then looked back at Cody, who said, "Trust me."

McCauley and Naomi moved to the right side of the crate and got into a crouch, ready to run.

"I'll buy you as much time as I can. Stay low and don't stop until you hit the door. Get ready."

Pop-pop-pop-pop!

Bullets from the fire team rang out, splintering the left side of the crate. They kept their fire focused on the left, where McCauley had just popped out and thwarted Russo's movements.

"Now!" Cody yelled.

Naomi and McCauley dashed from the right side of the crate as Cody stood over them, unloading both pistols at the fire team. He shifted his focus from man to man, making each one hesitate for just a moment.

Naomi was out in front, but McCauley was right on her heels, adrenaline pumping. Naomi's vision went dark along the periphery, giving her the sensation of running through a tunnel with the door behind the blue barrels sitting at the end of it.

Twenty yards.

Fifteen yards.

Ping, ping, ping. The bullets ricocheted off the concrete floor, nipping at their heels as the fire team shot at them erratically.

Ten yards.

Five yards.

Then both McCauley and Naomi dove toward the blue drums. They weren't sure why they dove, but the instinct to get to cover that seemed so close and so far at the same time overtook them.

Simultaneously, Russo and the team leader crossed the gap on the left side and made it to the next cover. Russo peeked out just in time to see the top of the door behind the drums open, and then he heard the clank of metal as it slammed shut.

"Shit," he muttered under his breath.

Cody looked at his Beretta. The slide was locked open, showing the top of the empty magazine. He set it down, then loaded the last magazine for McCauley's 1911.

"Where do they think they're going, Cody?" Russo shouted. "There's nothing out there for them. It's just a small loading dock that backs up to the river. Did you think they were going to swim for it? In this cold, they'll be dead before they make it halfway across."

"I bought them a chance, at least," Cody said, struggling for breath.

"No, Cody, you bought them a temporary reprieve. After we're done in here, they're next. You know I'm going to enjoy killing them too. They've been nothing but a pain in my ass the last twenty-four hours. How about you, Cody? You ever kill anyone up close before? It's a lot different than shooting them at five hundred yards. It's much more personal when you're face-to-face. Kind of like how it must have felt when you saw your friend die on that roof? What was his name? Martinez? Rodriguez? No, I remember...Hernandez. Evans and Hernandez, guardian angels to the jarheads on the ground. You guys were legends. So what happened to you? Couldn't take seeing your buddy's brains splatter all over your uniform?"

"You haven't earned the right to talk about him!"

"What's the matter? Did I hit a sensitive spot for you? Oh, I get it. Now I see what happened. You fell in love with him, didn't you? All those week-long missions, just the two of you. But he didn't love you back, did he? So you shot him in the head and blamed it on a sniper? That's cold, man, real cold. I knew there was something off about you from the second I met you."

Cody used his remaining energy to rise to a crouch and fire the last of his bullets at Russo, who hid safely behind cover.

Bang, for Nando.

Bang, for Chadwick.

Bang, for Eisner.

Bang, for McCauley.

Bang, for Naomi.

Bang, for honor.

Bang, for duty.

Bang, for Cody.

Another press of the trigger, but this time nothing happened. Cody crumpled back down to the ground in a seated position, his back pressed up against the crate and his feet sticking straight out in front of him. He looked at the empty gun with the slide locked back, then tossed it on the ground. It made a clattering noise as it hit the cement floor.

"You out, Cody?" Russo shouted, still behind cover.

"Looks that way."

"You wouldn't lie to me, would you?"

"Why don't you come over here and see for yourself?" Cody taunted back.

"Okay, let's move in," Russo said to the team lead. "Carefully."

The team lead whispered in his radio, then he and Russo made their way to the crate with their rifles up and the muzzles pointed at it. As he approached, Russo could see Cody's boots sticking out. He sidestepped right to see a wounded Cody, struggling for breath, the empty gun lying next to his hand. He walked up and kicked the gun away, still pointing his rifle at

Cody. The rest of the team filled in and surrounded him in a semicircle.

"Cody, that looks bad. I don't think you're gonna make it, bud," Russo said.

Cody tried to respond but couldn't catch his breath.

"Looks like that lung might've collapsed too. Don't worry, though, it will all be over soon."

Whitaker stepped from behind the mercenary team and put his hand on Russo's shoulder to stand down. He stood over Cody, who looked up at him.

"I'm afraid Russo is right, Cody. There's no place for your friends to hide out there. It was a noble effort, but futile nonetheless."

Cody wheezed and coughed.

"Look at you, my boy. A lion to the end. You truly are one of a kind. I will never forget what you did for us."

Cody struggled to lift his blood-soaked hand off the ground. The mercs' guns rattled as they raised them out of precaution. Cody crawled his fingers to the right cargo pocket of his pants and fumbled with the Velcro latch. Russo stepped on his hand, pinning it back to the floor, then reached into the pocket and pulled out a small brick of C4 with a detonator strapped to the top.

"You little sneak," Russo said. "Was that your plan? You were going to blow us up?"

Cody shook his head and drew what breath he could.

"No," he said, pointing his free arm in the direction of the blue drums, too weak to extend his hooked index finger. "They are."

Like a conspiracy of lemurs, Whitaker, Russo, and the mercs turned their heads simultaneously toward the threat. Naomi and McCauley peered out from behind the drums. Naomi held in her hand the black cylindrical tube Cody had given McCauley. Her thumb hovered above the glowing red button on top.

"Thank you, Cody," she whispered, then pressed the button.

Surprise and confusion were the last things the group huddled around Cody felt as the C4 in Russo's hand detonated a one-thousand-degree fireball that engulfed them all. The explosion sent a concussive wave in all directions. Naomi and McCauley felt the heat as it smashed against the wall of drums. A few cracked, spilling their liquid contents, but the wall stayed mostly intact, shielding them from the blast.

When the ringing in her ears stopped, Naomi rose to see the devastation. A crater in the floor where the men had stood was all that was left. The large wooden crate was simply gone. Small scattered fires glowed in the wake of the bomb. She was half-expecting to see Cody one more time, but she couldn't find his body as she scanned the warehouse for him.

"Cody," Naomi said.

"He's gone, Naomi," said McCauley. "No one could have survived that. It's a miracle we did."

"No, it wasn't a miracle. He saved us."

"Yes, he did. You were right about him. He was a good person. I didn't give him the benefit of the doubt."

"It's okay. I think he secretly respected you—liked you, even."

"You think so?"

"I don't know," said Naomi. "But I'm going to remember it that way."

The pair stood in silence for a moment, and then Naomi spoke. "What do we do now?"

"We do just what Cody said. Let's go get the files, and then we'll get your life back."

"Is it over?" Naomi asked.

"I hope so, Naomi. Come on, let's get out of here."

The duo navigated the debris field and made their way to the front of the warehouse. Naomi turned and took one last look around before stepping out into the cold night air. The beautifully lit Chicago skyline hung in the background as they heard the first sirens approaching.

CHAPTER THIRTY-EIGHT

Harrison Pennington sat in the back seat of his stretch limousine with the soundproof privacy wall raised, ensuring the driver was cut off from the conversation. The car had just pulled to the curb in front of Pennington's headquarters, and his assistant, Brandon Jacobs, sat across from him with a file open on his lap.

"And what about the properties?" Harrison asked. "How much will we recover?"

"The bulk of it. I estimate seventy to eighty percent. Technically it was our money that funded the purchases, so we will have the biggest claim. The sellers, though, are also viewed as victims. So if they come forward, they will likely receive compensation for their damages."

Jacobs was referring to Eclipse's bankruptcy litigation. With Whitaker as the sole owner, the lawyers were going to have a field day sifting through the records to figure out just who was entitled to the assets.

"Seventy percent is an acceptable number," Harrison said.

"It should be enough to ensure the plans for the Circle Line continue," Jacobs said.

"Don't be so sure, Brandon. Owning a critical mass of property isn't enough to ensure it moves forward. We also need politicians on board. A lot of our political capital died along with Brendt."

"Yes, sir," Jacobs said. "As for that, do you still want me to take care of the funeral arrangements for him? If it gets back to us, it could arouse suspicion."

"Yes, we take care of our own, so your job is to find the money for the arrangements in such a manner that ensures it doesn't get back to us. He was my best pupil. A brilliant tactician, but he never could get out of the way of his own ambition."

"There is another issue," Jacobs said.

"Oh?"

"Miss Archer, sir. Are you sure you want to involve her? She's obviously very capable. It could be dangerous."

"And what would you have me do instead?" Harrison asked.

"Whitaker would have found"—Jacobs paused—"another way."

"She's national news. A young, smart, beautiful rising star in the legal world. Every news outlet and magazine in the country wants a piece of her. Her disappearance would create just the kind of attention we are looking to avoid right now."

"Understood, sir. Still, there is perhaps a middle ground. We don't have to give her access. No one would think twice about it, given how close she is to all of this."

"Close is exactly where I want her. People like her never stop until it's over. If we push her away, it will only incite her that much more. This way we will be able to keep a watchful eye on her."

"Shall I call the law firm with our proposal, then?"

"Yes. They should jump at the opportunity to capitalize on her name," said Harrison.

"Yes, sir," Jacobs said as he reached for the door.

"But just in case," Harrison said, "make sure they know it's not a request."

CHAPTER THIRTY-NINE

Naomi stood behind the desk in her office. Sunlight streamed in through floor-to-ceiling glass windows that overlooked Lake Michigan and the Chicago River. Boxes of files were crammed in and stacked all over, making the office look small. Then a knock on the open door.

"Come in," Naomi said, still looking down at some papers she held in her hand.

"Hi, Naomi," said McCauley. He had a small butterfly bandage on his forehead covering a cut he'd received when he was struck by one of the blue drums in the blast.

"Detective McCauley!" She beamed with excitement. It had been weeks since they had walked out of the warehouse. In the whirlwind of the aftermath, they hadn't spoken much to each other. The local police were fighting with the FBI, the district attorney with the federal prosecutors, all were pulling Naomi and McCauley in different directions, looking for their piece of the headlines. The truth is, the cornucopia of evidence found at 1405 West Cortland would keep them all busy for months. Not to mention the journalists who called 24/7. Naomi hadn't turned her phone on in over a week, relying instead on a prepaid one she bought from her corner Walgreens. McCauley made his way along a small path carved out between the boxes to Naomi, who squeezed him in a tight embrace, her head against his shoulder.

"Pat," McCauley said. "My friends call me Pat."

"It's good to see you, Pat," she said. She scrunched her nose at the sound of it, "It doesn't suit. How about just McCauley?"

"That works too," he said, lifting the top off of one of the boxes and peering in. "So what's all this, a new case or something?"

"Cases, actually. Inside these boxes is every open legal matter for the Pennington Corporation. In the wake of everything that's happened and...Richard's death, Pennington has made Sloan MacIntyre exclusive counsel, provided I am the lead partner on it."

"So a promotion. That's great, I'm glad to hear it. You certainly deserve it. Maybe they can give you a bigger office, though," McCauley said, waving his hands at the sea of boxes.

"They did. Two, actually, up on the top floor. They're going to knock out a wall to join them, but it won't be ready until next week."

"Well, I'm really happy for you," McCauley said. He nervously spun the box top in his hand and stared at the floor. "You know, we never talked about it. I just wanted you to know, I could have pushed the button. You didn't have to do it."

Naomi turned and looked out over the lake in a thousand-yard stare. "Yes, I did."

"For Richard?"

"And for Cody." Naomi thought for a moment, then shook the memory from her mind. "How about you, what are you going to do now?"

"I've got a lot of vacation saved up. I think I'm going to finally take a chunk of it. We have a small cabin around the bend of the lake in Michigan City, Indiana. It's not much, but it's quiet. I'm going to take Emily there to get away from all the noise."

"That sounds nice. I guess we all deserve a little break. You know, I'm going to need a full-time investigator. I've already been authorized to hire one. When you get back, the job is yours, if you want it."

"You mean work for Pennington?"

"Well, technically you'd be working for the law firm, but

yes, you'd be working on the Pennington matters."

"I'm not sure that's for me. I'm a cop at heart. I'm better at dealing with the bodies and the bullets. I think this stuff is a little out of my league," McCauley said, gesturing at the files surrounding them. "Besides, my pension is vesting now, and every year I work kicks me up another two percent. I figure I still have a few good ones in front of me."

"You know this firm makes a lot of money. The pay would be a lot more than two percent of a cop's salary, but I don't suspect that will change your mind, will it?"

"No, you're right. It probably won't. I guess I'm not doing it for the money."

"Want to hear a secret?" Naomi asked, looking around her office and coyly waving McCauley in closer. "Neither am I."

"No? So why are you doing this, then?"

"Something Whitaker said at the steel mill didn't sit with me. He said, '*We* could never have afforded to buy all that property.' He was rich, for sure, but not that level of rich—not Pennington family rich."

"That's why he embezzled the money. At least that's what the prosecutors are saying. No one's found anything connecting the family to Whitaker's scheme. Officially, the Pennington family are victims in this."

"And you believe that?"

"Not for one second," McCauley said. "So, what, you think the answers are buried somewhere in the bottom of one of these banker's boxes?"

"Maybe, maybe not. But as the lead partner, I have unparalleled access to all the Pennington records. If the answers are out there, I'll find them."

"So it's a 'keep your friends close' type of a deal."

"Exactly."

"Well, in that case," McCauley said, clearing files off the chair across from Naomi's desk and sitting down. "Maybe you ought to tell me more about this job offer."

Naomi smiled.

END

<<<<>>>>

Thanks for reading. This project was a source of great joy for me, so I hope you got as much out of it reading it as I did writing it. If you enjoyed it, I would humbly ask that you tell your friends and family about the book. In addition to word of mouth, reviews are the lifeblood of independent authors, so taking just a few minutes to leave a review on Amazon would be a tremendous help. I have included a link to the book's page on Amazon below as well as a link to my website where you can subscribe for updates on future projects. Thanks for all your support, and happy reading.

-A. B.

Please leave a review here, or via your kindle app:

https://www.amazon.com//dp/B07QV41PQ5/

Subscribe (at the bottom of the page) for updates at my website:

https://www.ablevin.com/

Follow me on Facebook:

https://www.facebook.com/A.B.LevinAuthor/

44844407R00154